OTHER PROPER ROMANCES
BY SARAH M. EDEN

PROPER ROMANCE

THE GENTLEMAN

AND THE

THIEF

SARAH M. EDEN

SHADOW
MOUNTAIN

Library of Congress Cataloging-in-Publication Data
Names: Eden, Sarah M., author.
Title: The gentleman and the thief / Sarah M. Eden. Other titles: Proper romance.
Description: Salt Lake City : Shadow Mountain, [2020] | Series: Proper romance
    | Summary: "Ana Newport, ostensibly a music tutor, leads a secret life as a
    petty burglar, but then meets Hollis Darby, a gentleman who secretly writes
    penny dreadfuls. Can they successfully lead double lives and still find love
    together?"—Provided by publisher.
Identifiers: LCCN 2020016875 | ISBN 9781629727905 (trade paperback)
Subjects: LCSH: Music teachers—Fiction. | Burglars—Fiction. | Novelists—
    Fiction. | Man-woman relationships—Fiction. | Nineteenth century, setting. |
    London (England), setting. | LCGFT: Romance fiction. | Novels.
Classification: LCC PS3605.D45365 G46 2020 | DDC 813/.6—dc23
LC record available at https://lccn.loc.gov/2020016875

Printed in the United States of America
Lake Book Manufacturing LLC, Melrose Park, IL

10   9   8   7   6   5   4   3

To Melanie Jacobson,
who stepped up in the very moment
I needed her most

CHAPTER 1

London, 1865

Hollis Darby learned two things at the knee of his not-so-dear, long-departed, low-life, scoundrel of a father: how to gamble beyond what was advisable and how to be an utter disappointment to his family. He'd long ago given up cards. But, if his brother's ongoing rant was any indication, he continued to excel at being a disaster of a relative.

"Even in the leanest of times," Randolph continued, "a gentleman does not sink to some levels."

"Would those 'levels' exclude things such as having food to eat, clothing to wear . . . unacceptable behavior like that?" Hollis's brother had been harping on this particular topic from the moment they'd climbed into the carriage together.

Randolph's face twisted into the patient expression he'd perfected in their childhood. "I am not suggesting you cannot find means of supporting yourself. But there are some methods of doing so that would not bear scrutiny."

"Such as?" Hollis drawled a touch too innocently, but

he'd found playing the fool made his brother's posturing more bearable.

"Do you truly need me to delineate the acceptable professions for a gentleman?" Randolph skewered him with a look of utter annoyance.

Hollis popped up his gloved fingers, counting off options. "Making speeches in Parliament. Firing cannons during war. Something to do with horses."

"Do not be obtuse." Randolph swayed with the rattling of the carriage. "You receive no subsistence from the family coffers—those have been empty all our lives—and Society knows you haven't been secretary to Lord Whitley for at least a year now."

Two years, actually. The offer to come to London with Lord Whitley ten years earlier had been a godsend. Hollis had been nineteen, with no money for Cambridge, no place to go to escape his broken family, no desire to keep gambling for money to live on. Dogging Whitley's heels, Hollis had made connections and avoided starvation, all while keeping himself away from the card tables.

"Whitley has a secretary," Hollis said. "I believe his name is Carlton or Hepsworth or Nithercott. I can't ever keep those three straight."

"Those names are nothing alike." Randolph's gaze narrowed a moment before understanding filled his eyes and he shook his head. "Why do you always insist on jests when I am attempting to have an important discussion?"

"My apologies." He held back the bit of theatrical puffery he'd have liked to have tossed in.

"I have reason for concern regarding your public

activities," Randolph said. "This family's name has not precisely been free of stain these past years."

"These past *generations*," Hollis corrected.

Randolph ignored him and pressed on. "I am attempting to restore it and our fortunes at the same time. I cannot have even the slightest hope of success if you are undermining my efforts."

"Have you heard even the quietest whisper of scandal around me, Randolph?"

"I've heard plenty enough speculation." Randolph pulled his watch from his waistcoat pocket. "I'm to have luncheon with Barty Simmons at our club. He has the ear of a great many in Society. Wouldn't hurt the family cause to have you join us."

Hollis shook his head. "I have other obligations this afternoon."

"Why is it you always have other obligations when I'm going to the club?"

"Why is it you're always going to your club when I have other obligations?" He asked the question as if he were entirely in earnest.

Randolph was not put off his topic. "We're a legacy family at White's."

"Not all legacies demand preservation."

The carriage slowed, though not, as far as Hollis could tell, because of the press of traffic. "We must be approaching Hatchards." He snatched his hat from the bench beside him. "A thousand thank-yous, dear brother, for dropping me here."

"You would prefer an afternoon at a bookshop to one at a gentlemen's club?"

"Infinitely." Hollis moved to the end of the bench just as the carriage door opened. "Enjoy your very important luncheon."

"At least consider helping me restore this family's good name and standing," Randolph said as Hollis stepped down onto the walk. "My children's future depends upon it. All I ask is that you not do anything for which Eloise or Addison will suffer."

"I would never do anything to hurt my niece and nephew; I think you know that."

Some of Randolph's bluster died down. "I'm fighting an uphill battle; I think *you* know that."

Hollis popped his hat on his head. "I'll be the very portrait of propriety." As tedious as that would be.

Randolph looked the tiniest bit mollified. "You'll come take dinner with us soon?"

Hollis dipped his head in acknowledgment before motioning for the carriage door to be closed. He stood on the walk as the carriage rolled away down Piccadilly and turned off the street.

Free of his brother's scrutiny, Hollis walked with casual haste away from the bookshop. Hatchards was a fine place to spend an afternoon, but it was not actually his destination.

Randolph worried that Hollis might be involved in a profession that would cast a shadow on the family reputation. *Oh, Randolph. You ought to be fretting about so much more than that.*

Hollis pulled a penny from his pocket and spun it in

his fingers as he moved leisurely in the direction of Covent Garden. He had time enough to make his way at a pace that wouldn't draw notice.

Mongers hawked their wares. Customers with a few coins to rub together wandered in and out of the shops. A good number of people had, either in their hands or in their pockets, the familiar "penny dreadfuls"—serial stories sold for a penny and exceedingly popular among the poor and working class. They were considered a scandalous choice among the upper crust, one few admitted to but many indulged in.

Onward he went, spinning his penny, keenly aware of anyone and everyone around him. He would appear to them as a gentleman of means, of indifference, never knowing he tracked them like a pickpocket in a crowd of unguarded purses.

Among the penny serials, he spotted a good number sporting the teal cover of Mr. King's latest work. King was, in a bit of fitting name-play, the reigning monarch of the genre. Hollis also saw a smattering of the first installment of a new series by Lafayette Jones, a particular favorite of his.

He stopped and purchased a copy for himself. That'd put some truth to the bald-faced cropper he'd told Randolph about how he meant to spend his day. He tucked the light-weight booklet in his interior jacket pocket, keeping it hidden from prying eyes. They would see what he wanted them to see. Nothing more.

He kept his demeanor casual but his eyes sharp. He didn't usually get this close to his destination without spotting others tossing or spinning pennies about. It was a sign, an identifier, a calling card among them.

He didn't see any. *Hang it.* He'd be skinned if he was late.

Hollis turned up the steps of what, to a passerby, would look like an unassuming London townhome with an ordinary blue door. It wasn't locked; it never was on these crucial days. The entryway looked a bit shoddy compared to the polished stone floor and carved columns of his family's London home. Father had managed to complete the Darbys' descent into bankruptcy, but at least he hadn't taken a crowbar to the old place and sold it by bits. The vestibule was unexceptional. The sleeping butler, though, was an oddity.

Hollis laid the penny he had been spinning in his hand on the walnut end table alongside at least a dozen others.

The butler, head still hanging and heavy with sleep, reached out and pressed a specific flower in the decorative molding. The first time Hollis had seen the butler press that flower, triggering a nearby door to open all on its own, he'd been speechless. The wonder of it had faded over the years.

He moved with quick step into what, in any other home, would've been a parlor or sitting room or something painfully boring like that. Here, it was a small-scale recreation of the House of Commons. The room was abuzz, but the meeting hadn't started. He wouldn't be chewed up and spit out for tardiness. Not this time.

Brogan Donnelly greeted him as Hollis moved toward his usual seat. "I'd nearly given you up. 'Tisn't like you being the last to arrive."

"I didn't have the sun shining off your fiery hair lighting my way," he said.

Brogan shrugged. "I offered m'services to those who

came when they were meant to. Couldn't laze about waiting on you."

"My brother offered to drop me wherever I was going," Hollis said. "I had to formulate a likely story and destination that wouldn't garner suspicion."

"Where'd you choose, then? The 'I Don't Belong to a Secret Society of Renegades' shop? I hear one recently opened on the Strand."

Hollis sighed dramatically. "If only I'd thought of that. I chose Hatchards."

"A shame."

Fletcher Walker, Hollis's closest friend and the acting head of this organization, known amongst themselves and in whispered speculation around Town as "The Dread Penny Society," called out over the cacophony of voices. "Order, mates! Order."

With a degree of swagger even an American would have been hard-pressed to emulate, the membership made their way to their various seats. Fletcher, as always, occupied the throne that sat in the midst of them.

The society's newest member sat directly across from Hollis. Elizabeth Black, who wrote under the *nom de plume* "Mr. King," had made the most memorable application for membership in the history of the Dread Penny Society—cloaked in confidence and clad in trousers—and she had proven herself an invaluable addition during the two months she'd been one of them.

"With me," Fletcher instructed.

Every meeting began with a recitation of the society's oath: "For the poor and infirm, the hopeless and voiceless, we do not relent. We do not forget. We are the Dread Penny Society."

Fletcher sat with either elbow on a chair arm, his fingers entwined. "Penny for your thoughts, gen'lmen"—he tossed a flirtatious look to Elizabeth, the two of them being sweethearts—"and lady."

Elizabeth took the floor first. "The Barton School for Girls is open and running smoothly, but it will still need an influx of funds if it is to remain in operation. I'd like to see us secure another donor or two."

The Dreadfuls supported a lot of causes, but education was Hollis's personal passion. The Barton school focused on vocational training for young girls, many of whom the Dreadfuls had rescued from being forced into less savory occupations.

Fletcher turned his attention on Hollis. "Squeezing money out of the fine and fancy—that's why we keep you around."

Blast it if that wasn't truer than he wished it were. Until Elizabeth had joined, he'd been the only Dreadful with connections among the well-to-do. He regularly got the symbolic pat on the head as he was sent off to do the namby-pamby work the others were too rough-and-tough to bother with.

"My sister-in-law mentioned a musicale hosted by the Kennards," he said.

"What're the chances you'll know anyone there?" Fletcher asked.

Brogan jumped in. "Better'n the chances *you* would."

The group laughed. Fletcher took it in stride, as always.

"Thompson will likely be there," Hollis said. "He might

consider patronizing the Barton school. Lewiston might as well."

"I, too, received an invitation," Elizabeth said. "I might know some of those Hollis doesn't, though musical evenings aren't precisely my specialty."

"They're not mine, either," Hollis said.

A rare bit of quiet settled on the group as they all pondered the best means of chewing the fat with potential donors without drawing too much attention to their activities. Secrecy kept them in business. Kept them alive at times, too.

Stone spoke, which was a rare enough thing to draw the group's attention. He was only known by that single name, and other than having been a slave in America's South, no one knew anything about his past. Little was known of his present. But when Stone spoke, everyone listened.

"Convince Miss Newport to perform," he said.

Everyone looked to Elizabeth. Miss Newport was the music teacher at her school.

"An excellent suggestion," Elizabeth said.

"Brilliant," Fletcher said. "The four of us will see if we can't squeeze a few society types for a healthy stack of loot." To the room, he said again, "Penny for your thoughts."

Kumar spoke up. He had been born in India but had lived the entirety of his adult life in London. The penny serials he wrote were set in the land of his birth. That he never portrayed his fellow countrymen as caricatures or simpletons, shallow villains or helpless victims like far too many English writers did when setting stories in India made his stories all the more important and needed.

"Martin spotted our tiny thief," he said. "She was

slipping out of a house in Mayfair. Police haven't caught her yet, but neither have we."

The Dreadfuls had gotten wind of a small girl undertaking thefts at the homes of the upper class. Their estimations put her at eight or nine years old. They knew the Metropolitan Police were keen on apprehending her, but the DPS was determined to catch her first and give her a chance at a better life.

The business of searching out a slippery London urchin was discussed, though no strategy was formed other than keeping their eyes peeled and ears open. Other matters were discussed, everything from previous missions to whispers of criminal activity, from employment opportunities for some of the children they'd rescued to what supplies were needed at the schools for which they were silent patrons. Through it all, Hollis's thoughts never strayed from the upcoming musicale, but not because of his assignment.

Ana Newport would be in attendance. Ana Newport.

He'd met her months earlier when calling at Elizabeth's school. Though he would never have admitted it out loud, he'd been almost immediately smitten with the sweet-natured music teacher. He'd been by the school a few times since but received little more than a very kind, very vague greeting.

Spending an evening in her company would be both wonderful and torturous.

The DPS meeting wound to a close. Rather than wander back to his flat, Hollis retreated upstairs to the library. Dropping into a leather chair near the window, he pulled the penny dreadful he'd purchased earlier from his jacket pocket.

Holding one of Lafayette Jones's stories in its final form

hadn't yet stopped being a first-rate feeling. Randolph would be troubled if he knew his brother spent his days reading such uncivilized literature, especially considering Jones's work was meant more for children, and *working-class* children at that. Yes, Randolph would not like knowing Hollis had read it.

He grinned a touch wickedly. If only Randolph knew Hollis had *written* it.

HIGGLEBOTTOM'S SCHOOL FOR THE DEAD

A GHOST OF A CHANCE

by Lafayette Jones

Chapter I

Ace Bowen had been a student at Higglebottom's School for the Dead for a few months and was quickly becoming the school's most legendary pupil. He was learning the art of being a ghost faster than anyone before him, and he did it with flair.

He walked the corridors of Higglebottom's with an otherworldly strut. Ghosts *could* walk, no matter that the living seemed to think all they did was float. Floating, in fact, was more difficult.

The other students always waved to him as he passed. The staff shook their ghostly heads in amusement. He was the life of the school, so to speak. He, along with his friends, Bathwater and Snout, was also the source of most of its mischief.

"Pouring ink into the laundry cauldron so the haunting shrouds all turned light-blue. Tightening all the floorboards so none squeaked during the Third Form's 'Ghost Walking' exams." Professor Rattlebag had been listing the boys' pranks. He wasn't likely to finish before the end of the dinner hour. "Teaching the school parrot to mimic the sound of rattling chains so Professor Dankworth could not be heard during her 'Disguise Ghost Conversations with Sundry Sounds' lesson."

Oh, the parrot could mimic more sounds than just chains. Bathwater sputtered, trying to hold back a laugh. Ace lounged in a chair that wasn't there—a skill most students didn't master until at least Third Form.

"I think it best you three go directly to your dormitory," Rattlebag said. "There will be no dinner for you."

Skipping dinner wasn't much of a punishment as ghosts did not actually need to eat, but learning to pretend as if they did proved helpful when wanting to go unnoticed amongst hungry Perishables.

The boys rose and made their way toward the office door. Ace aimed his path toward the wall.

"Not through the wall, Mr. Bowen," Rattlebag said, sounding far too tired for a ghost who'd not needed sleep in nearly a millennium. "You haven't mastered the skill yet. Nurse Snodsbury was quite put out the last time she had to reassemble you."

Willing to save Snodsbury a bit of bother, Ace passed through the open door with his ghostly feet a few inches off the floor, another skill a First Form was not meant to have mastered.

No, Higglebottom's had never seen a student quite like him.

"Rattlebag has no sense of humor," Snout said as they walked toward their dormitory. "Those gags were brilliant."

Bathwater shrugged. "Maybe things stop being funny after you've been dead nine hundred years."

"Rattlebag certainly stopped being funny," Ace said.

They all laughed, not the least worried about punishments or expulsion. The teachers liked them, despite the havoc they wreaked.

"Two weeks until the Spirit Trials," Snout said. "Do you mean to ask Cropper to join our team?"

Ace was considering it. They needed a crack team for that term's trials.

For eight hundred years, school terms at Higglebottom's School for the Dead had ended with the Spirit Trials, a series of tests in which the students demonstrated all they had learned about being a proper ghost. A high enough score allowed the winning team to advance to the next Form early.

Ace was bored to death, as it were, of First Form studies. "Cropper's whip smart. But he's not a lot of fun."

Bathwater attempted to sit in an absent chair but mismanaged the thing, spilling onto and partway through the floor. "I guess I'm not so whip smart, myself," he said, pulling himself up with some effort. He managed to not leave any bits of himself behind.

Snout eyed Ace with curiosity. "Would you rather have a diverting teammate or a helpful one?"

"The three of us could do well enough to at least pass the Spirit Trials," Ace said. "Might as well have a lark doing it."

"Even if it means not skipping to Form Two?" Bathwater asked.

If ghosts had actual hearts, Ace's would've dropped

a bit at that question. He wanted to be challenged at Higglebottom's. But he'd not had much time for larks and absurdity in life. He meant to enjoy a hardy helping of both in the afterlife.

"If we don't qualify to skip ahead early, we can make the most of our final term in Form One."

"Rattlebag might advance us anyway," Snout said. "Anything to get us out of his classes."

"All the more reason to make certain the Spirit Trials are a highlight."

"Are you aiming for more mischief?" Bathwater sounded worried. Though he enjoyed their mischief and joined in eagerly, he did worry a bit over it.

"You bet your afterlife, I am."

Somewhere in the room something thudded, a common sound in a school full of ghosts learning to be proper haunters. But nothing had fallen or shifted or lay in a heap.

"What was that?" Bathwater asked.

"I don't know, but I mean to find out." Ace floated—a bit of showing off helped build a touch of confidence—to the noisy side of the room.

Nothing seemed amiss.

Then the bed skirt rustled. The wind wasn't blowing outside the ancient school. No one in the room was practicing making a draft.

Ace knelt on the floor, careful not to slip through, and peered under the bed, directly into the eyes of a boy. But not just any boy.

A *living* one.

CHAPTER 2

Ana Newport had attended very few Society gatherings in the past two years, and none away from Thurloe Collegiate School, where she was a teacher. She took a deep, reassuring breath as she waited to depart for a musicale.

"You needn't be worried, Ana," Elizabeth said. "You will play your violin beautifully and win the hearts of everyone there tonight."

That was not at all the reason for her nervousness, but it was a reason she could admit to. "I haven't played in public in years. And I'm hardly a regular on Society's guest list."

"Well, you're on this one," Elizabeth said.

At first, Ana had refused Elizabeth's suggestion that she attend. Society had not been kind when her family's fortunes had turned. That made her wary. But Elizabeth had let slip that Mrs. Sudworth would be in attendance, and there was no question of refusing after that. Ana needed to be there if that terrible, horrid, wretched woman was.

A knock sounded at the door. Elizabeth hadn't moved

far from the door in the past fifteen minutes, waiting for the gentlemen who were accompanying them that night.

A moment later, the men stepped inside. Fletcher Walker was a well-known author of penny dreadfuls, who had managed to gain something of a foothold in Society despite having spent his early life in the gutters. His close friend, Hollis Darby, came from an "old money" family. They'd been part of the upper crust for generations, and he was precisely the sort of refined and intimidating gentleman she'd been in awe of when she had still been part of that world, young and starry-eyed and naive.

Mr. Walker pulled Elizabeth into an embrace the moment the door was closed behind him. "I've missed you, dove."

"If you came by more often, you wouldn't have to miss me." Elizabeth threaded her fingers through his but addressed both of the gentlemen. "Shall we be on our way?"

Before Ana could take more than one step toward the door, however, Mr. Darby held out his hand. "Please, allow me to carry your violin. I promise to be very careful with it."

He was always the perfect gentleman. How well she remembered the strict propriety of those of his standing. She remembered nearly as well how hypocritical that often proved.

"I know it ain't proper," Mr. Walker said to the group as they approached the waiting hackney, "but I'd much prefer to sit with Elizabeth." He eyed Ana and Mr. Darby with an undeniably charming bit of pleading. "Have a heart? Do a bloke a favor?"

"I will not impose upon Miss Newport," Mr. Darby said.

"And neither should you, no matter your wish for a bit of sparking."

"If they are going to be sparking, I don't know that I want them in the same carriage regardless of where they're sitting," Ana said.

Mr. Darby smiled at her humor. No matter that he occupied an elevated rung on the ladder of Society, he had a way of setting her at ease.

"I will not be made uncomfortable by the arrangement Mr. Walker suggested," Ana said.

"Capital." Mr. Walker grinned.

They were soon inside and settled, and the hackney began its journey to the evening's destination. Across the carriage, Elizabeth and Mr. Walker spoke quietly, their heads pressed together. Mr. Darby sat beside Ana, her violin held carefully on his lap.

"I hope you will forgive me if this proves a bit of nosiness," he said, "but you seem anxious."

"I am." She clasped her gloved hands. "I have not been out in Society in years. And I've not played any instrument outside of Thurloe in at least that long. I have every expectation of things going terribly wrong tonight."

"I, for one, have every hope the evening will go wonderfully right." His voice was so soothing and calm, so very reassuring. "I cannot think of anyone more perfectly suited for a musicale. You won't want for topics to discuss, as music is your area of expertise. And you will impress all in attendance with your talent."

"You have never heard me play," she answered, amused. "I might be terrible at it."

His smile, dimly lit by the late-evening sun, blossomed. "Miss Black speaks very highly of your skills. I am not nearly brave enough to question her reliability."

Ana hazarded a glance across the way. Elizabeth and her beau weren't paying them the least heed. "She has been very kind to me."

"I cannot imagine anyone being anything but kind to you."

She didn't need to imagine it. Her family had once occupied a minor place amongst the influential. They were newly accepted in Society, not for their standing but for their growing wealth. Her mother had possessed flawless manners and grace. Father had been the epitome of a gentleman despite having earned his fortune. All of that had disappeared in an instant. The Society peacocks had turned to vultures.

"Merciful heavens, Miss Newport. You're growing paler by the moment."

She tried to smile, but the memories were not pleasant ones. "My family suffered a reversal of fortunes a few years ago. Based on how we were treated at the time, I am not entirely confident of my reception tonight."

"Society is a fickle beast." He leaned closer, though not so close as to be inappropriate. "I will be nearby all evening. Should anyone treat you with any degree of unkindness, I will gladly intervene on your behalf."

She could not afford to have anyone dogging her heels the entire evening. A lighthearted response would likely gain her a bit of freedom. "Perhaps we should engage Mr. Walker's help should fisticuffs be necessary."

Mr. Darby smiled at her once more. She did like his

smile; it was genuine and kind. "He would not need to be asked twice."

"How is it you came to be friends?" The two men were so drastically different.

"We met quite by accident and found we got on well. The rest simply happened."

"Are you the reason he goes about in Society?" she asked. "He wasn't born to it."

Anyone hearing Mr. Walker speak could easily sort his low origins.

"I suppose I am," Mr. Darby answered. "He was a good friend to me when I needed one. I hope I've proven the same to him."

From across the carriage, Mr. Walker answered. "You're certainly my *loudest* friend."

Good-natured as always, Mr. Darby grinned. "I wasn't being as stealthy as I thought, apparently."

"You could learn a thing or two from my literary works." Mr. Walker said the last two words with an impressive impersonation of an upper-class accent. "Quite the sneaky chaps, my characters."

"And they're children," Ana said. "Surely Mr. Darby wouldn't be bested by two little boys."

Everyone turned to her, including Elizabeth. "You've read Fletcher's penny dreadfuls?"

From any other employer, the question would have been filled with reprimand, but Ana happened to know her very exceptional friend and employer didn't disapprove of the low literature. "I have read them. I enjoy them, in fact."

"Do you read others?" Mr. Darby asked.

"A few. The daring adventures written by the author known as Stone. I haven't yet read the newest offering from Lafayette Jones, but I've heard it is delightful."

Elizabeth smiled. To the gentlemen, she explained, "We have several students who are fond of his and Mr. King's works."

"Everyone is fond of Mr. King's stories," Ana said. "I see them being read everywhere."

"If Mr. King weren't so blasted talented, I'd be fully jealous," Mr. Walker said. "But the fella can spin a tale."

The hackney came to a stop at their destination. Talk of authors and stories had distracted Ana for a moment, but now her nerves returned fully.

She was handed down from the carriage. Mr. Darby joined her in the next moment, her violin case still in his hand. He offered his free arm, and she wove hers through it.

The music room of the fine house was full to bursting. Mr. Darby did not abandon her. He walked with her to their hostess and made a charming and proper introduction.

"Ah, yes, Miss Newport," Mrs. Kennard said. "Miss Black said you would be favoring us with a performance."

"I will do my utmost to not be a disappointment."

Mrs. Kennard elegantly waved that off. "Your abilities are well spoken of by those whose word can be trusted."

"Miss Black is too kind," Ana said.

"Mr. Headley told me of your talent as well."

Mr. Headley. That was unexpected. He had, at one time, been a suitor of Elizabeth's, before she had revealed her preference for Mr. Walker. In all Mr. Headley's visits, he'd never shown himself to have taken the least notice of *her*.

"Thank you for inviting me this evening, Mrs. Kennard," Mr. Darby said.

"Of course. Perhaps in the future, you might convince your brother and sister-in-law to attend."

Mr. Darby dipped his head. "I will do my best to convince them."

A bit of tension touched the promise. Had Mrs. Kennard noticed? She didn't appear to.

Ana took a seat beside Elizabeth, waiting her turn to perform. Several others were called upon before she was: two young ladies on the pianoforte, another on the harp, a young gentleman on the cello, and an older gentleman who sang a fine rendition of a Mozart aria.

Then it was her turn. Elizabeth gave her arm an encouraging squeeze. The gathered attendees applauded politely as was expected. Mrs. Kennard waited in front of the group for Ana to join her.

After a quick check of the strings to make certain her violin was in tune, Ana gave Mrs. Kennard a nod. In an instant, she stood alone before them all. Her gaze met Mr. Darby's. He dipped his head almost imperceptibly and smiled reassuringly.

She set her violin on her shoulder and rested her chin in place. Her selection for the evening was a portion of Beethoven's Violin Concerto in D Major. She knew it well enough that she hardly needed to think in order to play, and the tune wasn't so emotive as to be scandalous nor so staid as to be boring.

As she played, she clandestinely searched the crowd for Mrs. Sudworth. One row at a time, she checked each face.

Near the end of the piece, Ana saw the woman she was looking for. Mrs. Sudworth sat nearer the back of the room where the chandelier light sparkled off the many jewels she wore. Ana remembered how that ghastly woman would trot out her entire collection of gemstones any time she was in Society. The result was far more gaudy than impressive, but no one doubted for a moment that the woman was wealthy. And Mrs. Sudworth never doubted that she was above her company.

She likely didn't even remember Ana or the harm she'd done to Ana's family. But Ana remembered. And that memory had brought her here tonight.

Ana finished her piece almost without realizing it. That's what came of choosing a selection she didn't have to pay attention to. The attendees applauded politely. She offered a curtsey and a smile before resuming her seat.

Elizabeth leaned closer. "Beautifully played."

"Thank you." Ana took a tight breath. Everyone would likely think it was a release of nerves, but her uneasiness was only just beginning.

From the other side of Mr. Walker, who sat beside Elizabeth, Mr. Darby leaned forward enough to meet her eye.

"Lovely." He mouthed the word, but she could clearly make it out.

She smiled her gratitude, and relaxed. Though Mr. Darby didn't know the entirety of what weighed on her, his support proved deeply reassuring.

The remaining performers were quite good, their selections pleasing and well-executed. At the conclusion of the performances, the gathering rose from their seats and began mingling as they made their way to the refreshment table.

Ana kept a tight hold on her violin case—she would need it—and made her way purposefully but unobtrusively to where Mrs. Sudworth had been sitting. Her quarry had risen along with the rest of the attendees but hadn't gone far.

A diamond necklace sparkled above her neckline. Rings adorned nearly every finger. A silver bracelet sat amongst a half dozen pearl ones. Gems even glittered in her hair. She could have been made a permanent exhibit in the Tower of London directly beside the Crown Jewels and would not have looked out of place.

The woman noticed her and offered a quick, clearly rehearsed smile.

Ana curtseyed. "Mrs. Sudworth."

No recognition touched the woman's face. Not even the tiniest glint of familiarity. This woman had actively participated in the destruction of Ana's family. Did she not remember her even the tiniest bit?

That was for the best, really.

"You played well," Mrs. Sudworth said, dipping her head before turning her attention pointedly to her more distinguished companions.

"Forgive me for the interruption," Ana said quietly and attempted to step around the group.

She bumped into Mrs. Sudworth, however, and not a light brush as she passed. Looks of disapproval and near disgust were cast at her, along with wrinkled noses and pursed lips.

Ana quickly regained her balance, offered a quick curtsey

and a barely audible plea for forgiveness, before rushing off. She found a quiet corner of the room and sat, her violin case on her lap. Mr. Darby found her there a moment later.

"You seem to have become separated from us in the press." He looked more closely at her. "Are you unwell? You seem shaken."

"I bumped into someone. The crowd was too close. I suppose I'm a little embarrassed. And I likely should check that my violin was not damaged."

"Make your inspection," he said. "I'll fetch you a glass of punch."

He was such a kind man. Thoughtful and generous. And he seemed to think well of her, which she likely ought not.

As he slipped from view, Ana opened her violin case. It was the perfect excuse and the perfect pretense. She opened the small compartment where she stored her rosin and her polishing cloth. She tucked underneath them what she'd come to this musicale for and had, by a near miracle, managed to secure: a single silver bracelet.

CHAPTER 3

Perhaps we should engage Mr. Walker's help should fisticuffs be necessary. Miss Newport's words from the evening before repeated in Hollis's mind as he trudged down Garrick Street toward Covent Garden. Boxing was not considered an ungentlemanly pursuit. Why, then, had Miss Newport assumed he would be inept at it? Fletcher was more obviously rough-and-tough, but Hollis could hold his own. Perhaps a round or two in the boxing salon at headquarters would put a bit of puff back in his pride. But first, he had a mission to undertake.

He spied Stone rounding the opposite corner. Hollis had bested Fletcher any number of times in the Dreadfuls' boxing salon, but no one bested Stone.

Hollis and Stone came up even with one another.

"Fine day," Hollis said.

"Care for a walk around the market?" Stone was not a man of many words. Speaking seven together at once was unusual for him.

"I'd fancy a stroll." Hollis matched his stride.

This was not one of those missions which required the Dreadfuls to not be seen together. Stone had determined this particular task was best accomplished in as simple and direct a way as possible.

"After a late night, my legs could use a bit of a jaunt to finish waking up this morning," Hollis said.

"Y'all shouldn't stay out so late."

"But if the evening is a fruitful one, the long hours are well worth it."

They made an odd pair walking into the Covent Garden marketplace. London was not entirely without a diversity of appearances and accents, allowing Stone, despite his words heavily flavored with the sound of America's South and his ancestry obvious at a glance, to not draw as much attention as he might have in a tiny hamlet tucked far from the roar of the metropolis. Yet, gentry coves—gentlemen of Hollis's station—weren't known for applauding that diversity.

"Was your evenin' fruitful?" Stone asked.

"Not in the expected way," Hollis said. "I'd hoped to see a couple of friends there, but they weren't in attendance."

The Dreadfuls were adept at discussing their secret activities without giving anything away. They could manage it even in a crowded marketplace.

"My friends' absence seemed to strike most in attendance as odd," Hollis added.

There was no verbal response; Hollis hadn't expected one. Stone simply walked beside him, hands tucked in the pockets of his navy-blue tailcoat, eyes focused ahead, mouth drawn in a tight line.

"One was meant to attend with his wife, but she wasn't there, either."

Stone's expression didn't change even the tiniest bit, but Hollis knew he was listening.

"Our poor hostess was baffled," Hollis said. "A few other people noted the absences as well."

"Unfortunate for you," Stone said.

From the other direction, Fletcher came walking toward them. The DPS generally avoided having three Dreadfuls out and about together, but fortunately, Hollis and Fletcher's friendship was well-known, which would make their greeting one another unremarkable.

"Well met." Hollis kept his tone light and unconcerned.

Fletcher held up the small bouquet of slightly wilted flowers in his hand. "Thought I'd take this humble offering to my lady love. Bought it off a little one not far from here."

Ah. One of Fletcher's rescued children, no doubt. He'd dedicated himself to saving London's urchins from the horrors he, himself, had lived through. In the process, he'd created a complex network of street children who kept their eyes open and their ears to the ground and told him anything he needed to know.

"Did you get your penny's worth?" Hollis asked, nodding toward the flowers.

"Got myself a *shilling's* worth." Fletcher walked with them. "My flower girl spotted our good friend Alistair, who disappointed Mrs. Kennard last night."

Hollis jumped in. "Another friend who was absent," he told Stone in a low voice.

The term "friend" was, of course, code. Most patrons

they sought were mere acquaintances. Alistair Headley fell more in the category of nuisance.

"Seems he's been seen about with Four-Finger Mike again, still up to his neck in something rotten," Fletcher continued. "That foozler has his fingers in a couple of rancid pies."

"And I'd guess gambling is part of the putrid recipe," Hollis said.

They'd discovered that gambling was not Headley's only questionable activity. He fraternized with a known criminal, Four-Finger Mike, who added to his list of crimes on a daily basis and had escaped police custody repeatedly.

"Perhaps Headley missed the musicale because he was at one of Four-Finger's gambling dens," Hollis said.

"Or up to somethin' worse." Fletcher's look was too pointed for the remark to have been offhand. "Monsieur Thorn-in-Our-Side is frequenting lower and lower places, but he ain't making his jaunts all by his lonesome."

"Who is he with?" Hollis asked.

"That's the million-guinea question, ain't it?"

Headley was connected to Four-Finger Mike, who was, in turn, connected to the notorious criminal mastermind, the Mastiff, a man even the police feared. Four-Finger's associations made Headley a source of suspicion.

"Maybe we need to walk on the man's heels a bit," Hollis said.

Fletcher shook his head. "You keep an ear to the ground in your circles. Leave the tailing to us."

"I think I've proven myself able to hold my own." He was

forever being relegated to the role of observer-at-a-distance. He knew he could be more, and it was time they let him.

"Headley frequents rungs on the Ladder of Importance above the rest of us," Fletcher said. "You're the only one with access."

Yes, but that didn't have to be the limit of his contribution. "In the meantime, though—"

"Flexing muscles don't do us a lick of good if we cain't follow through," Fletcher said.

A frustrating answer. "Maybe I could make a suggestion to the Dread Master."

Their organization was run behind-the-scenes by a man known only as the Dread Master. Fletcher alone knew his actual identity. He answered to the mysterious man—they all did—but he steadfastly refused to reveal who the Dread Master was. Hollis was Fletcher's best friend in all the world, and even he'd not been let in on the secret.

"I'll ask him," Fletcher said. "Meanwhile, best snuggle up to the fine and fancy. See what you can learn."

Hollis met Stone's eye but found no empathy there. He'd learned over the years that it did little good to press a matter if the majority of Dreadfuls present weren't on the same page. "Since our two friends were out of reach last evening, we're still short our goal for the Barton school. Shall we try again?"

Fletcher gave it a moment's thought before nodding. "See if you can sniff out another gathering they've been invited to and get yourself on the guest list."

Getting invited to parties—that was Fletcher's highly important role for Hollis. The others thwarted criminals, saved lives, uncovered vast and dangerous plots. He went to parties.

Pathetic.

"And if someone's being robbed at the next one, try to notice," Stone said.

Fletcher looked as confused as Hollis felt.

"Mrs. Sudworth claims a silver bracelet of hers got filched from right off her wrist."

"How could she tell?" Fletcher asked dryly.

Stone didn't appear to understand.

"Jewelry drips off that woman like water off a dog in a rainstorm," Fletcher explained.

Stone turned his attention to Hollis and, motioning to Fletcher with his head, said, "The reason he ain't invited nowhere."

"Fletch, you can't compare a lady to a dog."

Fletcher brushed that off with a smirk.

"She's sure the bracelet was stolen during the musicale?" Hollis pressed. "It seems more likely she simply thought she'd put the bracelet on but didn't. It's probably at her house."

"She says it ain't."

"Where does Mrs. Sudworth live?" Fletcher asked.

"Portland Place." Hollis was not merely their resident party attender, he was also their address book of the influential.

"And where did we last track our little thiefling?" Fletcher asked.

"Marylebone," Stone said.

In near perfect unison, they all nodded. Portland Place happened to be in the Marylebone area.

"We have to find that girl." Fletcher never sounded more worried than he did when fretting over one of his urchins.

"Getting more notice?" Stone asked.

Fletcher nodded. "My urchins are calling her the Phantom Fox. Slipping in and out of even the busiest fine houses, making off with jewels and silver snuffboxes. Never gets caught. Never even gets seen. The baby girl's good, but she's frying fish too big for her pan, and she's going to get burned."

Stone motioned ahead of them with a jut of his chin. "Our mark."

Huddled beside a fishmonger's cart, a ragged urchin, likely not yet seven years old, sat with his head hung, not looking at anyone who passed. They'd heard, thanks to the gossip of a few different muffin-wallopers and tea-talkers, that he was being starved and beaten by the monger who'd obtained him as an unpaid work boy. The law let masters treat their apprentices as badly as they chose. The Dreadfuls allowed no such thing.

Stone wandered down a side path, serving as lookout. Fletcher browsed the flowers on a nearby cart. Hollis approached the fishmonger, assuming an air of importance and prosperity. He eyed the fish with a critical eye.

"I've a fine catch this morning," the man said, motioning to a collection of river eel too slimy to have been caught within the last twenty-four hours. Hollis would be making no purchase, and not merely because his purpose in the mission was to distract the man.

"Anything other than eel?" he asked. "I'm not certain I trust eel from the Thames. It always seems to leave me green around the gills, as it were."

"Not *my* eels, guv'nuh."

"Tell me about them." It was not a request. Until he'd been required to "play" the role of fine gentleman, Hollis hadn't realized what a collection of puffed-up peacocks his fellow rung dwellers really were.

Beside him, Fletcher had hunched down next to the ragged child, completely hidden from the fishmonger's view. Fletcher had a way with the children. He had once been an urchin himself, after all. If Hollis kept the boy's master distracted long enough, Fletcher would slip him away. Stone would hang behind to make certain they weren't followed. Hollis would depart in a different direction.

While the scraggly man, whose odor rivaled that of his goods, waxed oddly poetic about his putrid fish, Hollis kept track of the others. Fletcher made off with the little boy during the portion of Hollis's eel-choosing lesson that covered the importance of bait. Stone followed their path as Hollis was learning about the man's theory on keeping fresh-caught fish fresh, the efficacy of which was called into question by the contents of his own cart.

"I will consider it." Hollis dropped the disingenuous remark—he'd also come to a harsh realization of how dishonest upper-class people could be—and went on his way. He'd every intention of exiting the market and doubling back to headquarters to debrief with Stone since Fletcher would be gone for a while taking the little boy to one of their safe houses.

But he didn't get that far. Randolph along with his wife, Cora, and their children, Eloise and Addison, were standing among the flower carts directly between him and his path out. It was a good thing Hollis was alone. His brother knew of and grudgingly accepted his friendship with Fletcher but had made clear his preference that his wife and children not be "exposed" to Fletcher's less-than-pristine manners and style of speaking. Heaven only knew what his reaction would be to Stone. Hollis didn't particularly care to find out.

He slipped a coin to the first flower seller he passed and purchased a small handful of pansies. With quick and quiet step, he managed to sneak up on his eight-year-old niece. Bending low enough to be nearly eye level with her, he offered the flowers. "For you, my dear."

"Uncle Hollis!" She wrapped her arms around his neck. "I asked Father 'Do you suppose we'll see Uncle Hollis at Covent Garden?' and he said he did not believe we would. But I knew we would. I knew!"

Hollis slipped her arms free of his neck and placed the pansies in her hand. He took her other hand in his own. "Seems to me, dear brother, you ought to have greater faith in your daughter's ability to predict the future."

Eloise had been a favorite of his ever since she was a baby. She had the Darby stubbornness but a healthy dose of her mother's more contemplative side.

"How are you, Hollis?" Cora asked. "I've not seen you this age."

"Randolph already scolded me for neglecting to come for dinner. I do intend to rectify that, I promise you." He looked to Eloise once more. "I attended a musicale last evening, and do you know what I thought to myself again and again?"

"What?"

"That, given ten years or so, I would be sitting in a fine room like that listening to my Eloise play music for everyone." He leaned closer. "Have you been practicing as your governess asked?"

"Miss Dowling has no musical ability." Eloise made the observation with the unmistakable inflection of someone repeating something they'd heard said a few times.

His gaze shifted to the girl's parents. Randolph nodded subtly but unmistakably, motioning them onward, toward the nearest end of the market. Little Addison walked with his hand firmly held by his mother. Hollis kept Eloise at his side.

"Miss Dowling is an excellent governess, but she is rather hopeless at musical instruction," Cora said. "I suppose we will have little choice but to employ a musical tutor."

The family's financial situation was not an easy one. Could they afford a tutor? Sweet Eloise received so much enjoyment from what little music she'd learned to play. It would be a shame to take that away from her.

"Perhaps if you had a teacher come in once a week to offer instruction," Hollis said. "That arrangement could likely be made for a reasonable—"

Randolph shot him a look of warning. Talking about money was considered rather lower-class. Ironic, really, considering money was a significant part of what separated the classes.

Hollis changed the ending of his sentence. "—effort. In fact, I know a teacher of music who would be an excellent choice."

"Do you?" Cora was clearly intrigued.

"She is a lady, by birth though no longer by fortune. She currently teaches at Thurloe Collegiate School, which is an excellent school for girls from respectable families. Her abilities and standing are so well regarded that she, just last evening, graced Mrs. Kennard's musicale with an astoundingly impressive performance."

"Oh, Randolph." Cora took hold of her husband's hand. "She sounds perfect."

Not many in their circles permitted public displays of affection, not even something as simple as holding hands. Hollis had always admired that Randolph and Cora did.

"Would you ask if she is interested or available for private lessons?" Randolph asked him. "I don't know what flexibility she has, already being employed as a teacher."

Hollis understood the question his brother also wished him to ask: What would her fee be? "If you would be willing to drop me at Thurloe, I would be happy to inquire this very day."

Not many minutes later, they did precisely that. With an acknowledgment of Cora's gratitude, Randolph's trust, Eloise's sweet kiss on his cheek, and Addison's continued wariness, Hollis climbed from the carriage and made his way to the door of the school. This was calling day for the teachers, so he would be permitted ample opportunity to visit with Ana. If he'd thought he could manage it without drawing too much attention, he would have called every week.

Randolph and Cora had given him the perfect excuse. He tipped his proverbial hat to them for that.

To his relief, Ana appeared pleased to see him. A young pup had come to call on her, something that never failed to be the case on the rare occasions he, himself, made an appearance. He motioned with his head toward the man. Her look of exhausted frustration told him all he needed to know. The

Dreadfuls might not have trusted him often with anything furtive, but he'd learned a thing or two about dispatching difficult people. With a quick dip of his head and a preemptive word of appreciation to the man for giving up his place, Hollis took the young gentleman's seat, leaving him standing about.

"What a pleasure to see you, Mr. Darby," Ana said, her gratitude apparent. "What brings you around?"

"It is calling day, is it not?" He offered his most winning smile.

"You do not always come on calling day. Something has brought you here this time."

She was astute; there was no mistaking that. "I have, indeed, come with a matter of business," he said. "But as I greatly enjoy your company, my business is not my only motivation in being here."

"You have piqued my interest, Mr. Darby. What is this business which compelled this visit?"

"Have you any interest in providing private music lessons?" he asked.

With a twinkle of mischief in her eye, she said, "Why, Mr. Darby. I had no idea you harbored musical ambitions."

If he thought for one moment she would be willing to teach him to play a musical instrument, he would have snatched up the nearest one and declared a lifelong desire to play it. "I have a niece—a delightful, somewhat precocious, tenderhearted girl of eight—who harbors a deep love of music. She has begun to learn the pianoforte, but her parents have discovered her governess—a paragon in all other respects—is dreadful as a music instructor."

"And her parents wish to ask me?" She seemed both flattered and confused.

"I told them of your performance last evening, of your impeccable manners, how highly the headmistress here speaks of your abilities as a teacher—"

She colored up beautifully. How could he have helped but fall top-over-tail in love with her? She was as lovely a person inside as out.

"They hope that, perhaps, you have the time and inclination to add our little Eloise to your list of students."

"Oh, Mr. Darby. You are too kind." She entwined her fingers, clutching her hands too tightly to fully hide her nervousness. "I fear they will be sorely disappointed when they actually make my acquaintance."

"No one who has ever met you could possibly be disappointed."

Her smiled warmed and softened. "I would have to ask Miss Black if it would be possible for me to accept your offer. But if she will permit it, I think I would enjoy that."

"You will love Eloise," he said. "She is an angel."

"How soon would your . . . *brother*—" She tilted her head in a question.

He nodded.

"—need an answer?"

"Whenever you have one for him," he said.

Another gentleman arrived, intent on being granted Ana's time and attention. The other teachers had their visitors as well. Hollis sat among them all, listening to the general conversation and feeling rather like a one-legged horse in a race.

He reminded himself what a lucky cove he was to simply be with her again—twice in two days, in fact.

On the side table near Ana, peeking out from underneath a shawl he knew to be hers, was the familiar teal cover of Mr. King's latest offering. She had already indicated she read and enjoyed the penny dreadfuls.

Perhaps if she enjoyed Mr. King's stories as much as she appeared to, there was some hope that his clandestine publishing life would not meet with her disapproval.

Perhaps.

THE GENTLEMAN AND THE THIEF

by Mr. King

Installment I,
in which our Hero enlists the help of a brave and kind
Neighbor and encounters a most dire Prediction!

The grand estate of Summerworth sat nestled between a raging river and the windswept moors. Its turrets and towers loomed large, declaring to all who drew near that this was the home of a noble and exalted family. Yet, within its palatial walls, a mournful sadness wrapped ice around the heart of the only person who lived therein.

After great tragedy and heartrending loss, only Mr. Wellington Quincey remained of those who had once made their home in the splendor of Summerworth. His family had dwindled to only one; the Summerworth staff had dwindled to only two.

Wellington's despondency had rendered the house an almost unbearably sad place to live. His sorrows were many. His companions were few.

For all his anguish, he was not an unkind gentleman. Those who knew him liked him. Many a heart ached at his suffering and isolation. His family was gone. His home was remote.

He had all but given up on finding companionship and love and a new beginning by the time he reached his twenty-fifth year. Loneliness was his lot in life, and he would endure it. But there was one thing he could not sort out. How was it that an estate as far from neighbors as his, so devoid of staff and visitors, was the victim of an unending string of thefts?

Jewelry had disappeared. Silver. Paintings. Priceless heirlooms. His trusted servants hadn't the least idea what precisely had befallen Summerworth. The missing items could not be located. No clues had been left behind. He was utterly and completely baffled.

It was with this mystery hanging heavy on his weary mind that he mounted his trusty steed and dedicated a morning to riding a circuit of the estate. He was not at risk of being beggared by the thefts, but neither could he ignore the growing list of pilfered items. Who could possibly be taking them? What ill-intentioned thief was bringing such misery to his already painful life?

He rounded a turn in the path as it passed the cottage of the estate steward. Elmore Combs had remained in his post after the death of Wellington's grandfather some fifteen years earlier, Wellington's father ten years after that, and Wellington's older brother a mere two years ago.

Combs's daughter, Tillie, stood outside, pulling laundry off the clothesline. Wellington had known Tillie since they had been children running and skipping and laughing through the meadows and lawns and streams of Summerworth. They had been dear friends during those long-ago days. He hadn't seen as much of her the past few years as he would have liked. Life had demanded too much of him.

"Good morning, Tillie." He pulled his horse to a halt beside the house. "How are you faring this fine day?"

She folded a sheet against herself and smiled at him. "I'm well, sir."

"You needn't call me 'sir,'" he said as he dismounted. "We have been friends all our lives."

Tillie laid the sheet in her large basket. "But you're grown now, and the master of the estate. Things ain't quite what they used to be."

He pulled another sheet from the line and began folding it himself. "Are we not still friends, Tillie?"

"You're hardly here anymore. I've a closer friendship with the hedgehog who lives in back of the cottage."

Her words struck deep. Heaven forgive him, he *had* been neglectful. He'd lost his grandparents, his parents, and his brother. He seldom saw his friends from Cambridge. He had no true friends amongst Society in London, merely a list of vague acquaintances. He kept to himself, a shield against the grief of losing people he felt close to. But it meant he remained painfully lonely.

"I could come help you fold laundry," he offered. "Then we could talk as we work."

Amusement danced in her eyes. "Folding laundry ain't for the master of the estate."

"I'm doing it now." He dropped the sheet into the basket. "Besides, who will even see me working other than you and your father? This needn't be a source of teasing, unless you mean to engage in jests at my expense."

"'Course not."

He took down a serviceable-looking apron and folded it as well. "If laundry is off-limits to me, what will you permit me to do? Sweep the front stoop? Weed the kitchen garden? Are either of those acceptable for a 'master of the estate'?"

She folded a shirt, no doubt her father's. "I suspect you've spent time weeding and sweeping at your own house, it being short-staffed like it is."

"Lately, I've invested most of my time attempting to locate a virtual treasure trove of missing things."

Nothing remained on the clothesline. She took up the basket and held it against her hip. "Things've been swiped?"

"Quite a number of things," he said. "Jewelry. Silver. Paintings."

"And you've not located any of it?"

He shook his head. "I fear this mystery will prove utterly unsolvable."

He walked beside her back to the quaint and inviting cottage. The door stood open, allowing them to enter without a pause.

Her father was inside and greeted Wellington. "Welcome, Mr. Quincey. Have you come on estate business?"

"I stopped to offer a good morning to my lifelong friend but have been rightly informed by your daughter that I have not been an attentive companion to her these years."

Mr. Combs turned wide eyes on his child. "Tillie. You'd

speak so critically to a gentleman of his standing? 'Ave you taken leave of your manners, girl?"

"Pray, do not scold her," Wellington insisted. "I was rightly chastised, and I mean to make amends."

"How?" Tillie never had lacked for boldness.

"We spend little time together, as you rightly observed, and I have a maddening riddle at the estate. Perhaps you might help me sort it."

She looked intrigued. If she agreed to join the hunt for the elusive thief, he would have her company again. The house would not be so empty. The joys of their childhood friendship would bring light back into his darkened world.

"Would you help?" he pressed. "I would be greatly obliged."

"I do have a knack for sorting mysteries." She carried her basket to the table. "We could solve this'n together."

"I would be deeply indebted to you." He turned to Mr. Combs. "A great many things have gone missing up at the manor house, odd bits and large pieces. I cannot for the life of me guess where they've gone or who might have taken them. You would not begrudge Tillie some time spent help-ing me discover what's happened to them, would you? I would not, for all the world, wish to add to your burdens here."

"We'll manage," Mr. Combs said. "Besides, I'm curious to know who—or what—has been making off with your things."

"'Or what'?" Wellington repeated.

Tillie nodded. "My father is quite well versed in all the old tales and creatures: pixies, fairies, changelings, redcaps."

"You suspect my thief is a mythical monster?" The moors were filled with mystery and magic, but Wellington hadn't thought such had bled onto his own estate. "Is that your theory as well, Tillie?"

"I think we'd best assume anythin' is possible."

"Mark me, children, there's more in this ol' world than can be seen or understood." Mr. Combs eyed them in turn. "Unless you proceed with a healthy dose of respect for what you can't explain, you'll forever be chasing what you can't foresee."

CHAPTER 4

If you have the least concern this will reflect poorly on Thurloe, I'll turn the Darbys down." Ana hoped that wouldn't prove necessary. Though she enjoyed her work at Thurloe, she hadn't always wished to be a school-teacher. Working as a private tutor, with more independence and greater control over her time and choices, was more to her liking.

Elizabeth nodded. "Providing musical instruction for a family of the Darbys' standing will not be looked down on in the least. Further, it will give you more income."

Ana smiled. "I do not consider my wages here to be miserly, I assure you."

"If you would prefer, I am certain Mr. Darby would agree to not pay you." Elizabeth's humor was often so subtle that those who didn't know her well missed it entirely.

"I would hate for him or his wife to be accused of being stingy," Ana said. "I shall accept payment for my efforts—for their sake, you understand."

"Very good of you." Elizabeth dipped the nib of her pen

into the inkwell. "Arrange with the Darbys to hold your lessons at a time when you aren't teaching here. That should allow you to accept their offer."

"How far away do they live from Thurloe?" Ana asked. "I'm not certain I can walk there and back and still have time for the lesson if I have to schedule it between my students here. And if I pay for a hansom cab, I'll spend all my extra income very quickly."

Elizabeth looked up from her pile of parchment—she was, no doubt, working on her next silver-fork novel. "I'm sure Mr. *Hollis* Darby would see to it you are fetched and returned without incurring the slightest expense."

"I don't wish to burden him. He's been very kind." More than she deserved.

Though she could not be entirely certain, Ana thought she saw Elizabeth actually roll her eyes. "Hollis Darby is the epitome of a gentleman. He asked you to do this for his family; he will not permit the doing of it to bankrupt you. Further, he would not wish you to exhaust your time and energy walking from here to his brother's home and back. Further still, I believe he would not feel the least put out spending the length of a drive in your company."

That was reassuring. "Of course, if it proves a burden to him, other arrangements can always be made."

"Certainly." Elizabeth offered an encouraging smile.

Ana carefully penned a note for Mr. Darby—the younger Mr. Darby as he had been the one to extend the opportunity—and gave it to Fanny, their chambermaid and sometimes errand girl, to deliver to him. Having finished all she needed to do for the day, Ana pulled on her dark wool coat and comfortably worn boots. She did up her hair in a flattering but modest chignon. She pulled a certain silver bracelet from her violin case and tucked it into a cleverly hidden pocket sewn into the lining of her coat.

Ana spent most of her evenings away from the school, undertaking important errands, but Fridays were set aside for her most important, most personal appointment.

The walk to Pimlico took nearly an hour, yet she made the walk every week, no matter the weather, no matter her exhaustion. She first stopped at various vegetable and fruit carts, then a local butcher who always had a small chicken or two for a reasonable price. With her basket heavy laden, she made her way down once-familiar streets, followed at every turn by memories and regrets. If any of the residents of the increasingly fine houses she passed recognized her, none said as much nor stopped her for a bit of reminiscing.

She reached the faded blue door on St. George's Road that she had once walked through every day and, using the old brass key she kept with her, let herself inside. The parquet floors in the entryway were dull and covered in a thin layer of dust. The faint trail of footsteps were hers, ghosts from a previous visit. She closed the door behind her and turned the bolt. Light filtered in through the dingy, arched transom window.

The doors she passed as she crossed the entryway were closed, as they had been for years. She climbed the once-carpeted stairs to the first-floor landing. It too had suffered the ill effects of neglect. The beautifully carved molding no longer drew the eye or elicited admiration. The house had once been a jewel; now it was a shell.

Ana stepped through the first door at the top of the landing, the only room still in use other than the kitchen. A tall, broad man at the far end of fifty sat in a straight-backed chair near the empty fireplace. He looked up as she stepped inside. He rose and crossed to her, took the basket of food, and left the room. The interaction was well known to them both.

She continued to the window seat, where another man, younger but more gaunt than the first, sat on the cushionless bench, looking out over St. George's Road.

He wore a tattered dressing gown over his threadbare clothes, several years out of fashion. His hair stuck out in all directions, clean but unkempt. He'd not shaved that morning, likely not the morning before either. His eyes were wide, anxious. A less charitable person might have insisted there was madness there. Ana knew better. He was not of unsound mind. He had simply given up on life.

"Good evening, Father."

"Mr. Thompson has been out at all hours. Up to nothing good. Society'll forgive him though, mark my words." His voice didn't hold quite the flavor of Mr. Walker's, but he'd never fully mastered the accent of the upper class. Mother had been better at that, and she'd insisted Ana behave and speak properly.

"Mr. Thompson doesn't usually garner your notice." Ana crossed to the small bedside table in the corner. It had once resided in Mother's rooms, its drawers proving a convenient place to store baubles. "What has our neighbor done differently today?"

"Not just today. He's in and out at all hours."

"Yes, you said that." She opened the top drawer and pushed aside a few folded handkerchiefs and light wraps. They had been Mother's more serviceable ones. Her finer silks and embroidered linens had been lost when Father's company faltered. "Many ladies and gentlemen are out late attending balls and soirees and such. No doubt, the Thompsons are simply doing the same."

Father stood and leaned closer to the window, his forehead nearly touching the glass. "He stumbles in. I'd wager the bruiser's drunk."

That *was* strange. Ana had known Mr. Thompson during her growing-up years. He was not a bounder nor a drunkard. Indeed, she'd always admired him, considered him an example of the sort of gentleman she would like to someday have as a permanent part of her life. She hoped he was not actually involved in anything disreputable. She'd been disillusioned enough the past three years.

"I attended a musicale two nights ago," she said as she pulled a small box from the back of the drawer to the front. "I played my violin."

His bushy brows drew together. He watched her a moment, as if sorting out what she'd said. "You were engaged as an entertainer?"

She often dug through this particular drawer. Father neither seemed to notice nor worry about it. "No, Father. I was there as a guest. Most Society musicales call upon the guests themselves to provide music."

He turned from the window, but his gaze wandered around the room rather than settling on her. "Were you looked down on?"

"No. I cannot say anyone was beside themselves with excitement to see me, but I was not treated poorly."

Father rubbed a hand over his forehead, leaving behind a smudge. "It wasn't my fault—you losing your place among them."

"I know. Mr. Darby says Society is fickle. I think he is correct."

"Darby?" He pouted fiercely, something he'd done all her life when he was thinking particularly hard. "I remember the Darbys. Two brothers, I remember."

Ana smiled and nodded. "You always did have a very good memory."

He looked back out the window, no doubt watching for Mr. Thompson.

Ana returned her attention to the box she'd pulled from the drawer, opening it carefully. It had once been full of the most beautiful jewelry: lovely, tasteful rings, pendants Mother wore on her favorite gold chain, necklaces boasting a variety of gems, earbobs, and bracelets. It was nearly empty now. Only two rings were there along with one necklace.

And, now, a single silver bracelet.

I will get them all back in time, Mother. She'd made the same silent vow on every visit since Mother died. She was slowly getting it all back from the people who'd taken so much from them. Jewelry, mementos, knickknacks, decorations. If she could have managed it, she would have reclaimed the furniture and paintings and books that had been snatched away as well. One could only hide so much in a violin case.

Wallace, Father's valet and the only servant left in the house, returned, having put away the food Ana brought.

She nodded toward her father. "He's very concerned about Mr. Thompson."

"I suspect he gets lonesome, miss. He watches the world around him, but he ain't part of it. Wears on a soul, that does."

"He has you," she said. "That's worth a great deal."

"Thank you, Miss Newport."

"I'll do a bit of straightening while I'm here. I have some time before I need to return to the school."

"I'm sorry I cain't keep the ol' place cleaner," Wallace said. "Too much for one person, it is."

"You take care of Father and keep him company. That is far more important."

She spent another hour there, sweeping and straightening. She cleaned Father's window, knowing how much time he spent there. He would be happier if he could see well.

The man he'd been before his fortunes failed would not have spent his days looking out at the world; he would have been out in the world. He had retreated, and she'd lost hope of tugging him back. She could restore some of the things that had been stolen from them, but she couldn't give him back his dignity or pride or good name.

Before leaving, she pressed a kiss to his sunken, stubbly cheek. "I will see you next Friday, Father."

He kept his gaze on the street below. Ana slipped out.

It wasn't my fault, he'd said. She knew it wasn't. He'd been blamed and scapegoated, and the entire family had paid the price for that injustice.

Society was fickle, yes. But so was Fate.

CHAPTER 5

ollis stood in the entryway of Thurloe, watching the lady who had claim on his affections rush down the stairs toward him. If only her excitement was from seeing him rather than her new position. He didn't mean to press his suit or want to cause her any degree of discomfort. They would make the journey to Randolph's home as comfortable acquaintances. He'd require himself to be satisfied with that.

"I am bringing with me a few sheets of very simple music that my beginning students use early in their lessons." She took a quick, somewhat tight breath. No matter that she was smiling and clearly eager, Ana hadn't entirely hidden her nervousness. "I'm not certain how much your niece has learned already. You said she has had *some* musical instruction." She pressed her lips together, brow suddenly drawing low. "Perhaps I ought to have selected a few more difficult pieces as well. Her governess might feel insulted if I've *under*estimated what has already been taught. Do you suppose she'll be upset? Eloise is only eight years old. My youngest students here are only a bit older than that. They are usually very amiable."

Hollis took her hand and held it gently. "My dear Miss Newport, set your mind at ease. Eloise loves music and will be delighted to continue learning to play her pianoforte. Her governess will be grateful to be relieved of responsibility for a subject matter on which she is not well versed. And know that I suggested you for the position because I have every confidence that you are equal to it."

Though her fingers were wrapped around his, he felt the warmth of her touch around his heart.

"If this goes terribly, will you solemnly vow to not laugh at me when I cry in the carriage all the way back?"

Did she truly think him so unfeeling as that? "I could never laugh at your tears."

"A gentleman through and through, I see."

His declaration was far more than the empty platitudes of social obligation. If only he were in a position to tell her as much.

He tucked her arm through his, another thing she likely thought was done strictly out of good manners. They stepped out of the school, and he handed her up into his brother's waiting carriage.

"My brother lives near Belgrave Square," he said, taking the rear-facing seat across from her. "The drive won't be overly long, but neither will it be mere moments."

"I know the area," she said. "I grew up in Pimlico."

Pimlico? The residents of that corner of London could be rather flush. And even those who weren't drowning in money were well-off. She had spoken how her family had once been part of Society, but he'd been under the impression theirs had been a tentative hold. He'd wager the Newports had money—or did at one point. There was a mystery there. He never could resist a mystery.

"My brother's home was our family's London home when we were children. If only we'd lived a bit further south, you and I might have known one another."

"I would have liked that," she said. "I had no brothers or sisters, and I was a little older than your niece when our family acquired the house I grew up in, so we hadn't any established connections. I had very few friends as a child."

"You must have been lonely." His heart ached for the little girl she'd once been.

"Terribly at times." Her fleeting smile was sweet but heavy. "Tell me about Eloise. I will be a better teacher if I know a little about my student."

Hollis accepted the change of topic. He shared insights with her about his eager and precocious niece. He also warned Ana that, should Addison leave the nursery and make an appearance, the little boy had a tendency to be standoffish.

"Does he share that trait with either of his parents?" she asked.

"His mother is a little timid, which can give the inaccurate impression of haughtiness." Cora was a fine person, but not everyone was permitted to see that about her. "My brother is . . ." How did he explain this without being disloyal? "He can be aloof, but you mustn't take that as a personal slight."

"He'll not be unkind, will he?"

He'd better not be. "No."

She wrapped her fingers more firmly around her small satchel containing her music. "I don't wish to disappoint them." Her eyes met his. "Or, goodness, *you.*"

He leaned forward, hoping his easy demeanor and quiet smile would reassure her. "I haven't the least worry on that score."

"I will enjoy being inside a home again," she said, "especially one so near to where I grew up. Thurloe is a lovely place, and I'm not unhappy there, but I miss the feeling of home and family."

Home and family. Hollis longed for those things as well. His rented rooms weren't exactly all the crack, but they'd not have put any sticklers to the blush. Considering his penniless, prospectless situation upon first arriving in Town, he wasn't ungrateful. But he lived alone. The Dreadfuls were something like a family, but it wasn't the same, likely because his place among them felt so trivial and unnecessary.

The carriage stopped directly in front of Randolph's house. Ana's shoulders squared, though Hollis could see her hands shaking as she took up her satchel.

"Courage, Miss Newport," he whispered. "You are equal to this."

The smile she bestowed on him would, he felt certain, make regular appearances in his thoughts and dreams.

The butler—newly installed after Randolph's marriage, their childhood butler having long ago quit his post for not being paid by their father—opened the door.

"Good afternoon, Parker," Hollis greeted. He pressed his gloved palm to Ana's back and nudged her inside. "Would you send word to the nursery that Miss Eloise's music instructor has arrived?"

"Very good, sir."

While the man went to deliver the message, Hollis accompanied his lovely companion to the music room. The space was less sparse and depressing than it had been during the years Hollis had lived there. Father had sold nearly all their belongings, but Randolph had managed to acquire some replacements.

Ana moved directly to the pianoforte. She set her satchel on the floor beside it and plunked a few of the keys. It was a smaller and more humble instrument than most houses in this area could boast. It was, no doubt, all his brother had been able to procure with his all-but-empty pockets.

Hollis wandered to the tall, curtained windows. The world outside was as quiet here as it was in his corner of London. He'd wanted to make his townhome in a more bustling and exciting location. Being part of the Dreadfuls had ruined him for peace and quiet. But Randolph had balked loudly and colorfully when he'd heard the address where Hollis had originally meant to live. Compromise had seemed best. It had also proved boring.

"Uncle Hollis!"

He spun around at the sound of Eloise's voice. "Sweetie!"

She rushed to him and jumped into his open arms. Soon enough she'd be too big for such things. He meant to cherish her littleness while it lasted.

"Have you brought me flowers?" she asked. "I like it when you bring me flowers."

"I have brought you Miss Newport. She is my friend and a music teacher."

Eloise turned bright eyes on Ana, who stood by the pianoforte, watching her newest student with unmistakable delight.

He set Eloise on her feet and pushed her toward Ana, though she didn't actually need the encouragement.

The little girl rushed to her new teacher. "Good morning, Miss Newport." She offered a very prettily executed courtesy.

"Good morning to you, Miss Eloise." Ana motioned to the stool. "Please have a seat, and let's begin."

For all her uncertainty during the journey from Thurloe, Ana was immediately in her element. Hollis sat in a chair under one of the windows as the lesson began.

Eloise plunked her way through a very simple piece she'd learned, while Ana listened with an encouraging smile. He could have happily sat there all day long, no matter the lack of polish in Eloise's performance, but he heard his brother's voice in the corridor and felt it best to offer a greeting.

He slipped from the music room and came face-to-face with more than he'd anticipated. Randolph was deep in conversation with Alistair Headley.

The two gentlemen noticed him at the same time, and the conversation immediately halted.

"Headley," Hollis greeted with the tiniest dip of his head.

"Darby," was the equally unenthusiastic reply.

"Mrs. Kennard was disappointed not to see you at her musicale."

Headley offered a small shrug. "I was otherwise occupied."

"Is that what it's being called now?" Four-Finger Mike was not known for the propriety of his pursuits.

"What *what* is being called?" Headley asked.

"Whatever it was you were doing." Hollis shrugged as if it were terribly unimportant. Playing the fool tended to upend people enough they often revealed more than they intended.

"I don't believe I said what I was doing."

"Odd." Hollis pretended to ponder the point. "I could have sworn I had an inkling what you've been up to."

Headley didn't answer. He turned his attention back to Randolph. "I'd best be on my way."

"I'll see you out," Randolph said. "You can tell me more of . . . what we were discussing."

Headley spared Hollis a quick glance as he stepped out. The man didn't seem truly suspicious, but there was definite concern in his expression. Interesting.

The butler stood near the now-closed door, watching through the narrow window so he could anticipate his employer's return.

"How often is Mr. Headley here?" Hollis asked, moving to join him.

"Increasingly often, sir."

Hollis didn't care for that answer. "Does he seem to be a bad influence on my brother?"

Parker's eyes darted to him. "Are you asking your brother's butler?"

"No, I'm asking one of my best spies."

Parker nodded once, firmly. "Oy, then." His posture

slumped from the rigidness required of a proper servant. "That bloke Headley's a rum customer if you're asking me."

"You think he's dangerous?" Hollis eyed Headley through the narrow window.

"I hear things." When Parker wasn't "on duty," he had as much swagger as any of the Dreadfuls, and a far more colorful vocabulary.

"I'm aware of your acute hearing, Parker. Thankful for it, even." While Fletcher had his network of street children who brought him word of difficulties and danger, Hollis knew almost everything going on in more exalted circles because he had his own network among the servants. "I've heard some whispers about Headley. Have you?"

Parker nodded. "His footman says he's hardly ever home. Out 'til all hours, he is."

"Not unheard-of for gentlemen of means."

"I asked the hack driver who comes by for him regular-like," Parker said. "Mr. Headley's not lazing about at any respectable places. Few days back, the driver dropped the gen'lman at a copper hell in Lambeth."

Lambeth? *Jumpin' Moses.* "Does he frequent the slums?"

Parker shook his head. "But wandering out to the seedier side of things even 'sometimes' ain't exactly the sort o' thing an up-and-upper oughtta be doing."

"Have you heard any whispers of him hanging about with a man called Four-Finger—"

"Mike." Parker nodded. "A shady bruiser if ever there was one."

"Keep your ears out, man," Hollis said. "I don't like that Headley's cozying up to my brother."

"You want me to send whispers your way?"

Hollis nodded. "Get word to my man, Ambrose." His valet was part of Hollis's network of serving-class spies. "You still have your penny?"

Parker pulled a coin from his waistcoat pocket and gave it a toss in the air. "I know what to do with a calling card."

As the butler, he'd likely collected thousands of *actual* calling cards. That the marked penny, an identifier used by nearly all the Dreadfuls' informants, had come to be called that amongst Hollis's servant spies delighted him to no end.

"If Headley makes any trouble for my sister-in-law or her children—"

"I ain't gonna stand back and watch any of 'em get hurt," Parker said.

Hollis nodded. He had every faith in the butler-turned-informant.

Outside, Randolph was walking back toward the house, alone.

"Summon your respectability, Parker. Time to play butler."

Though Hollis would have liked to discover what he could from his brother, Randolph was particular about appearances, and that bled into class distinctions. He would have been frustrated to know Hollis had spent the past minutes amiably chatting with the butler.

So he returned to the music room. Eloise was bouncing excitedly on her stool. Ana sat on a chair beside her, grinning from ear to ear. He'd known the two would take to each other straight off.

"I'm 'naturally inclined to music,' Uncle Hollis," Eloise said. "Miss Newport said so."

"If she said so, then it is most certainly true." He pressed a kiss to the top of Eloise's head as he passed.

"And Miss Eloise says I am the 'most pretty teacher in all of London,'" Ana said with a laugh.

"And *that* is most certainly true." He didn't kiss her—he hadn't that right by anyone's estimation—but he did wink. That was also a stretch of propriety, but switching quickly from "covert spy" to "unfailingly proper gentleman" was not always easily managed, especially when what he'd learned through his spying was worrisome.

Alistair Headley was in the stew up to his beady little eyeballs. And Randolph was spending time with the man. No good could come of that. No good whatsoever.

THE GENTLEMAN
AND THE THIEF

by Mr. King

Installment II,
in which our Hero begins an Investigation
and accepts a most unusual Challenge!

Wellington had all but forgotten what a mischievous delight Tillie was. She arrived at Summerworth for their investigation with a jest-filled list of suspects, including everything from "a dog with a poor upbringing" to "a flock of magpies with remarkable coordination."

Her laughter had ever been a source of utter delight to him—to *all*, in fact. Had ever the heavens blessed a soul with so happy a disposition as she?

"I believe we would do well to begin where the items have gone missing," he said. "Most have disappeared from my sitting area."

"Your private rooms?" She clasped a hand to her heart. "How very scandalous!" Amusement twinkled in her eyes.

"It is a fortunate thing this house is empty," Wellington said. "You would have all the countryside whispering about me."

"Is that why you never invite me up to the house any longer?" Though her humor remained, a touch of earnestness had entered her tone.

"I ought to have come by your cottage any number of times these past years," he said. "The weight of grief can crush one's judgment."

She took his hand, as she'd so often done in their younger years. "Don't you fret it, Welly. We've a mystery to solve, you and I. That'll lift your spirits."

Was ever a man so undeservedly blessed with so forgiving a friend? They walked hand in hand up the stairs and down the corridor. She turned toward what had been his rooms when they were children.

"No, Tillie. I am in the master's rooms now."

She laughed lightly. "I forget sometimes how very much has changed since we were children."

"*You* haven't changed," he said.

She pulled away, preceding him across the threshold of the master's chambers, but tossed back over her shoulder, "You might be surprised."

Wellington had spent his share of time amongst the ladies of Society and their practiced primness. Tillie was a breath of utterly and joyfully fresh air.

"Now." She stopped in the middle of the room. "What has gone missing?"

He joined her. "A painting off that wall." He pointed. "My father's pocket watch. Two necklaces that once belonged to my mother that I have kept in my bureau as a reminder of her. A pair of pearl cuff links."

"Blimey," she muttered. "You're being pillaged."

"I know it. And this isn't the only room from which items are missing."

"Mr. and Mrs. Smith would not have taken them." Tillie had known his two remaining servants her whole life and knew well their goodness and utter trustworthiness. No, there was no question of the Smiths being anything other than loyal and good and true.

"I've not had visitors in months," he said. "And no tradesmen have come to the door. I cannot sort it. Indeed, it is a question that sits heavy upon my mind."

"How large was the painting?" Tillie asked.

"One grown person could carry it," he said, "but not without effort."

Her face twisted in an expression of contemplation. Wellington smiled from his very heart at the once-familiar sight. While she had always been of a playful disposition, no one who had known her could doubt her intelligence.

"Were any other large items taken?" she asked.

"Yes. Some that would be difficult to sneak away with."

She turned to him, excitement sparkling in her deep-brown eyes. "Any too large to remove far without a cart?"

He thought over his list. "A heavy gilded mirror disappeared from my mother's room. That could not be carried far, even by several people."

"Do you realize what this means?" She took hold of his arm, bouncing in place. "No one has come or gone. The mirror, at least, must still be in this house. Your blighter likely tucked it away somewhere to nip off with later."

What a stroke of genius! What a needed bit of luck! "If

we discover where the things are hidden, we can reclaim them."

She nodded. "You'll have your treasures back and might even catch yourself a thief."

Oh, rapturous discovery! This time *he* seized *her* hand. "I know precisely where we ought to look first."

"We should do this more often, Wellington."

He laughed. How long had it been since he had well and truly laughed? Tillie had always been his sunshine on rainy days. He'd been a fool not to reach out to her during the storms of the past years.

They moved swiftly down the servants' stairs into the dim silence below.

"I thought we agreed Mr. and Mrs. Smith weren't our thieves," she said.

"They aren't. But most of the rooms on this level are shut up and never used. There is an exit on this floor of the house with no stairs to navigate."

"Ah." She nodded her understanding. "A perfect arrangement for slipping ill-gotten goods out unseen."

The belowstairs was quiet. Only the ever-blowing wind off the moors rattling the windows broke the silence. This had once been the bustling center of a lively household. Now it was little more than a cavern. Life too often demanded exacting tolls.

With an eager bounce to her step, Tillie began searching the rooms. "No pilfered goods in here, guv'nuh," she called out.

"I object to 'guv'nuh' as much as I did to 'sir,'" he said. "And, for the record, I'm no longer overly fond of 'Welly.'"

She plopped her fists on her hips and, standing outside the next room she meant to search, said, "You've become quite the pompous bore, Wellington Quincey."

"I have not."

Her head tipped to the side in a pose of theatrical disbelief. "Then prove it."

"And how would you propose I 'prove it'?"

A slow, sly grin spread over her face. "A race. I will check the rooms on this side of the corridor; you check the other side. The first one to the other end wins."

"A footrace?" He shook his head. "We are not eight years old any longer."

"Precisely what a pompous bore would say." Though she still smiled, unmistakable disappointment flickered across her face.

He could not bear to disappoint his oldest friend, not when she had just that day brought the first flicker of light back into his gloomy existence.

With an air of determination, he pulled off his jacket and hung it on the handle of the nearest door. "Prepare yourself for defeat, Tillie Combs."

"You did not best me when we were children, and you won't now."

She rushed to her first room. He did as well.

Nothing was amiss. The next room proved the same. As he stepped out into the corridor, Tillie was just slipping into her third room.

"You are falling behind," she called back.

Twice in one morning she had made him laugh. How he had needed her in his life!

MR. KING

He pulled open the door of the next room he was meant to check. Before he could so much as glance inside, a scream pierced the air.

Tillie!

CHAPTER 6

Ana set out late the next night, clad in a drab dress with only one thin petticoat and leather slippers. She had a secret pouch tucked in a well-hidden pocket in her skirt, one large enough to hold a porcelain figurine Mother had given her for her twelfth birthday. Her destination was the home of Mr. George Mortimer, the man who'd taken that treasure from her.

The Mortimers had been invited to a soiree in another area of Town. The house would be relatively quiet. She would have a small window of opportunity during which the servants would be abed but the family would not yet have returned. She'd watched the house enough the past weeks to know its routine.

Both servants' entrances, front and back, would be locked; they always were. But the door to the herb room never was, and it contained a door leading inside. She wasn't certain where that door lead precisely, but she'd been inside enough homes of this age to have a fairly good guess.

The aroma of rosemary and thyme, sage and dill filled

the room, offering an olfactory welcome to her, an uninvited woman. Her single petticoat let her dress hug her body more closely, allowing her to slip more easily through narrow spaces. It, along with her soft-soled shoes, kept her movements quiet.

She'd once been a lady of some standing and position. Now she was a thief. Fickle fate, indeed.

The interior door of the herb room opened to a dark, narrow corridor. A dim light at the end illuminated what she was certain was the main corridor of the servants' wing in the basement. She moved quickly but carefully.

Her guess proved bang-up.

The corridor was lit only by light spilling from a room at the other end of the main corridor, likely the housekeeper's or butler's room. She slipped silently to the first stairwell she found. It hadn't quite the noticeable wear marks one would find on the main servants' stairs, and while there'd be less risk of being caught if she took this path upward, she didn't dare take the chance that it led directly to a bedchamber or someplace else she'd be harder-pressed to escape.

A bit farther up the corridor she found the main stairs. She followed them up and around, emerging onto an unadorned landing on the ground level.

She felt certain her figurine would be in Mr. Mortimer's library or study. He'd been so gleefully smug when he'd taken it, calling it a "victory memento." He'd have placed it somewhere he could look at it with triumph every time he utilized the assets he'd seized from Father's company.

Some townhomes placed libraries on the ground level, some on the first floor. Some were at the front of the house, others were at the back. This retrieval might prove a multi-night endeavor, as too many had before.

She found a sitting room, a small coat closet, a drawing room. Nearly halfway to the back of the house, she came across the very room she was searching for. Luck was with her tonight.

Ana pulled the pouch from her pocket. She took out a small copper candleholder and fit a tiny candle in it. She set it on an obliging table and used the match she'd brought to light it. The tiny flicker of flame was enough for her to see what she needed without spilling light out of the room.

She stepped toward the large cherrywood desk, evaluating the space as she moved. Paintings in ornate frames. An intricate ormolu clock. A high-polished silver salver holding a collection of fine spirits in crystal decanters. On the desk sat a pair of casually discarded cuff links. This man, so wealthy he could leave diamonds lying about and surround himself with items of inarguable monetary value, had stolen a young girl's beloved figurine to be spiteful. He could have bought hundreds just like it. The knickknack had no value beyond the sentimental.

She set the candle on the desktop, then sat in his chair. He would have placed her figurine somewhere he could see it from that vantage point. Mr. Mortimer was taller than she, so she eyed the space a little higher than her gaze naturally fell. From left to right, she scanned each shelf, each tabletop, each cranny.

Her "adventures" had taught her to be patient and take her time. It paid off again. Her beloved figurine was on a midlevel shelf to the right of the desk, tucked amongst an odd assortment of other figurines, miniatures, and small knickknacks. Ana stood and crossed to it.

She reached for it without disturbing anything else. When her fingers wrapped around it, she swallowed back a lump of emotion. She'd missed this sweet, little reminder of her mother's love. Holding it carefully, Ana returned to the desk and the tiny light of her candle. The figurine was of a young woman in a colorful dress, reminiscent of the century before, holding a violin. She stood on a base of what was meant to look like a tree, but it wasn't very convincing. Nothing about it could have appealed to Mr. Mortimer other than the pain he knew losing it would inflict on Father's family.

"But I have it back now," she whispered.

She slipped it in her hidden pocket. Mission accomplished, she studied the library. A ground-floor exit would be easier than slipping back through the servants' wing. Sure enough, a set of French doors led out to what appeared to be a terrace.

Ana blew out the candle, then moved swiftly out the French doors. She closed them behind her, slowly enough the only sound was the tiny click of the latch.

The terrace was adequately shadowed. By keeping close to the house, she and her shapeless dress stayed hidden. She needed only to reach the side gate of the back garden and she could slip out and away without having been noted by anyone. Again, patience was the key.

She turned a corner. The gate was within sight. She was nearly out of danger.

Whispering voices broke the silence of the back garden. Men. At least two.

Ana hunched down, slipping behind a low shrub. It was entirely in shadow; she wasn't likely to be seen. Provided the men didn't remain in the garden all night, she could slip out once they left.

"Mortimers are gone for a few more hours at least," one of them said. "If the Phantom Fox is coming back, it'll be tonight, mark me."

Phantom Fox. That was the nickname whispered about the streets in reference to none other than herself. Her efforts had begun to draw notice. If her reclamations weren't so important, she might have given them up.

"The front door was locked," said the second man. Though Ana was no expert in the various accents of the world, she was relatively certain this man hailed from India.

"The rear door is as well." The first man spoke again. He was English, and she would guess he'd had some education. "A sneak thief with any degree of ability won't be stopped by that."

Certainly not.

"Test the windows and doors on that side," the Englishman said. "I'll check 'em here."

Ana's hiding spot was far enough from any windows or doors to keep her safely hidden. Still, it wasn't terribly comfortable. The candle had cooled enough to tuck it and the copper candleholder back in her carrying pouch and into her pocket. With her hands free, she tucked her legs against her chest and wrapped her arms around them, pulling herself into a tight, more fully concealed ball.

The silhouette of one of the searchers was visible from her hiding place. He was tall and leanly built. He wore a long, dark coat, and a misshapen hat pulled low on his head. He moved with confidence and agility. Were he to catch her, she would be hard-pressed to run fast enough to evade capture. Keeping still and silent was her best course of action.

The man tested one window after another without making the slightest noise. That didn't happen on accident. Who was this man? What was his connection to the Mortimer house?

He stepped onto the terrace and checked the French doors she had used to escape. She'd had no means of locking it behind her. As quietly as he had opened it, the man slid the door closed once more. He turned.

She held her breath.

After a moment, he moved to the next set of windows, checking each one. He moved past the shrub she hid behind.

His companion returned.

"The terrace door weren't locked," he reported. "All the windows were, though."

"The herb room door wasn't, either," his partner said. "A word of warning in the ears of the butler wouldn't go astray."

"And the house is quiet. Perhaps they dodged this particular train."

"For now," the other man said.

They made a slow circuit of the gardens, both eyeing the house. Ana's feet were growing tingly from being held in one place for so long, but she didn't dare adjust her position even the tiniest bit.

Even after the men had slipped through the garden gate,

she remained still. Autumn was newly arrived and the evenings were not terribly chilly. She could stay as long as she needed with no fear of freezing.

When she at last rose from her hiding spot, she moved with even more caution than before. Only when she reached the safety of her own room at Thurloe did she fully breathe again.

That had been a nearer run-in than most of her reacquisition missions. She had her figurine back, but the risk had been enormous.

No matter that the items she "stole" had been stolen from her in the first place, she knew enough of the inhumanity and injustice of the law to have any hope she would be heard or believed.

Her family deserved to have back what the leeches had robbed them of, but if she were caught righting that wrong, it would cost her absolutely everything she had left.

CHAPTER 7

'll pummel you," Fletcher offered Hollis as a friendly warning. It'd been a long time since they'd gone a round or two in the boxing salon at DPS headquarters. Fletcher never would admit that Hollis could hold his own.

"I'm not looking for a match," Hollis said. "I'm trying to think through some things."

Fletcher nodded. "Exertion clears the mind."

"Especially when that mind was empty to begin with," Brogan tossed out. The man never could resist a jest.

Stone, sitting in a well-worn chair in the far corner, watched without comment. But he was listening. Stone was always listening.

"What is it you're thinking through?" Fletcher asked, popping his fists into fighting position.

Hollis did the same. "According to the servants' grapevine, Alistair Headley's spending time in Lambeth."

The entire room seemed to pause. Even Stone, who was already perfectly still, somehow became even more still.

"Why Lambeth?" Brogan asked. "Does he consider purgatory too safe and uplifting a place?"

Brogan and his sister frequented London's poor and crime-riddled areas like Lambeth, helping those who needed it, offering hope to those without.

"What madness would send Headley to that corner of Town?" Fletcher wondered.

"Gambling," Stone said.

Hollis circled Fletcher, wanting to blow off a bit of steam. "That's the prevailing theory. And I'm hearing he's still seen about with Four-Finger Mike."

An uppercut from Fletcher preceded his answer. "Seems the police oughtta be following Headley around in their search for that fugitive."

Hollis raised his fists to better protect his face. "Following him, though, means they'd be following Randolph."

Fletcher jabbed. "Your brother ain't the sharpest knife in the drawer."

"But is he stupid enough to be wandering down to Lambeth?" Brogan pressed.

Hollis swung and dodged. "Blimey, I hope not."

Fletcher landed a fist on Hollis's left shoulder, sending him reeling back but not sprawling on the ground. "I'll see if any of my urchins know Headley's activities and if Randolph's been seen about with him."

Fletcher jabbed again but missed. Hollis swung before he could resume his protective stance and managed to land a solid jab.

Stone nodded his slow and rare approval.

In the next instant, Kumar stepped through the door. "Our little sneak thief's been spotted."

"The wee girl?" Brogan asked.

Kumar nodded. "She's in Pimlico."

"Which part?" Fletcher asked.

"St. George's Road."

"We'll let you know what we find, Hollis." Fletcher grinned before snatching up a towel and mopping the sweat from his face, neck, and chest.

"I can do more than saunter around being decorative," Hollis said, cleaning up as well.

Fletcher gave him a look of amused doubt. "You *do* dance a fine quadrille."

"Shove off."

"This baby girl's quick." Stone moved with determined step to the door. "We don't have time for your chest thumpin'."

The man had a point. They'd been trying to sweep up the Phantom Fox for weeks. The authorities weren't likely to show the kindercriminal any mercy, but the Dreadfuls knew too much of the desperation of street children to think she needed anything but compassion, especially since, half the time, she didn't steal anything of any actual value.

Stone led the way to the Costume Chamber, a room with wall-to-wall wardrobes each filled with clothing in near-countless varieties, designed to be used in whatever scenario the Dreadfuls might find themselves. Brogan—the Dreadful with the most experience in disguises—crossed directly to the tall, pale oak wardrobe that held clothing fit for tradesmen.

"Not the all-black collection?" Fletcher asked.

"'Tisn't night, lad. We'd stick out like fish on an apple cart."

They changed quickly before exiting out the back of the building. The tradespeople they were meant to be wouldn't come in and out the front. Obtaining a hack was out of character for their roles, but they hadn't time to *walk* all the way to Pimlico.

"This little one's jumpy as a cricket in a chicken coop," Fletcher reminded them as they rode toward their destination. "We tread swiftly but lightly. And we likely need to corner her."

"We don't hold the child against her will." Stone spoke firmly. None of them would have argued with him on that score, but his tone made certain they didn't even think about it.

The hackney driver let them down a couple of streets away from St. George's in order to not draw too much attention. In addition to his actual fee, Fletcher tossed him a penny. This was one of their informants, then. That'd make things even safer.

"Which house is our baby bandit likely to've set her sights on?" Brogan asked.

Of the five of them—Stone, Brogan, Kumar, Hollis, and Fletcher—only Fletch would know the answer from experience. "The quietest. Thievery in broad daylight is risky. She'll pick a house with fewer people."

"Any idea which house that would be?" Stone asked Hollis. He, after all, was more likely to know the homes of the wealthy.

He shook his head. "I'm not as familiar with Pimlico. It's a shame Miss Newport's not with us. She grew up in this area."

"Wouldn't she be confused to see the lot of us now?" Brogan laughed.

"Divide up," Fletcher said. "All of us eyeing houses together ain't likely to go unnoticed."

Brogan and Kumar headed to one side of the road. Fletcher, Hollis, and Stone walked down the other. None of the houses seemed overflowing with activity, but none seemed empty.

"Wait." Hollis held up a hand. "This one's knocker's down." A sure sign the resident family was gone from Town. "There'd be a bare-bones staff."

"The house wouldn't've been purged, though." Fletcher nodded. "Our little girl'd likely realize that."

"An easy target for the Phantom Fox." Hollis motioned them to the iron gate that opened to the steps leading down to the servants' front entrance. The road was empty, but still they stepped with the confidence of tradesmen who'd identified the house they were meant to call at. Few people would think twice about them being there if they looked like they had a purpose.

The doorway was dim, tucked in the corner of the belowground-level alcove, but it was lit enough for evaluating the state of things. The glass in the door was dingy. The ground beneath their feet was covered in old, brown leaves, cobwebs, and small branches probably blown in during a storm, though there'd not been one recently. This was not an entrance that'd been used recently. If there was a housekeeper in residence, it'd never have reached this state of untidiness.

"I think we have an empty house, blokes." Hollis looked through the smudged and dirty glass, searching for any sign of light beyond. "I'd guess not even servants."

"Baby girl wouldn't pass this up." Fletcher reached into the pocket of his outercoat. A less-than-polite word escaped. "Forgot to move my lock-picking kit into these clothes when I changed."

Hollis squatted in front of the door and pulled out *his* kit. He slipped the hook of his torsion wrench into the lock, carefully adjusting its position to create the right amount of tension.

"Didn't know you picked locks," Stone said.

"I don't 'quadrille' at them," Hollis said with a dry look in Fletcher's direction.

"That'd be fun to watch, though."

"Shove off," he said again, but this time with a laugh.

Fletcher sometimes drove him mad, but they *were* good friends. Probably the best of friends.

With a bit of effort and a few other necessary tools, Hollis manipulated the lock until it slid open. "Genn'lmen." He waved them inside.

"Impressive work," Fletcher said as he passed.

Stone didn't speak but eyed Hollis with curiosity. Did none of them believe he had any useful skills beyond scraping and bowing and speaking properly? How shocked they'd all be if they knew he'd gambled his way through school.

The corridor they stepped into was dark, with not a person in sight. They passed what appeared to be the butler's

SARAH M. EDEN

room and then the housekeeper's room, both empty. The wine cellar, farther down the long, unwinding corridor, was vacant as well. The servants' hall still had its long table and benches, but neither appeared to have been used recently.

"Are we sure this house ain't abandoned?" Fletcher kept his voice to a whisper.

"Ain't in disrepair," Stone said. "Looks fine as anything from the street."

"I side with Stone on this," Hollis said. "The house isn't abandoned, but something is decidedly odd here."

They continued forward, approaching the kitchen or butler's pantry, when something moved, the sound reminding Hollis of a chair leg scraping a flagstone floor.

"Our baby burglar?" Fletcher whispered.

"Or someone belonging to this house we've broken into," Hollis said.

They tucked themselves around a corner into a small area, one that had likely held household supplies at some point. It was now, unsurprisingly, empty.

The shuffle of quick, tiny feet broke the silence of the house. Their little thief. They tucked themselves up against the wall and deeper into the shadows.

Almost silently, Stone said, "Fletcher, slip out and head her off. I'll go behind. Hollis, guard doors."

They nodded their agreement. Fletcher moved without the slightest sound into the dim corridor.

A heartbreakingly tiny silhouette moved past the doorway. Stone slid out as quiet as a breeze. Hollis stepped into the doorway. He could see the girl, frozen in place, staring at Fletcher. They'd guessed, based on reports from Fletcher's

82

urchins and brief glimpses by a few Dreadfuls, that she was perhaps nine years old. Seeing her now, Hollis guessed she was closer to seven. The poor, tiny little robin. How desperate would she have to be to undertake this work at so tender an age?

"You'll be in the frying pan, sprout, if you're caught here," Fletcher said. "Quite a risk, quid fishing the Quality. They ain't so forgiving."

Hollis might have objected to the description, but he knew it to be true.

The girl spun, intent on heading back in the direction she'd come, only to stop in front of Stone. Her breath shook audibly.

"We ain't gonna hurt you, love," Hollis said gently. "The police're sniffing you out. We're hoping only to snatch you out of their grasp."

"An' into yours," she snapped, her voice fragile but fiery.

"Not a bit o' it," he said. "We know of a school that'd take you in sure as you're breathing. You could learn to be a shop girl or a servant. Somethin' other than thieving and sleeping on the street."

"I don't have no choice," she said. "The man what comes for my loot'll never let me go."

She had a thief master, then. That was hardly unheard of.

"We ain't meaning to ask his permission, sweetie," Fletcher said.

"He'll kill me. I know it." Not a bit of exaggeration touched the words. Hollis had learned enough of the plight of street children to know she was in earnest. And accurate.

"He'll not know where to find you, love." Hollis affected

an accent more in keeping with hers and Fletcher's. "This school'll tuck you away, keep you there 'til you're safe to take up work."

"Would they—" She stopped at the sudden sound of footsteps coming down the stairs.

They all held still.

"We'd best cut and run," Fletcher said. "Come along, sweetie. You'll be boiled in brine if you're caught here."

Hollis didn't for a minute think the girl had decided to actually trust them; she simply realized the danger of remaining.

The four of them moved quickly back down the deserted corridor toward the tradesman's door. Fletcher scooped the girl up, quickening his pace. They were out the door, closing it quickly but quietly behind them, and up the steps, through the iron gate, and around the corner before another word passed between them.

"Now, sweetie. What was it you meant to ask before we were interrupted?" Fletcher had a way with the children of London. Even this skittish child didn't try to squirm out of his hold, neither did she look scared.

"I wondered, sir, if they'd have a place I could sleep at their school. The man'll find me if I'm sleeping on the street. I don't want to keep smouging for him. But if he can find me—"

Fletcher squeezed the girl more tightly as they walked on. "I know what he'd do iffen he found you, sweetie. I'll not let him. None of us will."

The little girl looked over his shoulder at Hollis and

Stone. Her gaze didn't waste much time on *him*. Stone had every ounce of her curiosity.

"What's your name, love?" Hollis asked. She had to be called something other than the Phantom Fox.

"Very Merry."

Very Merry? He'd discovered during his years with the Dreadfuls that the London children often had odd names, names they'd given each other. This little sprite had two.

"Never fear, Very Merry," Fletcher said. "The school'll take you in, give you a bed, keep you away from that man, and teach you a job."

"Could I—?" She stopped, her tiny-girl face pulled in a look of contemplation. "When I'm taught enough to have a job, would I 'ave to stay in London?"

"When you've had all the learning you need," Fletcher said, "I'll find you a job anywhere in this country you'd care to go."

Her look of doubt was nearly sassy. "How'll you even know I've finished getting all m' learning?"

He reached into his coat pocket and pulled out a marked penny. "You keep this on you, sweetie. I'll tell you who at the school can get messages to me. You need only show 'em this penny, and they'll come for me straight off."

She held the penny, her eyes wide. A child this poor, this desperate might very well spend the penny, too deprived for patience.

Hollis pulled a farthing from his pocket and held it to her. "This one's for spending, love. But the school'll see to it you're fed and warm and all. You'll likely not even need it."

She held the two coins, breathless with amazement. Her eyes moved to Stone, hopeful.

Hollis had never heard the man laugh, but he did then, quiet and low. He pulled a coin from his pocket and held it out to her. Very Merry smiled at him.

The girl would receive a helpful education, which pleased Hollis to no end.

She was being given an escape from the cruelty of the streets, which would do Fletcher's heart a world of good.

And she would be free of the thief master who'd forced her into this dangerous and degrading existence, which would satisfy Stone to his very soul.

The Dreadfuls didn't always have good days. But, sometimes, they had nearly perfect ones.

HIGGLEBOTTOM'S SCHOOL FOR THE DEAD

A GHOST OF A CHANCE

by Lafayette Jones

Chapter II

"Blimey!" Snout declared over Ace's shoulder. "It's a Perishable."

"What's it doing here?" Bathwater asked.

Ace shrugged. "Beats me. I've never heard of a *living* person being at Higglebottom's." He eyed the terrified face under the bed. "What are you doing here?"

"I was caught in a storm," the boy said. "I came inside to get out of the rain."

"It hasn't rained since yesterday."

The boy rested his chin on his upturned fist. "I know."

"You've just been hiding?"

The boy's eyes darted around. "This place is full of *ghosts*."

Ace rested his ghostly chin on his ghostly fist, his position mirroring that of the boy's. "I know."

"Are you going to eat me?" the boy asked.

"Ghosts don't eat."

"Lock me up somewhere?"

Bathwater dropped onto the ground beside him, stopping his movement at the moment his spectral form would've stopped if he had a body. "Why didn't you just leave after the storm ended?"

The boy took a deep breath, something else ghosts didn't *have* to do but practiced as a way of either blending in or causing distress, whichever was needed. "I've nowhere to go."

"You don't have a family?" Bathwater asked.

The boy shook his head.

"A school of your own?" Snout asked.

Another headshake.

"A name?" Ace dropped in dryly.

"Frank," he said.

"Ace, Bathwater, Snout, and *Frank*?" Ace would have rolled his eyes if he'd learned the trick of it yet. Ghost bodies didn't work quite the same way Perishable bodies did. "You'll need a better name."

"Does that mean we're keeping him?" Snout asked.

"Where else is he going to go?" Ace motioned the boy out from under the bed. "No point hiding anymore."

"We should probably tell someone," Bathwater said. "We're only First Forms. We don't know what to do about something this big."

That was a temptation no ghost with ambition could pass up. Ace grinned. "Then let's be the only First Forms in the history of Higglebottom's to manage a *prank* this big."

Bathwater hesitated for a fraction of a moment, then both he and Snout turned to him eagerly. They were the best partners in crime a fellow could ask for.

Ace spoke to their newest arrival. "Would you like to stay at Higglebottom's, Frank?" *Frank.* He really needed a better name.

Frank nodded.

"That's our challenge, lads. We're going to pass off this Perishable as a ghost."

"To the professors, even?"

Ace nodded. "It wouldn't be much of a prank if we didn't pull the wool over *anyone's* eyes."

Bathwater circled Frank, eyeing him. "No one'll believe he's dead. He doesn't look it."

"Because I'm *not*," Frank tossed back.

"We can teach you to play the part," Ace said. "Learning how to be a ghost is what we're all here for anyway."

"You don't know how?" Frank asked.

"It ain't something you die knowing," Ace said.

"He has to have a uniform," Snout said. "Everyone'll know he's not a student if he's wearing that."

The boy wore high-collared shirtsleeves and buckled-at-the-knee trousers. Though both were crusted in mud, they weren't tattered and billowing like the Higglebottom's uniforms. He looked like a muddy Perishable, not a ghost.

"He's closest to your size, Snout. Fetch him an extra of yours."

But when Frank tried to put on the frayed shirt and trousers, they just floated through his arms and legs. It seemed Perishables couldn't wear ghost clothes.

"Well, there's that plan busted." Bathwater sounded as disappointed as Ace felt.

Ace, however, was not one to give up easily. "The

Hauntings Department has an entire storeroom of things that aren't made of phantom fabric. We could make him a uniform."

Snout nodded enthusiastically. "We could."

"How are you at walking quiet so you don't make a sound?" Ace asked Frank.

"Never tried it." The boy made a go of it.

His first few attempts were dismal. He'd make a rotten ghost as loud as he was. The element of surprise was key to any proper haunting. Stomping around would give him away straight off. But as he slowed down, he got quieter. After a lot of attempts and a lot of advice, Frank could move with an impressive degree of stealth.

When he spoke, he didn't sound much like a ghost, but Ace couldn't pin down what it was about his voice that gave him away. That bit of training would have to wait until he pieced the puzzle together. "Don't talk to anyone but us. That'll sort that difficulty."

"But we do have to worry about his face," Snout said.

"A fine thing to say," Frank said, "considering I know why they call you 'Snout.'"

Even Snout laughed at that. This Perishable was going to fit in nicely.

"I think he means your face isn't pale enough," Bathwater said. "We could tell you weren't a ghost right from the start, and we hadn't seen your clothes or heard you walking or anything."

Frank turned to Ace. "You're heading this expedition. What do *you* suggest?"

While Ace pondered the trouble of Frank's complexion, the

silence was broken by a sound never heard at Higglebottom's School for the Dead: a stomach growling.

Frank's already too-colorful face turned redder. "I'm a little hungry."

"We have food here," Ace said. "We don't have to eat it, but there's plenty around."

"I'd die for just a bite or two."

Ace chuckled. "Seems to me you'd die *without* a bite or two." He turned to Snout. "Could you sneak a bit of food up for Pudding, here?"

"Pudding?" Bathwater asked. "Is that his name now?"

"He's aching for food. Seems to me, naming him *for* food would be fitting." He held Frank's gaze. "What do you think?"

The Perishable shrugged. "I don't mind."

"'Pudding' it is."

Snout slipped from the room.

"I know why I'm called what I am, and where Snout's name came from." Pudding looked at Bathwater. "Why do they call you 'Bathwater'?"

Ace was the one who'd given him the name, so he was the one who answered. "Because he objected to being called 'Baby.'"

"So you threw out the 'Baby,'" Pudding said, "with the 'Bathwater.'"

"A brilliant solution if you ask me." Ace had figured out another "brilliant solution" for their current difficulty. "While Snout's fetching you food, let's see if we can't find a classroom with a good amount of chalk dust. We'll have you pale as death in no time."

"And then?" Pudding asked.

"As soon as we've got a uniform for you, we'll test your disguise with a stroll around the school."

Pudding looked intrigued but wary. "And if the disguise doesn't work?"

"Then Bathwater, Snout, and I won't be the only ones of the four of us who're dead."

CHAPTER 8

Ana visited her father on Thursday that week, which was unusual, but Elizabeth had invited her to attend the opera on Friday evening, and she had decided she would rather forgo the weekly teachers' calling time than miss a chance to enjoy an entire evening of music.

She let herself in, as always, and made her way to the empty bedchamber beside her father's. It had been her mother's, but now stood empty except for a curio cabinet in the corner and a small square table and slat-back chair in the center. All the other furniture had either been sold or stolen.

Careful not to make noise, she opened the cabinet. She pulled her recently reacquired figurine from its hiding place beneath a loaf of bread and a bundle of apples. Ana carefully placed it beside Grandfather's silver snuffbox and Mother's enameled opaline powder box. She turned it slightly, posing the porcelain girl so she kept her violin tucked a little out of sight, a bit coy and a bit shy. It had always stood that way in her bedchamber.

The curio cabinet held treasures she'd reacquired over the

past couple of years. Bits and pieces of her childhood, of her parents, of a life that had been stolen from them. She kept a list at Thurloe of the items she wanted back, who had taken them, and where they were now. She likely had years of questionable activities left before she marked off the final treasure.

If only Father hadn't entrusted his business to a corrupt partner. If only he'd realized his partner's crookedness sooner. If only polite society had proven truly polite instead of a flock of vultures.

She had enough "if onlys" to drown in. She'd far rather stay afloat.

Pasting a smile on her face, she slipped out once more, closing the door and moving into Father's room.

"Good evening, Father."

"Ana. You've come on a Thursday. What a treat."

That he was happy to see her did her heart good. A person living separate from her family, spending her free time attempting to undo the damage done to her loved ones by heartless people, could easily grow cynical. Ana did her utmost not to let that happen.

"I am engaged for tomorrow evening, and I could not go an entire week without seeing you."

He smiled at her, a sad but loving sort of smile. "You are a good girl, Ana."

"Is Mr. Thompson behaving himself?"

"The Thompsons left London. Wallace heard whispers amongst the neighborhood servants that the Thompsons have a cousin who'll be living there for a time."

"You'll still have plenty to watch, then."

Father's spirits must have been high that day. He shook

his head in amusement, something he did not always allow. "I will make you a full reporting next Friday."

Ana handed off her basket of foodstuffs to Wallace.

He lowered his voice to keep his next comment between the two of them. "Someone broke into the house yesterday."

Ana's stomach fell.

"Heard more'n one voice," Wallace said. "Lots of footprints in the dust. Two, prob'ly three thieves. Never came up the stairs."

"Did they steal anything?"

Wallace's brows shot up and his mouth turned in amusement. "There ain't nothing to steal."

There had been the last time thieves had descended upon this house. "Does my father know?"

"He'd only fret," Wallace said. "I ain't meaning to mention it."

"That is likely for the best."

Father wasn't senile or in a state of mental deterioration. His struggles were born of loneliness and isolation, guilt and bitterness. He hid from the world as a way of punishing them, and likely himself. It was both terribly complicated and painfully simple.

She crossed back to her father and sat on the ottoman near his chair. "What are you reading?"

He held up a penny dreadful.

"That is the newest by Lafayette Jones, I believe." She had read a few of his works. His tales were light and fun, perfect for younger readers. Indeed, she'd slipped a copy of the first installment of this most recent tale to one of her students who struggled to read.

"Wallace read Jones's work first. He introduced me to them." Father nodded. "A fine thing, that."

"What do you think of this school for ghosts he has concocted?" she asked.

"Brilliant. Children will find the idea vastly entertaining."

"Have you read any other of the penny dreadfuls?" She enjoyed having something pleasing to discuss with him.

"I like those 'Urchins of London' stories."

"By Fletcher Walker," Ana said with a nod.

"You've read them?"

She smiled. "I've met Mr. Walker."

Father took in a quick breath. "Truly? Is he a respectable sort? One hears whispers about these authors."

"His speech isn't overly proper, but neither is it offensive. He acted the perfect gentlemen at the musicale we both attended. And he is good friends with Mr. Hollis Darby, who comes from a notable family. In fact, I am to attend an opera tomorrow and sit in a box with both gentlemen and some other very fine people."

"Thompsons have a box at the opera." Father's eyes darted to the front-facing window as he spoke. "I wonder if these cousins taking up residence will use it."

"They well might."

Conversation shifted to the neighbors. Ana's father watched the world around him but never joined it. Ana wasn't certain he even knew how to do so anymore.

As she made to leave an hour or so later, she pulled Wallace aside. "If any other precautions are needed to secure the house, I will do my best to acquire the necessary funds as quickly as possible."

"You're a right'n, Miss Newport. Good to your father, you are. He oughtta tell you that more often." Wallace suddenly seemed to realize what he'd said. "Not that I think it m'place to criticize the man I work for, mind you."

"You didn't," she assured him. "You offered me a much-needed compliment. One, I assure you, I appreciate."

She left with only kind words to buoy her heavy spirits. Father seemed unlikely to emerge from his self-imposed exile, and she was living her life in the shadows.

But she had an opera to look forward to. Music had always been her escape. She would cling to it.

Ana donned the same gray silk gown she'd worn to the musicale. If Elizabeth noticed the fashion faux pas, she didn't say anything. When Mr. Walker arrived in the hackney and he didn't point out her repeated wardrobe either, Ana's nerves began to settle.

As they walked toward their box for the evening, Elizabeth whispered to Ana, "Fletcher has spoiled me for operas. We've attended several in this box, and I don't believe I could ever attend one sitting anywhere else."

"You have become very highbrow, Elizabeth," Ana said with a laugh.

"Apparently."

All around them, jewels glittered, and fine gowns swished about beside finely tailored jackets and silk top hats. Attendees discussed the finer points of that evening's opera or performances they'd recently enjoyed in this particular venue.

There were some aspects of Society Ana truly missed: trips to the theatre, musicales, conversation at soirees.

They stepped into the box to find Hollis already waiting. Since starting to work at the Darby house, she'd begun thinking of Hollis by his Christian name in an attempt to keep the Darby brothers straight.

"Miss Newport." He offered her a bow. "I had hoped you would be available to attend this evening. Miss Black said Fridays often see you occupied."

"I was able to rearrange my schedule," she said. "It has been an age since I attended the opera. I've missed it."

"Tonight's offering is *Fidelio*, Beethoven's only opera," Hollis said. "Considering you played one of *his* pieces at the musicale, I thought you would enjoy this night's selection."

"You are very thoughtful," she said.

He appeared to blush, but so slightly she couldn't be entirely certain. She liked that it was possible he, a gentleman of significant standing, could color up at a compliment. Too many thought approval was their right.

Before another word could be spoken, Alistair Headley stepped into the box. Mr. Headley had once been a regular caller at Thurloe, but he'd not been there even once since Elizabeth and Mr. Walker's mutual affection had become apparent. He was a touch too arrogant with a tendency to assume that every woman was, by default, intellectually inferior to him.

"Headley." Hollis's greeting was one of both surprise and displeasure.

Mr. Headley eyed Mr. Walker with the slightest pursing

of his lips. "I see the bar for opera attendees has been lowered."

Mr. Walker didn't give the least indication he'd been insulted. "And you saw that, when? Lookin' in the mirror?"

Elizabeth set her hand on Mr. Walker's arm. "Ana and I will take our seats. The three of you can fluff your feathers until the curtain raises."

Mr. Walker's smile was one of amused mischief. Ana suspected she would like him a great deal if she came to know him better.

She walked with Elizabeth to the chairs at the front of the box and took the middle two. Below, the pit was teeming with working-class people, some even lower class than that. If not for Hollis's generosity, she'd have been limited to watching the performance from there, if at all. The box was decidedly more comfortable and far more luxurious. It was a treat, indeed.

Behind them, the gentlemen had not ended their posturing.

"I thought your brother would be in his box tonight," Mr. Headley said.

"The box belongs to the Darby family, of which I am a part," Hollis answered. "*I* am using it this evening."

"A pity for the box," Mr. Headley drawled.

"Have you come strictly as a grievance monger?" Mr. Fletcher asked. "Or did you mean to jaw at us all night?"

"One would think an author would speak proper English," Mr. Headley said.

"What is it you want?" Hollis's question seemed equal parts invitation and exasperation.

"I needed to talk with your brother."

Ana looked to Elizabeth out of the corner of her eye. Her friend was clearly paying very close heed to the conversation behind them.

"I can relay a message to him," Hollis said.

"We were meant to meet tonight, have a bit of a lark. He said he had other plans."

"You want me to tell my brother that he wounded your feelings?"

Elizabeth barely held back a laugh. Ana found herself smiling as well.

"He agreed to—" Whatever Mr. Headley meant to say, he apparently thought better of it. "Do you know where he went this evening—since he's obviously not here?"

"Odd, Hollis," Mr. Walker said. "You never told me you were your brother's social secretary."

"I can think of no occupation I would rather have," Hollis answered dryly.

"You two are imbeciles." Footsteps sounded—frustrated, angry footsteps—fading into silence.

The two gentlemen joined them, Mr. Walker sitting on Elizabeth's other side, Hollis on Ana's.

"What is Mr. Headley's connection to your brother?" Elizabeth asked.

Hollis's gaze settled on the stage below but didn't seem to truly focus. "Randolph and Headley have known each other a couple of years, but only as passing acquaintances. Something has changed of late."

"I don't like it," Mr. Walker said.

In a mutter just above a whisper, Hollis said, "Neither do I."

The curtain rose, but Hollis seemed unable to focus. After a half hour of seeing his distraction, Ana leaned toward him. "Do you need to look in on your brother?"

That seemed to pull him back to the moment. "Forgive me, Miss Newport. I am proving a poor companion."

She shook her head. "My thoughts are seldom present with me when I am concerned for people I care about."

"Your students?"

"Always." They were seldom far from her thoughts, especially those who were struggling in some way. "And my fellow teachers, and my father."

"Worry over my father occupied the vast deal of my time in the last years of his life," Hollis said. "I hope yours is less of a weight on your mind."

Ana never discussed her father with anyone. How odd that she felt at ease doing so with Hollis.

"I would worry less if he needed me less," she said. "I am not often with him, and he is alone much of the time."

"I am sorry to hear that," he said. "Is your father ill?"

"Ill of heart."

Hollis nodded. "My late mother could have been described that way. The weight of the world eventually broke her heart."

"I am sorry to hear that." She set her hand in his, squeezing his fingers. "Losing my mother was one of the hardest things I ever experienced."

He wrapped his fingers warmly around hers. "Sometimes I feel very alone in my grief."

They sat there, hand in hand, as the opera continued. And, as they did, an odd thing happened. Ana's heart rested in a way it hadn't since before Father had told her his business had failed, all their money was gone, and he was likely to be prosecuted for fraud. She'd been, to some degree or another, fearful every moment since.

"Sometimes I feel very alone, too," she whispered.

"If you ever wish for a listening ear or a supportive shoulder, those happen to be my two best features."

She set her free hand on his arm, keeping their other hands entwined. For the length of this one evening, she would let herself find in him the support and understanding so often lacking in her life.

He was a member of a respected and elevated family, a welcome part of the very Society from which she was distanced. Her poverty and lowered status had created a chasm. The necessity of taking up sneak thievery to regain what had been taken only broadened that gap. There was no escaping that reality.

But for tonight, she would cherish the warmth and kindness of this gracious and considerate gentleman.

CHAPTER 9

Hollis walked down Fleet Street, having given his publisher the most recent installment of "Higglebottom's School for the Dead." The tale was doing well, though not on the level of Fletcher or Mr. King, but still, he was pleased.

His spirits were light, but not fully owing to his publishing successes. Ana had sat with him throughout the opera. They'd spoken in intimate whispers about their families and lives. She'd held his hand for hours.

She hadn't done so on Saturday morning during their ride to and from Randolph's house. But she had smiled at him in her soft and sincere way. That had done his heart good. The more he knew of her, the more he liked her. He did worry, though, what so soft-spoken and gentle a lady would think if she knew the roughness of his edges.

As he made his way along Fleet Street, he spied Fletcher. Hollis sometimes came across one of the Dreadfuls in this area of London, generally having just handed over manuscript pages. He checked quickly for carriages, then jaunted across the street.

Fletcher gave him a nod.

"Are you delivering your latest installment?" Hollis asked.

"No. Just wanderin' about, assessing the weather."

Ah. He was checking with his network of urchins.

"Will my being with you make the barometers more difficult to read?"

He gave a small shake of his head. "I don't have a single barometer that don't know you and I are chums. Likely, none of 'em can sort out why."

"*I* can't sort out why."

Fletcher laughed. For all the misery he'd known in life, the man's spirits never dropped permanently. Hollis tried to emulate that.

"Shine your shoes, guv?" A small bootblack—likely approaching eleven or twelve years old—called out as they approached.

"Could use a shine." Fletcher stopped.

"I ain't certain you have time, guv'nuh." The boy flipped a penny around before tossing it to Fletcher.

Fletcher eyed it close. "This one's Very Merry's."

"Li'l angel-face imp at Barton school?" the boy asked.

Fletcher nodded.

"She seems right anxious to see you."

"Any inkling why?" Fletcher asked.

"Near as I've heard, she ain't ill or injured."

That was a relief.

"Fancy a trek to Barton school?" Fletcher asked Hollis.

"There's nothing I'd rather spend my afternoon doing."

Fletcher tossed the bootblack a farthing. "Ears to the ground, boy."

"Always." He pulled his cap. "And give my greetings to that cunning lady of yours. Still cain't believe she gave me the slip."

Fletcher grinned. "Never underestimate a woman, Henry."

"Wise words," Hollis tossed in.

As they walked away, heading toward the Barton school, Fletcher slid easily into the role of spy. So subtly most would miss it, his gaze turned alert and aware. Hollis was not quite as adept at hiding his scrutiny, so he tucked his efforts behind an air of aristocratic superiority. He didn't particularly enjoy playing the arrogant gentleman, but it was the only ace he held at the moment.

"How do we mean to play this?" Hollis asked. "We can't snatch the girl out of the school like kidnappers. Marching in and demanding they hand her over wouldn't work much better."

"I thought gentlemen of means could walk in anywhere and have their run of the place." Fletcher's humor could be dry as dirt at times.

"*You* have more 'means' than *I* do," Hollis pointed out.

Fletcher nodded to a costermonger neglecting his cart of apples in favor of a spot of reading. "He's reading one of Elizabeth's."

He was, indeed. "How is her—er, *Mr. King's*—latest doing?"

"Better'n all of ours combined, likely."

"The King reigns over the penny dreadfuls," Hollis said,

"and I'm, apparently, meant to walk into Barton school like the blasted queen and demand to see a little girl who's probably been nipping off with everything in sight."

"You ain't dressed the part, mate."

Hollis rubbed at his jaw. "Perhaps there's something in the Wardrobe Room."

"As much as I'd enjoy seeing you dressed as Ol' Victoria, I think we'd best arrive at Barton school togged as we are."

They turned down Long Acre. Barton school wasn't far off.

"I came with Elizabeth when she brought Very Merry here," Fletcher said. "The headmistress knows I've a connection to the little guttersnipe. She'll allow me a visit with the girl."

They reached the unassuming building that housed the Barton School for Girls. Most people passing it wouldn't have the first idea what it truly was.

The click of the knocker was answered in due time by a girl of likely fourteen or fifteen in a plain dress and clean apron.

Fletcher offered his calling card with a flourish. "Fletcher Walker and Hollis Darby for the headmistress, please."

The girl dropped a curtsey. "I'll fetch—" She shook her head. Her lips moved silently a moment, then she curtseyed again. "If you will wait here, please, gentlemen." Her accent wasn't refined, but it wouldn't cause an uproar in a finer household. She stepped away, but stopped and turned back, then bobbed a third curtsey. With that, the girl all but ran from the room and up the nearby staircase.

"That poor dearie is still in training," Fletcher said. "She has a spot to learn yet."

Hollis eyed the entryway, impressed at how clean and well-maintained it was, no matter that the furnishings were simple and clearly secondhand. The maids-in-training were likely charged with the upkeep of the school. An ingenious arrangement. What better way to learn a skill than by practicing it?

"Education works miracles. It changes lives. I'll never stop fighting for more children to have that opportunity," he said.

A stout woman with a rounded puff of silver hair trumped down the stairs. She eyed the both of them, her expression welcoming but her gaze sharp.

"Mr. Walker," she said as she reached the bottom step and moved toward them. "What brings you around?"

"I'm wanting to look in on that little Major MacFluffer Miss Black and I brought to you a few days back. Just wishing to set my heart at ease over her."

The woman nodded. "Merry is something of a disruption, but a joyful one."

Merry. The headmistress, it seemed, was not calling the girl by the name she, herself, went by. Perhaps that was why Very Merry had sent for Fletcher. Being in an unfamiliar place and called by an unfamiliar name would be disconcerting for any child.

"Mrs. Hempstead, this here's Hollis Darby." Fletcher motioned to him. "He's a friend and a champion of educational causes. He heard about your school and wished to see your good work for his own self. And he's quite curious about your littlest student."

A genuine smile twitched on Mrs. Hempstead's face. "She's a rare one, Mr. Darby."

"That is my understanding."

"Merry is receiving sewing instruction at the moment. If you step inside here"—Mrs. Hempstead indicated a doorway on the left—"I will bring her down to visit with you."

Hollis offered a dip of his head, then followed Fletcher into a small sitting room, as tidy and simple as the entryway. He made a circuit of the room, impressed by what he saw. Girls trained to be maids here would do well in their eventual positions. Working in a household was far safer than working on the streets.

"We *have* to find people to help fund this school," Hollis said. "We can't allow this to simply disappear."

"Heyup, Mr. Walker," a little voice greeted.

Hollis kept himself turned away. Until he knew they were alone with the little sneak thief, he didn't dare let her know he was the other gentleman in the room. She might recognize him, and he was meant to not have ever met her.

He heard the door close and hazarded a peek. Only the three of them were in the room. Very Merry's eyes opened wide when she saw him.

"You're dressed quite fine," she said. "An' you look accustomed to it."

"Nothing slips past you, Very Merry."

"An' you sound it, too." Her mouth pursed, and her brows dipped. "Which are you, then? High or low?"

Hollis allowed a little shrug. "A bit of both, love."

She smiled. "Whatever you need to be."

He nodded.

Very Merry set her sights on Fletcher. "I sent my penny out to fetch you."

Fletcher pulled it from his pocket. "That's why I'm here, sweetie." He flipped it to her, and she caught it in her quick little hands. "What's tied you up in knots?"

"There ain't nothing makin' this school safe but a lock on the door." She shook her head. "I've picked it eighteen times just since coming here. Cain't expect me to stay in a place like this. It'd ruin m' reputation."

What a mischievous delight she was.

"What would you suggest?" Hollis asked. "A bar on the door? A guard?"

She popped her tiny fists on her hips. If not for her seven-year-old frame, she'd have passed for a fishwife. "Wouldn't hurt, now would it?"

"You truly think it necessary?" Fletcher pressed.

Very Merry's shoulders rose and fell with an impatient breath. "If the man finds out I'm here, that lock ain't gonna keep him out. He'll do me in for welchin' on what I owe him." She *had* mentioned something about the man she stole for when they'd first suggested she come to the Barton school. "All us children bring 'im what we nip every day. If we don't, he'll beat us or not let us eat or make us sleep on the street. And sometimes—" She paused a fraction of a moment, then pressed on. "Children disappear," she whispered. "We don't know where they go, but *he* knows."

"He kidnaps them?"

Her mouth pulled in a slash. She didn't answer, but she

didn't truly have to. Very Merry, it seemed, did not think this criminal ringleader was simply taking the children. Hollis would wager she and the other children believed the unnamed man was doing them in.

"Do you think he's searching for you, sweetie?" Fletcher asked.

"He doesn't want anyone sniffing out where he is. Those of us what know . . ."

It made sense. Horrible, heart-wrenching sense.

"This man wouldn't necessarily look for you here, but if he happened to find you . . . ?" Hollis let the sentence dangle, allowing her to finish it.

"*I* can break in or out of here. It'd be nothin' to him."

Yes, but how likely was this man to find her? "Is it only *children* that he makes steal things for him?"

She shook her head.

"And are there lots of people?" Fletcher asked.

She nodded.

This wasn't good at all.

"He had the dodos hot on him a couple months ago," she said. "Barely got away, he did."

"Dodos?" Hollis asked Fletcher under his breath.

"Police," Fletcher explained.

Very Merry continued, not noting the side conversation. "He's jumpy now, chivied. Rages at every little thing, thinking everyone's turning on 'im. More of us've been disappearing. Coming here made me hope some of 'em just escaped, but I'd guess not many."

A lowlife who had a vast group of people thieving on his

behalf, who was dangerous and violent, and who had barely escaped arrest two months earlier. That was awfully familiar.

Hollis glanced at Fletcher, who held up four fingers. Four-Finger Mike was not the largest threat in London, but he wasn't one to be taken lightly. And he was a known associate of the Mastiff, a criminal so brutal even the Metropolitan Police were afraid of him.

"If we step over a bit and leave you here," Fletcher said to the little girl, "do you promise not to nip off with anything?"

She rolled her eyes. "I ain't gonna filch nothing."

Whether or not that was true, the girl climbed onto the threadbare settee to wait for them.

Fletcher and Hollis positioned themselves by the far wall.

"I hate to admit we've been outsmarted by a seven-year-old," Fletcher said, "but she's got the right of it. She cain't stay here."

"If we'd realized Four-Finger Mike was her taskmaster, we wouldn't have brought her here to begin with." Hollis rubbed at his mouth, thinking. "Could Elizabeth keep her at Thurloe? She has Ol' Joe there, keeping watch. And that little Daniel of his doesn't miss a thing."

Fletcher shook his head. "She already has two girls on Four-Finger's list. Three would be pushing our luck beyond reason." His expression pinched. "I'd take her in myself, but I've only me and my manservant in the house. Adding a little girl would be uncomfortable for all of us, most of all her."

"I can take her," Hollis said. "I have Ambrose and Libby. They'd look after the girl. Being one-time criminals themselves, they'd not turn their noses up at her. And, seeing as they've been informants for the DPS for ages, they can be trusted to know what to do should things grow precarious."

"What about her education?" Fletcher asked.

"Oh, I'm fully confident she'll receive a thorough education," he answered dryly.

Fletcher grinned. "You might be creating an unbeatable team with those three."

"I'm willing to take that chance if it'll keep our little Phantom Fox safe. She steals hearts as easily as everything else."

Fletcher sent a fond look in the girl's direction. "The urchins have a way of doing that. They fight hard to survive; a person can't help admirin' that."

"All us Dreadfuls are survivors," Hollis said. "She'll be one of us in no time."

"More likely, she'll be running us all ragged. Probably could even manage to sniff out the Dread Master and unthrone him."

"If having her wreak havoc in my house means I'll finally know the identity of our mysterious leader, then my only question is why didn't I bring her home ages ago?"

Fletcher mimicked Very Merry's theatrical eye roll. "I'm not tellin' you the Dread Master's identity."

"I know. I'm pinning my hopes on that little one."

Fletcher slapped him on the shoulder. "I wish you luck, my friend. I suspect life is about to get mighty chaotic."

THE GENTLEMAN AND THE THIEF

by Mr. King

Installment III,
in which our Hero finds himself in a
most uncomfortable Situation!

Wellington rushed in the direction of Tillie's terrified scream. The room was dim but not dark to the point of blackness. Thank the heavens he could see her. He ran directly to her, putting his arms around her and tucking her behind him. His eyes scanned the room, searching for the threat.

"It was over there." Her voice shook.

"What was?" The room was empty—not even a stick of furniture.

"A flame. A bl—blue flame."

"The room was on fire?"

She clutched his arm, trembling. "No. It was floating in the air. Away from the walls. Away from the floor. No candle. No torch. Just a flame."

His gaze turned from the room to her. "Floating?"

"Don't look at me like I'm mad." She pointed near the

window. "A floating flame. It was there, and then, *poof*, it blew out. But there was no one who'd been holdin' it. There was just . . . nothing."

She still held his arm, like it was a lifeline in a raging sea. Wellington didn't know what she'd seen, perhaps something outside that, when glimpsed through the high, dingy window, had seemed to be inside.

He stepped toward the window, meaning to see if he couldn't solve the mystery. She didn't release her white-knuckle grip on his arm. "You are well and truly frightened."

"You'd be as well if you'd seen what I did."

"A flame? The flicker of a candle?"

"It was too large for a candle." Her voice still shook. "It moved about all on its own. Nothin' to explain how it could possibly be there."

He unwrapped her fingers from his forearm and took her hand in his instead. He saw no singe marks on the walls, no indication that anything had been aflame. He spied nothing outside the high window that might have been mistaken for a flame. Would the mysteries never cease?

"I cannot explain it, Tillie." He looked to her. "Are you certain you didn't—"

"It weren't my imagination." Her eyes filled with growing panic.

Wellington tugged her toward the door. "Let us go back to the cottage. We can save our search efforts for another day."

She nodded, still shaken. "I think that'd be best."

Hardly another word was spoken as they crossed the

estate grounds. She was pale, bless her, and very quiet, a rarity for Tillie Combs.

Her father took note of her condition immediately. "What's happened?"

Tillie dropped onto a spindle-back chair, apparently not able or ready to answer. Wellington did so instead.

"During our search for the missing things, she saw something she cannot explain."

"What?" Mr. Combs looked from one of them to the other.

"A blue flame," Wellington said. "It floated with no explanation."

"A blue flame?" He repeated the description in a tone of awe, his wide eyes falling fully on his daughter. "Moved about, did it?"

Tillie took a shaking breath. "It was unnerving, Papa. Cold and . . ." She shook her head. "I didn't like it."

Mr. Combs rubbed at his unshaven chin as he paced away. "Odd, bein' where we are. Odd, indeed."

"You know what it was?" Wellington asked. What a boon it would be if he could, indeed, explain it.

"I've a notion." Mr. Combs motioned him out of the house. "I'll give it some thought, sir. If m' Tillie saw what I think she saw, you've a bigger mystery on your hands than you realize."

He was offered no further explanation than that. In a moment's time, Wellington was outside the cottage, alone, confused, and already longing for the return of Tillie's smiles and spirit-lifting company.

Two days after the blue-flame encounter, Mrs. Smith rushed into Wellington's library, a mixture of excitement and panic on her face. "You've visitors, sir!"

"Visitors?" He very seldom had anyone call on him at Summerworth. It was an isolated estate, and his period of mourning for his parents had necessitated the estate be quiet and lifeless. Even with that period past, nothing much had changed.

"Two carriages, sir," she said. "And the young people spilling out look fine indeed."

He rose from his desk and crossed to the window. Two carriages sat in the drive, but both appeared to be empty.

"The visitors are in the drawing room, Mr. Quincey," Mrs. Smith said.

The house was so out of practice with visitors, Mrs. Smith had managed the thing in quite the wrong order. "I will be there directly," he said.

She nodded and rushed from the room.

Visitors. He didn't know whether to feel pleased or concerned. What if his as-yet-unidentified thief had made off with the tea set or the chairs in the drawing room? What if these new arrivals were hoping for a place to stop their journey for the night and they, too, found themselves victims of this thief?

Wellington made himself presentable and joined his guests in the drawing room. One mystery solved itself immediately. Two of the gentlemen—Alsop and Henson—were known to him, they having been acquaintances at school. Perhaps not truly close friends, but near enough to make a call, even an unexpected one, completely acceptable.

Bows and curtsies preceded formal introductions. His one-time chums had brought with them a Mr. Fairbanks, his sister, Miss Fairbanks, and Miss Porter, an acquaintance of the Fairbanks family. Their manner of speaking and dress marked them all as residing firmly in the upper class. There would be no footraces among this lot.

"You've not been to London in ages, Quincey," Alsop said.

"I have been in mourning," he reminded them.

"Not for the last six months."

The truth of that could not be argued. "The estate has occupied much of my time of late. Leaving it unattended has not been an option."

Henson was walking the length of the drawing room. "The place seems nearly abandoned. Has some tragedy befallen the area?"

"Many of the servants left after my parents' passing." That was all the more detail he meant to furnish them with on that score. "As for tragedies, would a string of thefts suffice?"

The ladies pressed shocked hands to their hearts—not the theatrical jest Tillie had employed, but a gesture made in earnest. The gentlemen looked to him with alarm.

"Thefts?" Mr. Fairbanks clicked his tongue and shook his head. "What is this world coming to?"

"I believe I will catch out the culprit soon enough," Wellington said. "But at the moment I am baffled."

Mrs. Smith appeared quite suddenly in the doorway, a frantic expression on her aging face. "Another visitor, sir. Miss Combs."

Tillie slipped inside with her usual adventurous spirit firmly in place. "I've a notion to search again if you're—" Her gaze fell on the others. "Oh. You've callers."

Wellington waved her closer. "Miss Combs, this is Miss Fairbanks and Miss Porter. Mr. Alsop, Mr. Henson, and Mr. Fairbanks."

They offered half-hearted bows and curtsies. Tillie's effort was a touch less refined than was generally seen in more exalted circles, but there was no malice in it, no disrespect. She was a good soul.

"How do you two know one another?" Miss Fairbanks asked.

"Miss Combs"—it felt odd referring to Tillie so formally; they'd been friends so long, he struggled to think of her as anything but his one-time playmate—"grew up on the estate. Her father is the Summerworth steward."

"Ah." More than one of the visitors made the exact same noise of dawning understanding.

"Do you still live on the estate?" Miss Fairbanks asked Tillie. "Few people do, as I understand it."

"The butler and housekeeper and m'father and I are the only ones left," Tillie said. "We see to it the grand ol' place keeps standing."

"Mr. Quincey is fortunate to have all of you," Miss Porter's words were kind, but something in her tone was not.

Tillie seemed to notice it as well. Her brow drew down,

and she watched the gathering with more wariness than before.

Alsop returned his attention to Wellington. "We're bound for a house party at George Berkley's estate. You remember him from Cambridge. He said he'd be most pleased to have you there."

An invitation to a house party. This was the first he'd had since leaving behind his mourning period. When first he'd finished school and entered Society, he would have jumped at the opportunity, but now he found himself hesitant.

"Do come, Mr. Quincy," Miss Fairbanks said. "It promises to be a very enjoyable week in the country."

"While I am grateful for the invitation, I do need to sort out the matter of these thefts. Else, I might return home to find the house entirely empty."

Tillie still hadn't moved from her spot. Her eyes darted from one person to the next, her concern and confusion clearly growing. What had her so frozen? Tillie was not usually one to be rendered so withdrawn.

Mrs. Smith arrived with a heavily laden tray. She set it on a nearby table, then tossed him a look of apology. "I'll be back with the actual tea, sir. I'm a bit at loose ends, being out of practice and such."

Before he could reassure her, Tillie spoke. "I'll help you."

"Oh, bless you, Tillie."

The two women slipped out, but Tillie looked back, meeting his eye before dropping her gaze and hurrying from the room. Where had her unflagging spirit gone?

"Does Miss Combs often make herself so at home here?" Henson asked. "Seems a bit forward for a servant."

"She's not a servant," Wellington insisted. "She's the daughter of the estate steward."

"A minor difference," Miss Fairbanks said. "She is most decidedly bold."

"She is helping me search for the thief."

"Helping you *find* the thief?" Alsop shook his head. "Has it occurred to you, my friend, that she might *be* the thief?"

"Tillie?" He guffawed. "She would not steal so much as a dandelion from a meadow much less items belonging to another person."

Alsop shrugged. Henson gave Wellington a look of pity.

"I do hope we are wrong, Mr. Quincey," Miss Fairbanks said, "but you would be well-advised to keep a close eye on her."

"I will take your advice into consideration," he said through tight teeth.

"I see we have offended you." Miss Fairbanks fluttered over to him, all solicitousness. "That was not our intention. Do come to the house party with us. Allow us to show you we hold no ill will."

"Again, I thank you." He addressed them all. "But I will have to decline. Estate matters require my attention."

Conversation grew more general, ranging from topics of Society to the weather. The visitors were not unpleasant, neither had they been outright rude, yet Wellington felt dissatisfied with their company. He missed Tillie. He had missed her the past two days. Heavens, he had missed her the past two years. If only she hadn't run off to the kitchens.

If only this group hadn't sent her fleeing there. If only, if only, if only!

Tea was brought up, but by Mrs. Smith alone. Tillie, it seemed, did not mean to make another appearance.

The callers prepared to depart, insisting they needed to be on their way if they were to reach their stop for the night, the last before arriving at their final destination. Farewells were exchanged as were hopes that they would meet again, perhaps in Town.

"Do think on what we said," Alsop offered, one step from the front portico. "You may be chasing a thief who knows where you are looking. When one hands an arsonist matches, one is playing with fire."

Wellington motioned him on. "I will bear that in mind."

A moment later, they were gone, yet Wellington did not rest easy. He hadn't even a moment in which to do so before Tillie spoke from behind him.

"They think I am your thief, don't they?"

He spun about. There she stood, looking somehow both hurt and defiant. "They don't know you."

"But *you* do, and you gave some thought to their warning."

"Tillie—"

She pushed past him. "You didn't believe me 'bout that flame, and you don't full believe me that I'm not thieving from you." She pointed a finger at him. "We're friends, Wellington Quincy. Perhaps it's time you treated me like we were."

CHAPTER 10

"I've a bee to tuck up your bonnet." Ambrose was only this informal when interacting with Hollis on Dreadfuls business. He and his wife, Libby, were the apex of Hollis's servants' network pyramid. They knew absolutely everything.

Hollis carefully set aside the manuscript page he was working on and gave the man his full attention.

"It's Very Merry," he said.

"Is she giving you difficulty?"

Ambrose shook his head. "She's a little devil, but we're keepin' pace with her."

"Then what's the trouble?"

"She's said things that have my ears perked." Ambrose leaned his shoulder against the nearby wall. "Told us you and your chums found her belowstairs in some fine house in Pimlico."

Hollis nodded. "A nearly empty house where she'd not have found much of value to filch. While we were tracking her through London, we had report of her stealing little figurines and worthless bits of costume jewelry and such."

"She seems more knowin' than that," Ambrose said.

Hollis shrugged. "She *is* little yet. Maybe she hasn't sorted it all."

Ambrose folded his arms across his chest. "She told my Libby that she weren't in that Pimlico house to steal anything. She was hiding, but she won't tell either of us what or who she was hiding from. The closest we've come to an answer was 'He weren't supposed to be there.'" Ambrose pushed out a breath. "And it weren't a casual thing. Someone was where he oughtn't be, and that someone has her terrified."

"That someone is likely Four-Finger Mike," Hollis said.

Ambrose stood straight, his face pale. "What connection does she have to that whisht cove?"

"She was one of his underlings, stealing because he required it of her."

Ambrose whistled low. "I understand being terrified of that bloke. But he'd not be in that part of Pimlico. He'd be as out of place there as a badger in a horse race. No slippery fellow of his ilk would toss himself where he'd be so quickly sniffed out."

Ambrose was dead on the money there.

"He must have a reason for taking such a risk," Hollis said.

"A matter that crushing cain't be small, and our Very Merry likely knows more than she ought."

Which meant she was still in danger.

Hollis stood. "I'm going to grab one of the lads and take

a stroll down St. George's—see if we can't sort out what might send a rat to a tea party."

"I'll drop it in your ear if I hear anything through the network," Ambrose said. "Or if that demon child you stuck on us says anything more."

"You can't fool me, man. You're fond of that 'demon child.'"

Ambrose laughed. "We are that."

Hollis snatched his tall hat off the table beside the door. He looked back at Ambrose. "Keep an eye on the place."

"Keep an eye on yourself." He nodded toward the desk. "And don't neglect your writing. I need to know what happens with that Pudding fella."

Hollis popped his hat on his head, dipped his chin, and slipped from the room.

O———

Dreadfuls' headquarters was bustling when Hollis arrived. No meeting had been called; it was simply a popular spot that day. Luck seemed to be on his side as the one he most needed to find was already there, reading in the library.

"Ah, Brogan. Just who I was looking for."

Brogan flipped a page of his book. "Why is it I can't get any of the lasses to say that?"

"Your ugly mug, probably."

His mouth tipped at the corner. "I've not had many complaints."

"Or, apparently, many requests."

Brogan's smile formed fully. "What brings you 'round?"

"What do you know of the poorer areas of Pimlico? St. George's Road, in particular."

Brogan chuckled. "That ain't a poorer area by anyone's estimation."

That had been Hollis's assessment as well. "Do you remember the house on St. George's Road? The one where we found our tiny thief?"

"I do."

"She wasn't there trying to rob the place. She was hiding. From Four-Finger Mike."

The Irishman's ginger brows shot upward. "Boil m'bones," he whispered.

Hollis rubbed at his mouth. "I can't sort out why he would've been there. I suppose he could have been thieving, but there's a reason these slippery fellows piece together teams of crooks: saves them the trouble and the risk."

"'Tis an oddity, for sure." Brogan crossed his arms over his chest. "He'd be sorted out quickly amongst the Quality."

"And, yet, he was there. The man who escaped the police, who's masterminded kidnappings and robberies and arsons, was in a place he shouldn't have been. That worries me."

"Worries me, as well." Brogan rose slowly. "Fancy a stroll around Pimlico?"

"Only a stroll?"

Brogan made a small gesture of casual dismissal. "Perhaps a touch of spying, if we've a spare minute or two."

Hollis eyed Brogan's working-class togs. He'd likely come directly from one of his missions of mercy. "We need to be dressed at the same level, though. Otherwise we'll draw notice."

"For St. George's in Pimlico?" Brogan chuckled. "I'll dress *up*."

Another testament to how strange the idea of Four-Finger Mike being in that spot truly was.

A quick trip to the Wardrobe Room saw Brogan strutting about in the weeds of the upper classes. They passed Irving and Kumar, who both ribbed him thoroughly for his fanciness. As they approached the front door, they passed Stone.

The man looked them over quickly but thoroughly. "Cutting a dash."

"I make a fine aristocratic type, if I do say so." Brogan's attempt at an upper-class accent emerged far more like drunk Cockney.

"Maybe you'd best let me do the talking." Hollis slapped a hand on Brogan's shoulder. "Or at least agree to pretend to be Irish."

"I *am* Irish."

Hollis nodded, lips twisted outward in exaggerated doubt. "Sure you are. Stick with that."

"You know, you're a powerful lot funnier when you're not with Fletcher."

Hollis bowed with a flourish.

"Where're you off to?" Stone asked.

"Pimlico," Brogan said. "Four-Finger Mike was spotted there a bit back. We're goin' to sniff out a clue."

"Keep the rest of us in the know."

"We will."

In a bit of déjà vu, they took a hack to a spot a bit removed from St. George's and walked the rest of the way.

Instead of assuming the purposeful saunter of tradesmen, they walked with the easy assurance of the gentry.

Everything seemed exactly as expected. The homes were well-kept. The street was quiet. Of the two people they passed, neither had shifty eyes or held up a sign saying "I have nefarious intentions."

They were nearly to the house where they'd found Very Merry. She must've ducked into that particular spot for a reason. Hollis eyed the homes on either side of it, the park across the street and down a pace, the homes facing it. Nothing was odd or unusual. And nothing offered a place for someone as out of place as Four-Finger Mike to hide.

"I wish I knew what'd been happening before we arrived that day," Hollis said. "I'm beginning to suspect there was some sort of distraction that let him go unnoticed."

"I'd wager the same, but it'd need to've been something known ahead of time for him to've come here."

Yes, but what?

Hollis's attention settled on the house directly across from the one Very Merry had been in. A servant stepped out the front door and began screwing in the door knocker.

"Someone's newly arrived," Hollis noted.

Brogan made a sound of realization. "The comings and goings of moving in could distract from someone sneaking about."

"Do you suppose he stole anything from the new arrivals?" Hollis knew the answer.

"And took the lay of the land so he could send his minions back for more." Brogan rolled onto the balls of his feet a couple of times, watching the street. "We'd best discover who lives there and see if a warning ought to be whispered in their ears."

"My servants' network can find that out," Hollis said.

"Brilliant."

Hollis straightened his cuffs in a show of pleased arrogance. "That's a quick mystery solved. What shall we sort out next?"

"I know you're jesting, but we do have something else to wonder on. There've been more thefts matching Very Merry's style: nothing disturbed, no one taking notice, making off with small items that ain't worth a lick."

"Some of what she stole had value," Hollis said.

Brogan nodded. "But some had none at all."

"What's disappeared since we snatched the girl off the street?"

"Most recently, a leather manicure box. Ivory-handled tools."

A manicure box. And not even a silver-plated one. That, combined with the figurines and trinket boxes that had been nipped, amounted to little more than nothing. Four-Finger Mike didn't seem the type to let such "mistakes" go uncorrected.

"Is it possible," he wondered aloud, "that Very Merry is not actually the Phantom Fox, and we've another thief on our hands?"

"If I were you," Brogan said, "I'd worry less about the little thieflings and set m' sights instead on discovering why Miss Newport is letting herself into the very house where you found the urchin who's now living under your roof."

Hollis's head snapped in that direction. Sure enough,

Ana stood at the front door of Very Merry's hiding place—a house without a knocker up, a house that had seemed empty. And Ana was unlocking the door.

Brogan inched in that direction. "I can't let a peculiarity on this scale go unexplored."

"She doesn't know that I have any friends amongst the penny dreadful writers other than Fletcher," Hollis warned.

"So use any one of my aliases." With that, the Irishman moved directly toward Ana. Whatever she was up to, they were about to find out.

CHAPTER 11

"Miss Newport?"

Ana jumped at the sound of Hollis Darby's voice. Never in all her visits to her father had someone she knew stumbled upon her there. She stood frozen, unable to push the door open, unable to turn to look at him.

He knew her family lived in Pimlico. He knew they had fallen on difficult times; she had told him bits of it during their evening at the opera. But the neglect and poverty and bitterness he would find in this house would reveal the enormity of the situation. And should he catch her placing her most recent repossession in the curio cabinet, she would never manage to explain how she had acquired it.

She forced herself to breathe as she turned toward him. "Mr. Darby."

She didn't recognize the man next to him, though his finely tailored coat and high-polished watch fob spoke of a higher rung on the ladder.

Hollis's gaze slid up the façade of the house. "Is this where you live?"

"I live at Thurloe."

He smiled and rephrased the question. "Is this your family's home? You said you grew up in Pimlico."

She could hardly lie about that. He had seen her unlocking the door, after all. "Yes. My father lives here still."

There was no means of sending the gentlemen on their way, yet inviting them in would be too humiliating. She hadn't the strength for that degree of exposure, having spent every bit of vulnerability she could endure during their very personal moments at the theatre.

"Miss Newport," Hollis said, "this is my good friend, Ganor O'Donnell."

"A pleasure to meet you," she said.

"And I you, Miss Newport."

"I would invite you in, but the house hasn't any rooms prepared for receiving visitors," she said.

"We're not finicky, Miss Newport," Hollis's apparently Irish friend said. "I'd enjoy spending a moment or two coming to know you better, whether the doing of that happens in a gilded sitting room or a quiet, simple corner."

She suspected the man was something of a charmer.

"If we assure you we will not turn our noses up at anything, may we come in?" Hollis asked the question kindly, yet it was still embarrassing. Callers didn't generally have to beg their hostesses to permit them to enter.

She could only manage to answer in a miserable whisper. "It is likely worse than you are anticipating."

He smiled gently. "I believe I can safely assure you that we have seen worse."

"He's not wrong, Miss Newport," Mr. O'Donnell said. "We've spent time in some questionable places."

Odd. "Which places?"

"We'd tell you, but we've been sworn to secrecy." Mischief danced in Mr. O'Donnell's eyes. He was teasing her. She greatly appreciated it in that moment.

"I should also warn you that I haven't the least idea how my father will receive you. He's not violent or dangerous or anything of that nature, but he is a little . . . prickly at times."

They appeared undeterred.

She squared her shoulders and set her chin. "Well, then, gentlemen. Consider yourself warned."

"We do." Hollis dipped his head.

She pushed open the door and cringed at the strong smell of dust in the air. They followed her inside, one of them closing the door behind him. Ana didn't say a word as she led the way through the dingy entry to the bare stairs and began to climb. The gentlemen behind her didn't speak. The house wasn't filthy, simply neglected. With only Wallace on staff, the house couldn't be maintained as well as it ought to be. It was in desperate need of dusting and airing out—perhaps a new piece of furniture here or there.

They climbed the stairs, and Ana inched open the door to Father's rooms. She caught Wallace's eye and waved him over.

"We have visitors," she whispered.

Wallace sputtered but didn't manage to answer.

"I know one of the gentlemen," she said. "He will, I'm

sure, be kind. His friend likely will be too. But how is Father today?"

Wallace shrugged. "Seems in good enough spirits."

"Let us hope that proves true." She sighed and turned back to her guests. "My father's room is the only one with furniture or any degree of cleanliness. Your visit will have to happen in here."

Both men nodded their understanding.

Wallace opened the door fully and stood back to allow entry. Ana set her usual Friday basket on the table in the middle of the sitting area. Father was at the window, looking down on the street below.

"Good afternoon, Father. We've two gentlemen here wishing to make your acquaintance."

He turned. His pulled brow spoke of confusion but not dissatisfaction. Thank the heavens he appeared to have shaved that morning and was wearing an unobjectionable, if outdated, set of morning clothes instead of his dressing gown. The room even appeared to have been straightened recently.

"Father, this is Mr. Darby and Mr. O'Donnell. Gentlemen, this is my father, Mr. Newport."

Bows were exchanged.

Father greeted the gentlemen with grace. Wallace procured chairs and, somehow, a bit of brandy. With a silent sigh of relief, Ana lowered herself onto the window seat.

"I grew up near Belgrave Square," Hollis said. "I have a few acquaintances in Pimlico."

"A fine area, Pimlico," Father said. "Mrs. Newport and I were overjoyed when we were able to secure this home. Our daughter would have every advantage. A father could hardly want more for his child."

"And you have an *exceptional* child," Hollis said. "All who know her think highly of her."

Father tipped his chin upward and pulled his shoulders back. She'd not seen pride in his expression in such a long time that she hardly recognized the emotion.

"How fortunate you were able to find a property to purchase on St. George's," Mr. O'Donnell said. "I don't believe they come available very often."

"The house across the street switched hands recently, I believe," Hollis said.

Father nodded, his posture growing a touch more agitated. The gentlemen would soon realize what a sore topic this was. "Thompson had to retrench."

"*Charles* Thompson?" Hollis asked. "I hadn't heard his finances were in disarray."

"Wallace says his servants said he beggared himself gambling." Father let out a tense breath. "Some lose fortunes. Others have their fortunes snatched away."

"Frightening how fast things can change," Mr. O'Donnell agreed with a nod. "For his sake, I hope Mr. Thompson can't find himself a single card game in the country."

The briefest hint of amusement touched Father's face, something that happened as seldom as his pride. "His cousin likely hopes he doesn't manage to rebuild his accounts."

"Did his cousin take possession of his London house?" Hollis asked.

Father nodded. "An odd one, he is. I can't sort him in the

least. He has a great many callers, and at all hours—morning, afternoon, evening. Nothing seems untoward, simply strangely constant."

Ana turned enough on the window seat to look across the street. Two men knocked at the Thompsons' door. Ana couldn't see their faces, couldn't have even guessed at their ages, but they were gentlemen by the look of their clothes. They were ushered inside. No carriage appeared to have dropped them there.

Strange. She turned back toward the room.

"This is one of Lafayette Jones's," Mr. O'Donnell said, holding up a penny dreadful. "How are you enjoying it?"

"Immensely. Ana enjoys his work as well."

"Does she?" Hollis knew her enjoyment of them—they had discussed the penny dreadfuls before—but was making kind conversation with her Father.

The gentlemen discussed various authors: Fletcher Walker, Mr. King, Brogan Donnelly, Stone, Lafayette Jones. Father was more widely read in the area of penny dreadful serials than Ana had realized.

After a moment, Hollis joined her at the window.

Voice lowered, she said, "Thank you for being kind to him. So many in Society rejected him after his fortunes turned. He's hidden out here ever since."

"And you have been struggling to make ends meet." He spoke as quietly as she. Mr. O'Donnell and Father were too engrossed in their discussion of stories to pay much heed.

"We've had a difficult few years."

"Yes, you spoke of that during our time at the opera." He

set his hand gently on hers. "I hadn't realized how difficult those years apparently were."

"And now that you know?"

He threaded his fingers through hers, the simple touch reassuring her even before he spoke. "I only wish we had become friends sooner. Passing through difficulties is made harder by passing through them alone."

"You have passed through difficulties, yourself." She remembered well from their very personal conversation.

"It seems you and I have a great deal in common, Ana Newport."

But, oh, so much about them was more painfully different than he could possibly realize. He was a respected gentleman. She was a sneak thief.

Movement on the street below pulled her attention. She leaned closer to the glass, narrowing her gaze on the Thompsons' house. "That is the second pair of men to knock in the last few minutes."

Hollis looked down. "Were the others finely dressed as well?"

"They were. And like these, there was no carriage dropping them there."

"Hmm." He seemed even more curious than she was. "I wonder how often this scene plays out."

"I would ask my father, but he is calm and pleased just now." She looked back at the two men, bent over a copy of Lafayette Jones's latest work. "I'd rather not rile him up again, not when he's having such a nice visit."

Hollis continued to watch the street below. Ana slipped away and, with a quick check to make certain her father and their visitors were content, stepped from the room and into the one next to it. There, she opened the curio cabinet and set inside it a small, hinged, leather box—small enough to have been tucked in her drawstring wrist bag.

Ana opened the box, displaying the ivory-handled manicure set inside. It was not the finest example of such a thing—far from it, in fact—but it had been her mother's.

A mere moment after Ana returned to Father's room, Wallace did as well, having delivered her weekly basket of foodstuffs to the kitchen.

"Good of these genn'lmen to show kindness to Mr. Newport. He oughtn't be so lonely as he is." Wallace eyed both visitors, but not with suspicion. "What brought them 'round, I wonder?"

"They likely know someone in the area," Ana said. "Pimlico boasts many people of their station."

Wallace nodded. "Perhaps they'll bring others around to visit. That'd be a fine thing."

It would be nice for her father, yes. But she had concerns. "Perhaps we might see if we could get the small sitting room on the ground floor cleaned up. I don't know where we might get furniture, but—"

"I could repair a few of the broken bits in the attic, likely. Wouldn't be anything too fine."

It was a promising start. "There is a disused but still serviceable rug in the attic at Thurloe. Miss Black might allow me to have the use of it."

A twinkle of hope entered Wallace's expression. She felt the same touch hers.

"I'll come a few extra times in the next little while," she

said. "We can have the sitting room ready for visitors, I'm sure. In time, Father might even decide to leave the house."

"That would be a regular miracle, Miss Newport."

She moved over to the window where Hollis still sat, though he didn't watch the Thompsons' place any longer. He had taken up one of Father's copies of the most recent Lafayette Jones penny serial.

Ana sat beside the handsome and considerate gentleman. He looked up at her and smiled. "Welcome back, Miss Ana Newport."

"You missed me, did you?"

His expression turned warm and tender. "I did, indeed."

In that moment, her heart utterly melted.

CHAPTER 12

The Dread Penny Society's interest in Charles Thompson had been nothing more than the hope he would invest in the Barton School for Girls. Now it seemed he was involved in something much deeper. He, who had never before been associated with even casual gambling, had lost his fortune at the card tables. His home in Town was being let to what was said to be a cousin, whose guests' comings and goings were odd by all accounts.

What had truly unnerved Hollis, however, was seeing someone he knew all too well entering that suspicious house: Alistair Headley.

The man spent more and more time with Randolph. Hollis was worried, and he felt in his gut he had reason to be.

Across from him in the carriage, Ana sat in uneasy silence, clutching her usual Saturday satchel and watching him with her brows low and her forehead creased in confused concern.

"I am not being very personable, am I?" He offered a

quick smile of apology. "I've something to discuss with my brother, and I'm not looking forward to it."

"Your topic is a difficult one?"

"*Every* topic is a difficult one with him."

The morning light spilled through the carriage windows, illuminating her in a glow of gold. "You are very different from him in that respect. I find you quite easy to talk with."

"Why is it, then, you told me so little of your father's situation?"

Her gaze dropped to her hands. "Our family has passed through enough humiliations without making them even more widely known."

"What, precisely, happened?" He wouldn't press her to share but hoped she would. He knew the misery of carrying unseen burdens alone.

"Father made his fortune in trade, primarily shipping. He took on a partner as his business grew, but he didn't realize that partner was stealing funds from the company. Then the man disappeared, leaving behind empty coffers and defrauded investors."

A disaster by all accounts.

"We sold the things we had that were of any value," she said. "That saved Father from debtors' prison, but the damage to his reputation could not be undone. His partner was the fraudster, but Father was the one ruined by it."

"I enjoyed our visit with him yesterday. Ganor said the same several times after we dropped you at Thurloe."

"You were both very kind to him." She clearly had expected something other than kindness, yet there was nothing personal in the underlying accusation.

"He has a quick wit and a sharp mind. It is a shame few people have the opportunity to enjoy his company."

"His one-time 'friends' and associates turned on him when his fortunes fell. The things they said about him and to him were terrible. They exacted revenge in painful and personal ways." The sadness in her expression spoke volumes. That revenge, Hollis would wager, had been exacted against her, as well.

Hollis reached across and took her hand. She had allowed him to do that several times of late. "If he will allow us to visit again, Ganor and I would enjoy doing so."

"I hope you will."

The carriage stopped in front of Randolph's house. Hollis and Ana had made this trip several Saturdays in a row. Alighting and making their way to the music room was habit as much as anything now.

Eloise was waiting for them. She greeted them with enthusiasm. He'd known his little niece would love Ana. How could she not?

"I've practiced and practiced," Eloise told her music teacher.

"I am pleased to hear that. Would you like to play for your uncle?"

Eloise nodded eagerly.

Hollis took her hand and walked with her to the pianoforte. "I have always enjoyed hearing you play, love."

"No, you haven't, silly. I used to pound on the keys and make Miss Dowling have megrims."

Oh, sweet Eloise. So innocently entertaining.

She climbed onto the piano stool and, after smiling at

him, plunked out a tune. She already played better than she had only a few short weeks earlier. And her joy as she played was contagious. Hollis glanced at Ana and saw tender pride in her expression.

Eloise finished her piece and spun on the stool to face him. "Did I play well, Uncle Hollis?"

"You played brilliantly." He pressed a kiss to her forehead. He turned to Ana and took her hand in his. He raised it to his lips. "Thank you."

She blushed. "Thank you for recommending me for this position. I have loved it."

"Hollis, do release the teacher's hand," Randolph said from the doorway. "She needs to be getting on with the lessons."

Ana's color deepened, but it no longer looked like a blush born of pleasure.

"Ignore him," Hollis whispered. "It is what I prefer to do."

"Except when you need to 'discuss something' with him," she whispered, a glint in her eyes.

"Pity me, Ana. I'm about to suffer greatly."

She smiled. He released her hand and crossed to his brother.

When he was far enough from the instrument to not be overheard if he kept his voice low, Hollis asked, "Do you have a moment, Randolph?"

"I had hoped to slip out for a moment, see to a bit of business."

"This is important. We can talk in your library or here in

the corridor, wherever you prefer to discuss your close association with a known inveterate gambler."

Randolph's expression grew immediately strained. "Library."

Hollis motioned for him to lead the way.

They walked in silence to the room their father had once ruled from. He had been a hard and difficult man to live with in addition to being a selfish wastrel.

Randolph snapped the door shut behind them. "Inveterate gambler?"

"You know as well as I do who I am referring to and why."

"Alistair does gamble," Randolph said, "but I don't engage in games of chance as often as he, neither do I participate in games with the high stakes he does."

Hollis could have throttled him. "After all the lectures you have given me about our family reputation and your backbreaking efforts to restore the Darby fortune and name . . . you are *gambling*?"

"That is rich coming from the person who gambled his way through Eton."

Hollis forced a calming breath. "I never had the neediness for it you did. That Father did. That Grandfather did."

"I have done more to refill the family coffers in the last three weeks than I have in the last three years," Randolph said. "I have always been skilled with cards."

"Every Darby who ever lived was skilled with cards," Hollis drawled. "And far too many are slaves to them. Alistair Headley is known to frequent dens where that enslavement will be used against you in devastating ways."

Randolph's face twisted in a pointedly patient expression. "I don't go with him to those places. I'm not a fool."

"If you are gambling with what little financial stability you have, you are precisely that."

Randolph paced away angrily. "I am not in over my head, Hollis. I only play with other gentlemen, only low-stakes games, and only now and then. I have turned down most of Alistair's invitations to various card games. I am being responsible."

Oddly enough, Hollis believed him. He seemed entirely in earnest. "Did you ever play with George Thompson?"

Wariness touched the lines of Randolph's face.

"Thompson had to retrench due to gambling debts," Hollis said. "He was a responsible sort, not a known gambler like those in our family. I couldn't imagine him following Headley to one of the copper dens he's been spotted at, nor undertaking games with enormous stakes. Yet, he's ruined."

Randolph swallowed thickly. "I'm more careful than he was."

"Does Cora know?"

Tension seized Randolph's posture. "Are you threatening to tell her?"

"No." Hollis shook his head. "But Society is a small circle. She will hear it from someone eventually, and I don't know that she will be comforted by how 'careful' you've been. Games of chance are what started our family down this road sixty years ago."

"Don't lecture me," Randolph said. "Everyone assumes the Darby estate pays you like a good younger son, but I know that's not true."

"Have you spotted me at any of these games you frequent?"

Randolph pointedly didn't answer.

"Have I come to you even once in my entire life begging for funds?"

Again, no answer.

"Have I embarrassed you in public? Sullied the family name? Caused whispers beyond the idle gossip Society indulges in no matter the circumspect nature of a person's life?"

Begrudgingly, Randolph said, "No."

"Then save your posturing, Randolph. I gambled in school like you did. I was better at it, yet you'll not see me at a card table. I have too much respect for our mother's pain to cavalierly take up the cause of it for my own gain." He reached for the library door. "And I care too much about my sister-in-law and my niece and nephew to stand back and watch them suffer the way Mother did—the way *we* did. I'll keep an eye on things."

"Do you fancy yourself a spy?" Randolph scoffed.

"I fancy myself a great many things, none of which you should underestimate."

With that, he left, snapping the door behind him and trudging all the way out of the house. Returning on foot to his rented flat would take the better part of an hour, but he knew his frustration would benefit from the exertion.

Randolph was a fool.

Hollis refused to see his family destroyed by one again.

CHAPTER 13

More tiny thieflings were at work in the finer neighborhoods of London, with a high concentration near Pimlico. The DPS no longer believed Very Merry was the one known as the Phantom Fox, because that elusive thief was still whispered about on the streets.

When word reached the Dreadfuls of a new young thief, known among the urchins as Blue Bill, they sprang into action. Hollis joined the evening's search, though no one had indicated he was needed. He was determined to show them he was useful.

Hollis made his way to the area around Belgrave Square under the cover of nightfall. He knew the homes and families there better than any of the other Dreadfuls.

The Rollinses appeared to be having a soiree. Their house was lit and bustling. The Phantom Fox had been known to undertake thefts in homes right under the noses of dozens of people. The Rollinses' home would bear watching.

Eaton Place was quiet, as was Chester Street and Wilton Street. Hollis even slipped past his brother's house. Knowing

Randolph was not associating with the best sort of people lately, Hollis made a quick check of the ground-level doors and windows. The home was secure and peaceful, reassuring him for the moment.

Onward he walked, taking stock of one home after another. All was as it should be. When his steps took him past the Rollinses' house for the third time, he decided to stop ignoring his instincts and make a more thorough inspection.

If I were attempting to pilfer something from a house this busy, how would I go about it?

From the back, for one thing. And by way of the shadows.

Hollis slipped around the side of the house, slowly and cautiously, keeping close watch on every corner, every dark path, every window. Nothing was out of the ordinary. A terrace led off the home's drawing room. It was lit and in use.

Around a corner, fully in shadow, sat a quiet wing of the house that didn't appear to be part of the evening's festivities. A rather perfect arrangement for a thief as slippery as the Phantom Fox.

Hollis kept to the shadows. He studied the small nooks and hiding spaces a child-thief could easily slip in and out of. No one was there. He rounded the corner of the dark wing of the house, intending to simply watch a while. The chances of actually catching their little thief were slim, though the current situation at the Rollinses' house did increase the odds.

He found a dim, quiet corner and leaned against the brick wall, hidden from view by both the darkness and a tall, thick shrub. He waited. Not ten minutes after arriving at his chosen post, he spotted movement. A nearby window had been opened, and someone was climbing out.

He studied the shadowy figure. Clad all in black. Too tall for a child, but small for a full-grown man. Perhaps the Dreadfuls had been misinformed about the age of Blue Bill. Or perhaps, like Very Merry, Blue Bill was not the Phantom Fox.

Hollis inched toward the escapee. They were far enough from the bustling area of the house to go unnoted but only if they were both quiet. *He* planned to be.

Feet on the ground, the thief tiptoed away from the house. The man moved with undeniable grace. It was little wonder he'd managed to slip in and out of so many homes undetected. Quiet agility was invaluable to a sneak thief.

Moonlight caught on a flash of silver as the thief slipped something into the pocket of his close-fitted overcoat. What had he stolen this time?

The Phantom Fox, if that was who this was, turned from the house, affording Hollis a better look. For a moment, he couldn't make sense of the conflicting information he saw.

Trousers. A man's coat. Head and face covered by a stocking cap with eyeholes. A telltale lump at the back of the head consistent with a large knot of hair. A figure not well enough hidden to be mistaken for a man's.

The thief wasn't a child *or* a man. The Phantom Fox was a woman.

Hollis positioned himself along her escape route, ready to do battle if need be but hoping it wouldn't prove necessary. She spotted him and stopped at a distance near enough for conversation but too far away to offer any further clues as to her identity.

"The Phantom Fox, I believe." He chose a lower-class accent to match his clothes. "People're whisperin' about you."

She offered an abbreviated bow. Why a bow and not a curtsey? Surely she knew he could tell she was female.

"You're causing a heap of trouble for the little ones hereabout," he said,

Her head tipped to one side, a gesture that communicated confusion.

"They're being blamed for your thievery," he explained. "I ain't saying they haven't dirt on their hands, mind. But you're adding mud upon mud, and they're too little to wash it off."

He hadn't the first idea if she would even care about the plight of the urchins, but he had to try. "Take a bit of the heat off 'em, will ya? Lay low a while, or give off thieving altogether."

The Phantom Fox shook her head, silent. There were so few clues to identify her—intentional, no doubt.

A noise sounded in the direction of the busier part of the house. The Phantom Fox glanced that way, posture wary and alert. Hollis felt equally ill at ease. Being caught out would be a disaster.

They'd both have to move quickly toward the gate at the back of the garden. He only had a moment in which to decide if he ought to appeal to her conscience more or try to convince her to turn herself in.

She turned to look at him once more. Before he could say a word, she snapped a saucy salute. Quick as a cat after a mouse, she leapt onto a nearby stone bench, then onto a decorative pillar, its top ending a bit short of the wall, then onto the wall itself. She perched there. Nothing lay on the other side. How did she mean to climb down?

After the length of a breath, she jumped, disappearing from view behind the wall.

Hollis darted to the gate and around the back side, fully expecting to find her there, limping, if she was lucky. But she was gone, without leaving so much as a footprint in the grass or a smudge on the paving stones. He hadn't the first idea what direction she'd gone.

The DPS had been in search of an eight- or nine-year-old urchin. They would soon realize their search was far more complicated.

THE GENTLEMAN AND THE THIEF

by Mr. King

Installment IV,
in which our Hero makes a most gentlemanly
Apology and a shocking Discovery!

The house was far too quiet. For two days, not a sound had been heard. Mrs. Smith, Wellington suspected, was upset with him. Mr. Smith, who was seldom seen as it was, made not a single appearance. The most glaring absence of all, though, was Tillie's.

Wellington had gone by her house repeatedly, but she hadn't answered his knock, neither had she come by the manor house. How was he to apologize, to convince her that he did not, in fact, believe her capable of anything so underhanded as thievery if she would not allow him a moment in which to do so? His visitors had cast that aspersion, yes, but he had not. He would not. He could not.

Oh, was ever a man so vexed with the impossible task of apologizing to a woman?

Some three days after he'd last had a conversation with anyone inside the walls of his house, Wellington walked the corridors with his hands tucked in his pockets. His shoulders drooped under the burden of his loneliness. Even the elusive thief had abandoned him. Not a single item had gone missing in the past few days.

"I haven't a single soul with whom to share my change of fortune." It was his own fault, truly. He ought to have immediately risen to Tillie's defense. He ought to have said more to discount the hints of accusation his visitors had lobbed in her direction. The weight of regret only added to the stooped nature of his posture.

On and on he walked, making one lonely circuit after another. Minutes passed. His mind did not clear. If only Tillie would return and be his friend once more.

Into the cavernous quiet came the sound of footfalls, not rushed or threatening, but at ease and at home. Wellington kept perfectly still, listening and pondering. The steps drew closer. He stood his ground, unwilling to cede more of his peace of mind than the thief had already taken from him.

But it was no thief who appeared from around a bend in the corridor; it was Tillie.

So surprised was he that Wellington could not even manage a greeting. Fortunately for him, she did not appear to need one.

"Things are being stolen from our cottage," she said without preamble. "Unless you think I am thieving my own things, I'd say your mystery thief has changed locations."

"I don't think you are stealing from yourself."

She folded her arms across her chest and tipped her head to the side. "Only from *you*."

"I don't think you're stealing from anyone," he insisted. "Those visitors said that; I didn't."

"You didn't disagree with 'em," she said. "You said you would think on it. That ain't a vote of confidence, is it?"

"I was trying to get them to leave faster," he said. "Arguing the point would have prolonged their visit."

She lost a bit of bluster. "I know I ain't fine and proper like they are."

"And I far prefer your company to theirs." He reached out to take her hand, but she stepped back. The rejection was warranted, yet still it stung. He took a breath and re-gained his footing. The business at hand would be his best step forward. "What has been taken from your home?"

"A few coins," she said. "My little amber cross that I wear on the chain your mother gave me. A spade."

"A spade?" That was a decidedly odd thing for a thief to make off with.

She shrugged. "That one didn't make sense to us either."

"You helped me search my house for clues," he said. "Might I be permitted to offer the same assistance?"

"I'd not object." She jerked her head toward the front of the house. "Shall we?"

He walked at her side all the way to the front drive, then along the path that would take them to her cottage. A fair stretch of moorland separated their two homes. They would have time and plenty for either talking and repairing things between them or sinking ever further into the awkward silence between them.

"I am sorry for what happened with my guests," he said.

She shook her head. "I forget sometimes how much

things have changed over the past years. You're a distinguished gentleman; I'm still the steward's daughter."

"You are my favorite steward's daughter."

"My father is your favorite steward?" A hint of her usual mischief returned to her tone.

Wellington bumped her lightly with his shoulder. "I believe you know perfectly well what I meant."

She smiled fleetingly. "We have always been good friends, have we not?"

"The very best."

She looked up at him. "Then why is it you didn't believe me about the blue flame? You didn't ridicule me for it, but I could tell you thought I had cobwebs in m' attic."

"I thought no such thing," he said with a laugh. "I don't doubt what you saw. It was simply unexpected, and I hadn't an explanation for it."

Tillie stopped in her tracks, eyes trained up ahead. She pointed a slightly shaky finger. "Perhaps that will shed a bit of light on the matter."

Up ahead, floating above the ground, moving back and forth, not diminishing, not growing, was a light. Not any light. A blue one.

A blue flame.

Tillie's shoulders set. "After it!"

And she ran.

CHAPTER 14

Ana had never been caught making a repossession, though it had been a near-run thing a couple of times. That she'd been found out was unnerving enough. That the one who'd caught her had been none other than Hollis Darby had left her utterly upended.

Had he recognized her? Had she given herself away?

He would condemn her for certain. If he told Elizabeth, Ana would be fired. He wouldn't permit her to continue tutoring his niece. The characters in Mr. King's latest story might have been able to find common ground between a gentleman with Society connections and a woman suspected of thievery, but she had no hope that such a thing was actually possible.

When Thursday visiting hours arrived at Thurloe, Ana found herself too distracted and worried to engage in any of the conversations or enjoy their usual visitors.

As if her anxieties had summoned him, Hollis arrived, dressed to the nines in a finely fashioned, green driving coat and matching gloves. He cut quite the figure; there was no denying that. And she was terrified to see him; there was no denying that either.

"Might I convince you to abandon your calling hours and join me for a drive through Hyde Park?" His eyes sparkled with charm. Was that sincere, or was he playing a part for the sake of the onlookers?

"I have not driven out during the fashionable hour in years," she said.

"I suspected as much." He held out his hand to her. "I think it is time you made a return trip."

She could feel the other teachers around her silently urging her to accept. Elizabeth's subtle nod held a note of emphasis. There would be no way of refusing without raising suspicions.

"I believe you are correct." She set her hand in his and allowed him to pull her to her feet, praying he couldn't tell she was shaking. "Do you mind waiting while I put on my coat?"

"My dear Miss Newport," he said, "I would wait a lifetime for you."

No one in the room could have missed her blush. She dipped a quick curtsey and hurried up to her room. She hadn't a proper driving coat, but her serviceable brown one would do. If she was about to endure a dressing down, being unfashionable was the least of her worries.

When she returned to the sitting room, he rose and offered his arm. They walked together from the sitting room into the entryway.

"I haven't had a caller ask me to drive at the fashionable hour," she said. "I admit I'm a little nervous."

Hollis paused on the front walk and turned to face her

directly. "If you would rather not, I will understand. But I do think it would be an enjoyable way to spend the afternoon. And we would be afforded a rare opportunity for some privacy."

She suspected she knew what he wanted to discuss in private. At least he was doing her that courtesy, rather than revealing what he knew in front of her colleagues and friends. She allowed a slow breath. "A ride sounds lovely."

He motioned to the open-top carriage waiting for them. It was not the staid and sedate enclosed carriage that belonged to his brother. They would cut quite a dash in this vehicle.

He handed her up, then assumed his place in the driver's seat. She adjusted her skirts, smoothing and straightening them. Heavens, she was nervous. More than that, she was afraid. Some legendary sneak thief she was, trembling at the prospect of a conversation.

With a flick, he set the horse to a leisurely walk. They weren't far from Hyde Park, and there was no need to hurry.

"Have you forgiven me yet for Saturday?" Hollis asked. "I am beyond upset with myself for not realizing I'd left you at my brother's home with no explanation of my departure. I was upset with him—our conversation didn't go well—and I left without thinking."

That was the least of her concerns. "I assumed as much. No harm done, I assure you."

He smiled, and they continued on. Hollis didn't seem upset or disapproving. He didn't even look like he had anything serious to discuss with her. Had he not realized she was the Phantom Fox? Was it possible she'd escaped detection?

They reached the crush of the park. Plenty of other fine

carriages and smartly dressed people wound their way around the large green. After a few minutes with nothing but innocuous conversation, she began to relax and let herself enjoy yet another unexpected step back into the world she'd once known.

"Is something the matter?" Hollis asked.

She tucked her hand into the crook of his arm, as was customary. "I was only thinking how very long it's been since I did anything like this. Money gave my family entry into this world of fine carriages and high-class people, but it proved a feeble connection."

"I have experienced Society's fickleness like a dagger at times."

"Then why do you continue being part of it?" She hoped he didn't read any accusation into her words; she didn't intend for there to be any.

"Because I love Eloise and Addison too much to take away their choices in life. Our family's hold on this world is more precarious than anyone realizes. If their odd Uncle Hollis turns his back on it entirely, that might very well sever that hold."

She hadn't expected that answer. "But if they weren't a consideration? If you could choose the life you wanted based on nothing more than your heart?"

An almost sly smile spread across his face. "I'd do what I do now when Society isn't watching."

Nervousness pulsed in her chest. "And what is that?" The question emerged in a whisper.

"Can you keep a secret, Ana?"

She nodded, her fears growing.

A gentleman hailed them as his vehicle approached, then slowed. "Mr. Darby."

Hollis greeted him in return. "Mr. Lewiston. I've not seen you about recently."

"Perhaps you've been looking in the wrong places." The man clearly meant the observation as something of a lighthearted jest, but there was a heaviness in the bags under his eyes that belied his tone.

"Miss Newport," Hollis said, "might I make known to you Mr. Lewiston. Lewiston, this is Miss Newport."

Mr. Lewiston's bushy brow pulled together and his jowls puffed a moment. "I knew a Newport several years back. He had a daughter who'd likely be about your age now."

Oh, dear. "That might be my father."

"*Crawford* Newport?" Mr. Lewiston guessed.

Ana nodded, then braced herself for the inevitable dismissal or insult.

But Hollis spoke first. "I have had the pleasure of meeting Mr. Newport. Delightful gentleman, nearly as delightful as his daughter."

Mr. Lewiston's eyes darted from Hollis to Ana and back again. "Isn't he the one who—"

"You didn't tell me where it was I ought to have been looking for you," Hollis said. "Obviously not at soirees or musicales or the theatre, as those are places I have been and you have not."

Mr. Lewiston assumed an expression of great secrecy. "Ask your brother. He knows."

"He might very well." Hollis offered Mr. Lewiston a brief

dip of his head before making a quick farewell and resuming their drive.

"It is likely uncouth of me to say as much," Ana said, "but there was something very off-putting about him."

"Agreed. Even more odd, he didn't used to have that air about him."

Ana resisted the urge to look over her shoulder at the man. "What did he mean 'your brother knows'? That sounded unsavory."

"I believe his comment touches on the topic I was discussing with Randolph on Saturday."

"A topic so upsetting it made you forget about my very existence?"

With his eyes still on the road, he said, "Forgetting about your existence has proven utterly impossible for months."

It was not a sentiment he would express if he knew who she really was.

They were hailed several more times as they made their circuit of the park. Only one other of those they spoke with pieced together who she was and who her father was. And, once again, Hollis made it quite clear that she and her family had his approval. To those who hadn't a history to connect to her, he treated her as one would a lady of full standing in Society. He was gentle and tender, respectful and kind.

Hollis Darby was a comforting person to be with. He set her at ease. He offered her a measure of peace that she desperately needed. If he hadn't pieced together her secret life as a thief, she couldn't afford for him to. He would turn on her as everyone else had.

"You never did tell me what it was you would do with your life if you had your choice," she said.

His expression turned serious. "The first bit is that my grandfather gambled away most of our family's fortune years ago. My father then made short work of nearly all the rest. Randolph has done a remarkable job of accumulating enough to begin pulling the family out of dangerous financial waters, but the empty family coffers have required that I earn my living."

"I've not heard your name attached to an occupation," she said.

He smiled at her, the same almost sly smile she'd seen before. "There are things I do when Society is not looking."

She swallowed. "What—What things?"

He laughed. "Now you are imagining something dangerous and possibly criminal, aren't you?"

He might have been describing what *she* did when Society wasn't looking. Something he didn't seem to have realized he'd discovered.

"I know you enjoy Mr. King's work," he said. "Those stories would make *anyone* assume criminality lurked in the heart of every nobleman."

She found she could laugh. "I know you enjoy the works of your friend, Mr. Walker. His books paint a compassionate picture of the little criminals in London."

"I've come to know one of those criminals quite well," he said.

She swallowed. "You have?"

"Yes. A little urchin by the name of Very Merry. She had been stealing as a matter of survival, but the police, unfortunately, do not always see things that way. She is now living at my house, under the watchful eye of my housekeeper and valet."

"You've taken in an urchin?"

He nodded. "She is an absolute demon. And I adore her."

"You are a remarkable sort of gentleman, Hollis Darby. I've found few of your station are so accepting of those who've fallen from grace."

"I was raised in poverty," he said. "My family resides within a breath of returning there. That has made my brother fearful, but it has taught me empathy."

How far could that empathy stretch, though? The secret he'd shared with her was nothing compared to the one she held back from him. Society might look askance if his family's financial situation were revealed. If her secret were made known, she might very well be hanged.

Even the most remarkable sort of gentleman would draw a line there.

HIGGLEBOTTOM'S SCHOOL FOR THE DEAD

A GHOST OF A CHANCE

by Lafayette Jones

Chapter III

The more time Ace spent with Pudding, the more he liked him. He had gumption. He was funny. And, Ace suspected, he would always be up for a prank or two.

It was a deuced shame the boy wasn't dead.

"Is that enough chalk?" Bathwater eyed Pudding's pale face.

"Can't be," Pudding said. "I can still breathe."

"Are you accusing us of trying to kill you?" Snout laughed.

"It'd make this transformation easier."

Ah, yes, Pudding was funny.

Snout had sewn a uniform for Pudding, a feat that had amazed all of them—including *Snout*. He hadn't been a tailor's apprentice or anything like that during his Perishable years.

"Do you think we're ready?" Bathwater asked. "If he's caught out, we're all in the wringer."

The risk was most of the fun. "We're ready," Ace declared.

Pudding stepped lightly as they made for the dormitory door. He'd been practicing and could move almost as silently as the others. If only Ace could figure a way to make it seem as if, now and then, Pudding unintentionally slipped through the ground like First Forms so often did.

They took the stairs down to the ground level and sauntered out into the open-air commons. The school didn't hold classes one day each week, giving the students some leisure time. This was one of those days, so the commons was busy.

Students took note of Ace as he passed; they always did. He was always about with friends, so that didn't cause much of a stir. One of the four of them held his breath each time someone looked too closely. The scrutiny, though, always ended with the other student moving along.

"We're managing it," Snout said.

"The 'we' feels questionable." Pudding kept his voice low, apparently remembering that he didn't sound quite like he ought.

"You could always saunter about on your own," Ace said.

"We could always saunter to wherever the food is," Pudding tossed back.

Ace shook his head, managing not to accidentally spin it all the way around. "You Perishables and your obsession with food."

Pudding shrugged. "It's more an obsession with staying . . . perishable."

"Hush, lads," Snout growled. "Rattlebag's coming this way."

They formed something of a clump, chatting like nothing was odd about them. Pudding tucked himself a little behind Bathwater. It'd be best if he weren't too easy to see.

"Professor Rattlebag," Ace greeted. "I hope you're proud of us; we haven't made any mischief lately."

"Proud?" Rattlebag hitched a pearly eyebrow. "I think the better word is suspicious."

"Of us?" Ace used his most innocent voice. "We've been perfect angels."

"I doubt that." Rattlebag glanced over the others before returning his gaze to Ace. "Remember, I have my eyes on you."

He floated away. The professors had been practicing ghostliness for centuries and could manage all the tricks with hardly any effort. Someday Ace would as well.

The other three were grinning broadly when Ace looked in their direction.

"We snuck Pudding past Rattlebag," Ace said. He'd have given them a one-ghost round of applause if he'd learned yet how to make actual noise that way. That was a Second Form skill. "We're well on our way to becoming legends, my friends."

"Including me?" Pudding asked.

"The only Perishable to 'attend' Higglebottom's? That's legendary in anyone's book."

From across the lawn, Cropper approached. He wasn't a regular in their group, but he wasn't an enemy either.

Further, he was clever. Would he see through Pudding's disguise?

"Who's the newdead?" Cropper asked, nodding toward Pudding.

"Not entirely newdead," Ace said. "But still fresh. We're taking him under our shroud, so to speak."

Cropper watched Pudding a moment longer. "How far under your shroud?"

"What do you mean?" Bathwater asked.

"Whispers around Higglebottom's is that you need a fourth for your Spirit Trials team."

A Perishable on their Spirit Trials team? That would be the prank of the millennium. But it also might cost them the opportunity to skip ahead to Second Form. Another term in First Form would be a dead bore. Literally.

"That explains the addition," Cropper said, nodding like he'd just answered a puzzling question. "We'd all wondered why the Gang of Three now had four. He's your new teammate."

Snout and Bathwater looked to Ace, keeping their expressions unreadable to anyone who didn't know them as well as Ace did. If they said Pudding *wasn't* their new teammate, those wondering about him would wonder more. They'd be caught out for sure and certain.

"We're being charitable," Ace told Cropper. "Showing up newdead so close to the Spirit Trials is a recipe for failure. We're going to save this new arrival from that fate."

"That'll cost you the top prize," Cropper warned.

He knew it. He knew everyone else knew it. But knowing something was impossible had never stopped Ace before.

"Oh, we'll take the top prize. And we'll be the first team to manage it with a newdead."

Cropper shrugged. "I wish you luck, then."

"We won't need it."

Cropper walked away, only slipping a foot through the ground twice—not too rubbish for a First Form.

"Pudding's going to be on our team?" Snout asked.

"He'll have to be, or this whole thing'll fall apart." Ace eyed them all, including their chalk-covered new friend. "It'll be the most ambitious prank we've pulled yet. And we only need one thing to make it work."

"What's that?" Pudding asked.

"A whole heap of luck."

CHAPTER 15

"For the poor and infirm, the hopeless and voiceless, we do not relent. We do not forget. We are the Dread Penny Society."

Hollis dropped back into his seat in the Parliamentary room at headquarters, feeling quite pleased with the world.

"A penny for your thoughts, genn'lmen." Fletcher made the expected call for business.

Hollis did his best to pay attention, but his thoughts were on Ana. Their ride in the park had been heavenly. He'd shared aspects of his life that he never told anyone, and she hadn't balked or dismissed him. He'd made no real effort to hide his partiality for her, and he felt certain he'd seen that same preference reflected in her eyes.

He hoped to be able to share more of what he kept hidden, to trust her with the bits he hadn't told her yet: that he worked for his living, and that work was crafting low literature. She would understand; he felt certain she would.

"Blue Bill was taken in by the police two days ago," Martin said to the group. "They got him first."

"Did he prove to be as young as Very Merry?" Fletcher asked.

"A little older, but not much."

Fletcher looked to Brogan. "What does Parkington say?" Parkington was their contact at the Metropolitan Police.

"They found the lad with enough pilfered loot that there was no question what he'd been up to, and they're certain he'd been doing so on behalf of someone else."

Just like Very Merry. How many urchins were being forced to work for Four-Finger Mike, risking so much with so little hope of escape?

"Which area of Town?" Hollis asked.

"Don't worry," Irving tossed out. "I'm sure that bull of a valet of yours won't let anyone break into your flat."

The Dreadfuls laughed. Hollis knew it was all a friendly roasting and didn't take offense. They'd eventually take him more seriously.

Martin answered Hollis's question. "The boy was taken up in Pimlico."

Pimlico. Just like Very Merry. He met Fletcher's eye, then Stone's. They both realized the significance of that.

"Did Blue Bill tell the police who he was stealing for?" Hollis asked.

Martin shook his head.

"Parkington asked him, but the boy wouldn't tell," Brogan said. "Said he'd never seen a street child that terrified before. Whoever his overseer is, the lad's scared near to death of him, and very little shakes a London urchin."

"Four-Finger Mike has been spotted in Pimlico lately,"

Hollis said, "in connection to child thieves. I'd guess that's who this boy is tethered to."

Martin nodded. "Makes sense. He's a known thief boss and has shown himself to have little regard for children."

"But Pimlico?" Irving shook his head. "He's not been known to frequent that corner of London before."

"Pimlico's full of strange happenings," Hollis said, drawing everyone's attention. "Charles Thompson, whom we'd hoped to convince to invest in the Barton school, retrenched to the country on account of gambling debts. His house, *in Pimlico*, has been let to a cousin. I have reason to believe the house is being used to host games of chance, which feels odd considering the reason for its owner's quick removal from Town."

"Games of chance amongst gentlemen ain't unheard of," Fletcher said.

"Respectable games aren't kept secret," Hollis said. "Those participating don't sneak about to be part of them. And I can't say with any degree of confidence that a respectable game would include the likes of Alistair Headley."

That set off a chain of comments.

"I think Thompson's downfall is connected," Hollis said. "Mr. Lewiston, whom we also meant to ask for patronage of Barton school, is involved. And, though I hate to admit it, likely so is my brother."

A hush fell over the room.

"Something untoward is happening in that house. And if Four-Finger Mike is involved, then we need to be as well." Hollis leaned forward, sweeping a look across all of them.

"This might be our best chance to find him. Getting him off the streets would save countless children."

"Including the Phantom Fox," Fletcher said. "We haven't cornered that urchin yet."

Hollis hadn't told them what he'd discovered about her yet. Every time he opened his mouth to do so, he hesitated. He wasn't sure why. Something about it, something about *her*, made him suspect there was more to the situation than he realized.

"If the police can catch hold of Four-Finger Mike," Irving said, "he might help them find the Mastiff."

The hush of a moment earlier turned to the icy stillness of a glacier. Four-Finger Mike scared the children of London, but the Mastiff terrified *everyone*.

"I have a connection on St. George's Road directly across from the Thompsons' house," Hollis said. "From there, we can see most everything down on the street. I believe we'd be permitted to set up a lookout."

"Perfect," Stone said.

"But it'd have to be Brogan and me. We're the only ones known there."

Fletcher nodded. "Find out what you can. I'll see if the police'll let me have custody of their newest baby thief. I'll find a safe place for him."

And, quick as that, the Dread Penny Society had trusted Hollis for the first time with something other than being their connection in Society. He didn't mean to squander the rare opportunity.

Hollis let himself and Brogan into the Newport house the same way he had the day they'd tracked Very Merry to the basement.

"Should've told us you had this talent years ago," Brogan said. "'Tis a handy one."

"I've a great many talents, my man. I look forward to introducing the lot of you to all of them."

They closed the door behind them. This was a fine house. It was truly a shame it wasn't fully lived in. It was even more of a shame that Ana no longer had a home here. If Hollis had money enough and the right to be of help to her, he'd do all he could to give her back her home.

"I've my doubts this is the best way to secure the cooperation of the house," Brogan said. "Sneaking about is more likely to see us tossed out on our ears."

"Wallace might not want his employer to know we're about," Hollis explained.

"Ah. Your connection isn't the master of the house, but the staff."

"My connection is always the staff, no matter that the Dreadfuls think I can't function outside of a ballroom."

"We've been codding you a bit too much over the years, haven't we?"

"If that means 'heckling me,' then, yes."

They climbed the servants' stairs past the ground floor, all the way to the first-floor corridor. Mr. Newport was talking from within his room. Wallace would be in there. They'd simply have to wait for him to step out.

A moment later, he did.

Hollis flipped a penny to him. He caught it, eyed it

quickly, then motioned with his head toward the servants' stairwell. The three of them crowded in there.

"Something rumblin'?" Wallace asked.

"We think there's trouble brewing at the Thompsons' place, likely involves the gentry as well as the criminal world," Hollis said.

Wallace nodded. "Been watching them, both the master and I. Cain't say I like what we see."

"There must be another window in the house facing the same direction."

"Oy."

"Can the two of us"—he motioned to himself and Brogan—"set up a lookout there? We're wanting to sniff out a pattern or a connection. It's something bad; we can feel it in our bones."

Wallace scratched at his whiskers. "It'd upset Mr. Newport if he knew you was spying from his house. I only just managed to keep quiet that 'break-in' a couple weeks ago." Wallace tossed him a look of annoyance. "The lot of you are on my blacklist already for that."

"We were saving a child."

"I know it." Wallace appeared to be hiding a smile. "I'm overlooking the trouble you've caused me on that girl's account. I've known too many urchins to not be worried for the littlest ones."

"Couldn't've said it better m' own self," Brogan tossed in.

"Miss Newport wouldn't be happy 'bout this neither," Wallace said. "Suppose you give yourselves away?"

"We won't," Hollis said. "With a front-facing window,

curtains to tuck behind, and maybe a couple of blankets, we can do our work without the least sound or notice. Your employer and his daughter will be none the wiser."

Wallace nodded. "And you'd be ridding us of the trouble across the street."

"That is the goal."

"The room next to Mr. Newport's faces the street. You'll have to keep quiet, it being so close. There's an old table and chair in there. And I can fetch you blankets."

"Brilliant," Brogan said. "We'll settle in there. And we'll not make difficulty for you."

Wallace gave a quick nod. The three of them tiptoed down the corridor, past Mr. Newport's room, and to the empty bedchamber beside it. The curtains in the window were faded and dusty, but thick enough to obscure Hollis and Brogan's presence there. The table and chair had seen better days. Against the opposite wall stood a narrow curio cabinet. Outside of that, the room was empty. They could make this do.

Brogan had more experience in this area than Hollis did, so he tossed his question in that direction.

"Anything else you recommend for our 'spy lookout'?" Hollis asked in a whisper.

Brogan looked to Wallace. "Do you happen to have a rug? Bare floors are louder than carpeted ones."

"There's one in the attics. It's moth-eaten and faded nearly colorless, so it ain't ever used. Could move it here."

Hollis knew of at least one need they'd come head-to-head with soon enough. "If I give you a spot of brass, would

you fetch us some food? Simple things we don't need to prepare: fruit and veg, bread."

"Oy. I'm off to grab things for Mr. Newport this afternoon. I'll do for you then."

"Capital." Hollis gave him money enough to bring back
a couple of days' worth. After Wallace left, they settled in,
keeping their voices low and their movements to a minimum.

"Ambrose told him you broke into this house?" Brogan
asked.

Hollis nodded. "When he recruited him to the cause."

"Did you tell him Stone was part of it as well?"

"Are you out of your skull? Stone would kill me."

Brogan nodded. "True."

Hollis unbuttoned his shoes and set them carefully in the
corner. He'd make less noise in his stockinged feet.

"If the curio's near empty, it'd do for tucking away whatever food Wallace brings us," Brogan said.

Not a bad idea. Hollis crossed to it and noiselessly opened
the doors. Holding only a small but eclectic collection of trinkets and knickknacks, the curio shelves were relatively empty.
"There'll be space in here."

A little porcelain figurine held a violin, smiling sweetly
over her shoulder, putting him in mind of Ana. It was likely
hers. How many of the other things were as well?

He spied a silver snuffbox. An ormolu clock. Other figurines. A leather box containing an ivory-handled manicure
set.

A manicure set.

Hollis stood in front of the cabinet, eyeing the contents

while crossing off a list in his head. Figurines. Trinket box. Snuffbox. Manicure set.

"Find something interesting, did you?" Brogan joined him there.

"All those odd things the elusive Phantom Fox has been swiping—what are the chances nearly every item on that list would be in this curio?"

Brogan looked more closely. "There's no saying they're the *same* odd things."

"What was it Kumar said about the silver snuffbox the thief made off with?"

"Only the top was silver, and plate at that. The plating had rubbed off entirely at the hinges, so no one seeing it would ever believe it was solid silver."

Hollis took the box from the cabinet. The bottom and sides were wood. Only the top was silver. He turned it to examine the hinges in the back. All the plating was rubbed off.

"Blimey," Brogan whispered.

"Why would these things be here?" Hollis asked.

"Seems to me our tiny thieves weren't the ones lifting worthless bits."

Hollis already knew that. The next logical conclusion wasn't comforting. "Someone in this house must be the actual thief."

"Mr. Newport moved with too much stiffness to be in the business of slipping in and out of houses," Brogan said.

"And Wallace hasn't the grace or agility for it," Hollis said. "Ambrose told me the man was a pugilist."

"That leaves only one person," Brogan said.

Hollis paced away. "Can you picture quiet, fragile Ana working as a thief in the dark of night?"

"Might be she's not so fragile as she seems."

Hollis rubbed at the back of his neck. He could see in his mind's eye the thief he'd cornered. A small-framed woman. Moving quietly and gracefully. The same height and build as Ana.

Was it possible? Had he fallen top-over-tail in love with a thief?

CHAPTER 16

"Elizabeth has been contacted by two families looking for a private music tutor." Ana poured tea for her father. "She thinks, in time, I might find enough pupils to be an independent teacher. I could choose when and who I teach. I could live here again."

Father looked to his ever-faithful valet. "What do you say to that, Wallace? Ana could live here, perhaps chase away the specters that have you so alarmed."

Though Father's tone held mountains of teasing, Wallace didn't look amused.

"Specters?" Ana looked from one to the other a few times.

"There have been odd noises around the house." Father took a sip of tea. "I'm convinced we have a draft or a squirrel or mouse. Wallace, though, has taken Lafayette Jones's stories a bit too much to heart."

The man remained as stalwart as ever, not blushing or cringing at the teasing. "I ain't saying it couldn't be vermin or wind, only that I ain't one to ignore possibilities."

Ana poured Wallace a cup of tea as well. He was a

servant, yes, but he was also a friend. Without Wallace, this house would be in shambles and her father would be alone. She treasured him for his efforts to help.

"If Mr. Jones's depiction of ghosts is accurate," Ana said, "we needn't be overly alarmed should our noises prove to be supernatural. Ghosts are, apparently, quite friendly to us 'Perishables.'"

"I am looking forward to seeing how those ghost boys manage to keep their new friend hidden," Father said. "That Jones weaves an entertaining tale."

"He does, indeed," she said.

"Would you truly come back home if you found enough students?" Father asked.

She smiled at him over her cup. "In a heartbeat. I've missed home. I've missed seeing you every day."

His eyes wandered to the low-burning embers. "It's hardly a home now."

Ana rose and crossed to the table. She set her teacup on the table. "I would require you to read to me every evening, to provide copies of the latest penny dreadfuls, and point out each and every interesting thing occurring on the street below so I could spy on the neighbors as adeptly as you do."

"Impossible," Father said. "No one spies as well as I do."

Wallace choked on his tea. Ana tossed him a laughing smile. Father did not always tease or jest, so when he did, it was surprising in the best way.

"This does make me hesitate." Ana pretended to be concerned. "If I have gentlemen callers here, you will no doubt spy on them."

"We both will," Wallace said. "Cain't have anyone importuning you, Miss Newport."

"Your last gentlemen callers were perfectly acceptable," Father said. "*More* than acceptable."

"Oh, Father." She shook her head as she passed his chair on her way to the window. "I had very few callers all those years ago, certainly none who stood out enough to still remember."

"I meant Mr. Darby and Mr. O'Donnell."

That stopped Ana briefly in her tracks. "They weren't callers, Father. Not in that sense."

He turned in his chair enough to look at her. "Why shouldn't they be? They're young and handsome. You're young and beautiful."

"Bless you, Father." She had regained enough of her equilibrium to close the distance to the window.

"It's only the truth." He had emerged from his shell more and more the last weeks. Since the gentlemen's visit, in fact. "Mr. O'Donnell was witty and entertaining. He knew absolutely everything about the penny dreadfuls. And neither of them seemed to disapprove of me reading them."

"Do you suppose they'll come by again?"

"I'm certain Mr. Darby will," Father said.

Again, Wallace choked back a laugh. And, again, Ana eyed the both of them with what she hoped would prove a powerful enough glare that they would explain their amusement.

"Mr. O'Donnell was a chance-met visitor who enjoyed a discussion," Father said. "Mr. Darby, however, has a strong motivation for returning."

"And what might that be?"

Father looked at her, then at Wallace. With a hint of a smile on his stubbly face, he took up his teacup and sipped instead of answering.

Ana turned her gaze to Wallace.

"Oh, no, miss. I ain't spilling his secrets."

"What secret are you keeping, Father?"

Wallace shook his head. "Mr. Newport ain't the one I mean."

Her pulse, quite without warning, leapt to her temples. "You mean Mr. Darby, then?"

"I ain't saying another word." Wallace began a focused cleaning effort across the room.

"Father?" Ana turned to him, but he only shook his head.

Hollis has motivation. She knew what she wanted that motivation to be. The man showed her undeniable affection. He spoke tenderly and personally to her. She had reason to hope he was as partial to her as she was to him.

She sat on the window seat, looking out over the street below. Just as the last time she'd watched the Thompsons' house, two smartly dressed gentlemen, having arrived apparently without a carriage, knocked at the door. A moment later, they were let in, and the door closed behind them. At first glance, it seemed normal. But this was the *only* way anyone ever arrived there.

"There is something odd about that," she whispered.

"Watching the Thompsons' place?" Wallace asked from the nearby bureau. "Definitely something odd there."

"Have you been watching the comings and goings as well?"

"They're being thoroughly watched, I will tell you that."

Ana looked back once more to the front step of the Thompsons' house. Two more gentlemen had appeared. One of them wore trousers and a coat in matching blue-and-green plaid. She'd seen plaid before, but not in so large a pattern. It was memorable, she would grant the gentleman that. The other gentleman looked back toward the empty street, and when he turned, she recognized him.

Mr. Lewiston. The gentleman she and Hollis had spoken to briefly in Hyde Park. The one who had invoked Mr. Randolph Darby in a discussion of something Hollis hadn't approved of.

Ana didn't know what was happening at the Thompsons' house, but she was absolutely certain about one thing: when Hollis came to fetch her for his niece's music lessons the next day, she needed to tell him who she'd seen there.

O—🎹

Ana rode alone to the Darby house. The carriage had arrived unoccupied. Neither was Hollis at his brother's house when she arrived. The butler let her in, and a chambermaid escorted her to the music room.

She missed Hollis, and not merely because she needed to tell him what she'd seen. Her *heart* missed him.

Eloise was ushered inside not long after Ana arrived. She trudged to the piano.

"Is something the matter, sweetheart?" she asked. The little girl was usually enthusiastic about her lessons.

Her shoulders hunched. "Mama and Addison have gone

to visit Grandmother and Grandfather, and I didn't get to go with them."

"Because of your music lesson?"

Eloise nodded.

"We could have changed your lesson to another day."

Her pout was both heartbreaking and adorable. "I told Mama, but she said no."

"Would you like me to tell her, when next I see her, that in the future, you should be permitted to skip your lessons in order to visit with your grandparents?"

"Yes, please, Miss Newport." Her spirits appeared to lift. She climbed onto the stool. "I didn't practice on Wednesday or Thursday. I was going to tell you I did, but Mama says I'm not supposed to tell fibs." Eloise shrugged. "And Uncle Hollis says I'm supposed to be nice to you."

"Your uncle Hollis is a very kind gentleman."

"He says you're the prettiest music teacher in England." Eloise made the declaration quite seriously and quite without realizing her uncle might not appreciate her sharing that particular idea. "And he says you play the violin brilliantly. And he says he likes to talk with you. And he says you don't complain about being cold when you ride with him in the park, even though he didn't bring a carriage blanket for you."

"Good heavens, Eloise." She didn't know whether to laugh or dissolve into a puddle of embarrassment. "How often does your uncle talk with you about me?"

"Sometimes." Eloise plunked a few keys with her right index finger. "He came to see Mama yesterday. Mama was sad about Papa—I don't know why—and Uncle Hollis said he was angry with Papa—I don't know that why either—and they talked."

"About *me*?"

Eloise kicked her feet back and forth. "And Papa. And me. And sharp cards."

"Sharp cards?"

"I don't know what that is. Mama didn't know, either."

A suspicion formed in Ana's mind, one revolving around a word she'd read about in a penny dreadful. Fitting, really. "Do you think your uncle might have said 'card sharps'?"

Eloise thought a moment, then nodded.

A "card sharp," Ana understood, was an American term for someone who cheated at cards. Hollis was worried about something underhanded his brother was involved in, and he had been discussing his brother whilst referencing card sharps. The puzzle pieces slipped quickly into place.

His family's finances were precarious as it was, and his brother was risking it all by gambling.

Mr. Lewiston was involved in the same, and he had been at the Thompsons' house only the day before. Perhaps *that* was the reason for the constant flow of visitors there. It had been turned into an upper-class gambling establishment.

Eloise made a half-hearted attempt at playing the practice piece she'd been assigned for that week. Ana had the distinct impression the girl *could* play it better than she was, but her heart wasn't in it. She'd seen it happen to other girls at Thurloe now and then.

"Sweetheart," she said, "would you like to do something other than play the piano today?"

"Oh, yes, please." She spun and faced Ana. "Could we

read a story? Uncle Hollis tells me stories about a school where ghosts learn to be ghosts and the teachers are all ghosts, but now there's a real boy at the school."

Ana bit back a smile.

Eloise sighed contentedly. "He tells me the best stories."

What would the famous Lafayette Jones think if he knew this little girl gave her uncle credit for *his* stories? If the man had a heart at all, he would be happy to know his tales brought joy to this family.

At the sound of footsteps, they both turned toward the door. Mr. Randolph Darby stood in the doorway, eyes wide. He wore a blue-and-green plaid suit. Bright colors. Large pattern.

Mercy.

"Is Hollis here?" He sounded panicked.

"N—No, sir," Ana said. "He didn't come with me today."

Mr. Darby muttered something and turned to leave.

He had been at Thompsons'. He was Mr. Lewiston's companion. *Mercy.*

"Parker!" Mr. Darby's roar echoed from down the corridor. "Lock the doors, Parker!"

Eloise's sweet face held confusion and worry. Ana put her arm around the little girl.

"Papa sounds scared, Miss Newport."

He did, indeed.

Someone pounded at the front door. Not an ordinary knock, not even an anxious one. Pounding. Fearsome, angry, threatening pounding.

"Parker!" Mr. Darby bellowed.

"Miss Newport," Eloise whimpered.

Ana took the girl's hand and helped her off the piano stool. Together, they tiptoed toward the door of the music room. The front door rattled so hard Ana swore she heard splintering.

"Miss Newport." Parker, the butler, came running down the corridor. "Get Miss Eloise out. Get her away from here, wherever you can take her."

Good heavens.

"And Mr. Darby?"

"I'll look after him, miss." Parker pulled her out of the music room and nudged her toward the back of the house. "There's a set of French doors at the back of the ballroom. Slip out that way and get far from here."

The sound of wood breaking sent Ana into a near-panic.

Parker set something in her hand. "Find Mr. Hollis. Give him this and tell him what's happened. Go."

He shoved her. She gripped Eloise's hand tighter, and they ran.

THE GENTLEMAN AND THE THIEF

by Mr. King

Installment V,
in which our intrepid Couple give chase
and discover more than Expected!

Tillie was going to land herself in deep trouble chasing after a mystery on the moors. Many a soul had grown hopelessly lost in the vast nothingness of the wild hills.

Wellington called her name, but the wind carried it away. He ran after her, reaching her just as she reached the blue flame. But it had disappeared without a trace. No one stood where the flame had been, carrying a candle or torch or lantern.

"You saw it this time, di'n't you?" She looked up at him.

"I did." He stared at the spot where the flame had vanished.

She nodded again and again. "And you can see for yourself there ain't nothing it could've been a reflection of or anything we might've simply mis-seen."

"We didn't mis-see. But what *did* we see?" He turned his head, slowly, searching.

Tillie looked around as well. "There." She pointed into the distance. "It's there."

And so it was. A blue flame, just far enough to be barely visible. If he wasn't mistaken, it was moving.

"We'll catch it this time, Tillie." He snatched up her hand and ran with her out onto the moors.

On and on they went. Whenever they drew closer, the flame disappeared, only to reappear elsewhere a moment later. The mystic blue flame led them on a chase over hills, down rounded valleys. Over and over and over. Still, it eluded them.

Exhaustion was setting in, mingled with a heavy dose of frustration. What if their quarry proved uncatchable? How could they endure endless years of pilfering and thievery?

They stood breathless on the gaping moors, waiting for their prey to reappear. How long had they been chasing it? How far afield would it lead them?

"Why hasn't it come back?" Tillie whispered, spinning about, eyeing the landscape. "It's been gone longer this time."

The flame was nowhere to be seen. But something could be heard.

"What was that?" He turned in the direction of the sound.

"It sounded like a child cryin'."

"Out here?" Merciful heavens, a child lost on the moors was in danger indeed. "Hulloo?" he called out. "Where are you, child?"

A whimper answered, one hardly loud enough to be heard. But hear it, they did. Tillie, her hand still in his, pulled him around more bends and over a hill as they followed the heartrending cries.

"We have to find the poor child, Wellington."

"We will," he vowed.

And they did. A tiny, shivering boy, likely no more than six or seven years old, cowered behind a large rock, eyes wide with fear.

Tillie approached first. She could be mischievous and adventurous. Her temper could flare hot, or she could be tender as a newborn lamb. In that moment, she was soft and quiet and still.

She knelt beside the boy and gently, slowly, set her hand on his arm. "Are you lost, dearie?"

"I were running away." Tears clogged the child's voice.

Wellington knelt next to Tillie. "Why were you running?"

"I'd've been in a heap o' trouble."

Tillie sat beside the child. "You'll be in a mountain of it if you're out here when it grows dark. Come with us, dearie. We'll see to it you have food in your belly and a warm fire."

"I'll be in trouble."

"You won't be, I swear to it." Tillie looked to Wellington. "Will he?"

"Not a bit of trouble," Wellington said. "We'll take good care of you."

The boy shook his head. "You'll be angry at me."

"Why would we be angry with you?" Wellington could not ignore the real worry in the child's expression.

The boy took a shaky breath. "Because I stole it."

Wellington met Tillie's eye. Could this little slip of a child be their elusive thief?

"It's not him," Tillie whispered, apparently understanding his unspoken question.

"He's just said he stole something."

She shook her head firmly. "It's not him."

The little boy whimpered. His safety needed to come first.

"Come along," Wellington said. "We'll see to it you're fed and warm, then we'll settle whatever needs settling."

He agreed, but clearly wasn't at all convinced he was safe. Tillie took the boy's hand and smiled reassuringly. The child walked alongside them but didn't speak. Wellington kept a weather eye out, watching for the elusive blue flame, but it made no return appearance. He suspected Tillie was keeping close watch as well.

They arrived at the Combses' cottage just as the sky was turning pink with the first blush of the coming sunset.

Mr. Combs was home and eyed them with curiosity. "You've found a child."

"On the moors," Tillie said, leading their new addition to the low-burning fire. "We were chasing the same phantom I saw at Summerworth."

"You were?" Mr. Combs looked to Wellington. "Did you see it as well?"

"I did. We attempted to catch it, but it proved too fast and agile."

"Of course it did." Mr. Combs actually snorted with disdain, though there was no unkindness in the sound. "No one can catch a bluecap."

A bluecap? Wellington had heard of redcaps, murderous little goblins, but he was not familiar with this variety of spirit. "I don't know what that is."

"A little creature that appears as a blue flame, wandering about on its own, popping from place to place."

Precisely what they'd seen.

"Is it known to steal things?" Wellington asked.

Mr. Combs shook his head. "Not generally, but it expects to be paid. If no one is paying it, the sprite might be . . . collecting payment on its own."

"What would I be paying this creature for?" Wellington could not make sense of it at all.

"The bluecap is found in mines," Mr. Combs said. "The miners pay it for warning them about cave-ins."

"My house is not a mine, and there is no danger of a cave-in."

"It may be doing something else," Tillie said. "Something it thinks it ought to be paid to do."

Could this truly be the cause of his difficulties? A little creature that ought not to be anywhere near his house?

He motioned subtly to the little boy, huddled under a blanket near the fire. "The little one confessed to stealing."

Tillie shook her head. "It isn't him. He couldn't have moved the mirror or the painting."

"But the other things, maybe?" Heavens, did he have more than one thief?

"I didn't steal anything from you, sir." The little boy's voice was filled with misery.

"Then what *did* you steal?" Wellington asked.

The child took a quavering breath. "The blue flame."

CHAPTER 17

The Thompsons' place grew busier every day, practically every minute. Though the gentlemen still arrived in pairs, they now came practically on each other's heels. The comings and goings never stopped, not late at night, not early in the morning, not at midday.

"With Headley part of it all, it has to be gambling." Hollis made the whispered observation for likely the twentieth time since he and Brogan had come to the Newport home. He wanted to believe ill-advised games of chance were all that was happening across the street, but his gut insisted there was more to it than that.

"'Tis only gentlemen going in and out the front, but I'd be surprised if they were the only ones taking part." Brogan kept his voice quiet, as well. They never spoke above a whisper, not wanting to give their presence away.

"I'm picturing a seedy copper hell inside." He handed Brogan the telescope, relinquishing his place at the window.

"Even after seeing your brother there yesterday?"

Hollis shook his head. "I'm not convinced that was my

brother." He hadn't been the one on lookout when Brogan thought he'd seen Randolph.

"You're also not convinced your lady love is a sticky-fingered thief."

"I've told you I'll not discuss that." Until he could formulate a reasonable explanation, he refused to even think about Ana's involvement in all this.

Brogan watched the street through the handheld telescope. "I'd say they're near to doubling the in-and-out over there."

"That doesn't make sense," Hollis said. "If they're playing high-stakes games that are ruining people, they'd have few takers for future games."

"They have takers—and plenty." Brogan lowered the telescope. Though his gaze remained on the street, his thoughts appeared to be on something else. "For a time, while Móirín and I were giving aid in Maida Hill, there was a house that always seemed busy. The local working people knew it to be one where unsavory things were happening. Everyone knew it, but the flow of people never slowed."

Brogan and his sister frequented the poor neighborhoods, helping people, bringing food and supplies, teaching them skills to help them find work. They spent a fair amount of time in some very questionable areas of Town.

"Did you ever discover why people kept coming to that house?"

Brogan looked back at him. "Same thing that kept the little chimney sweep we rescued last year with his master for so long."

"Violence."

Brogan nodded. "And threats."

Hollis crossed back to the window. Two more gentlemen were waiting at the door. "There's a tangled web on the other side of that door; I know it."

"And a four-fingered spider, I'd wager."

Hollis rubbed the back of his neck. "Very Merry still doesn't sleep well at night. And she won't talk in any detail about him."

"'Tis a deuced shame he escaped the police after that fire. I thought we'd cleared the streets of him."

Hollis sighed. "So did I."

Voices broke the silence in the next room. Wallace and Mr. Newport were generally quiet. Hollis listened more closely.

"Is that a woman's voice?"

Brogan shrugged. "I didn't see Ana arrive."

"Who else could it be?"

The voices stopped. Then footsteps sounded. Growing closer. Too close.

Brogan and Hollis moved quickly and quietly in their stockinged feet and tucked themselves into the dark corner on the other side of the curio. They'd not be spotted should the door open.

Which it did.

Wallace stepped inside. He looked around the room, turning, until he spotted them. His gaze stopped on Hollis. He held up a penny between his thumb and forefinger, just long enough for Hollis to take note of it, then tossed it to him.

Hollis caught it. He checked the markings. "This is Parker's."

Wallace nodded.

"Is he here?"

"He ain't. But he sent it."

"With whom?"

"Miss Newport. And your niece."

"Eloise?" Worry surged.

"Little one's been cryin'. Miss Newport looks to be in a full blue funk."

Eloise was here, and Ana was terrified? This bordered on disaster.

"Did you tell her we were in here?" Brogan asked.

Wallace shook his head. "Only said I'd get the penny to Mr. Hollis."

"Something terrible must've happened. I can't waste time pretending I'm being fetched."

Brogan moved toward the window. "Think of something to tell her. Keep mum about me being in here."

Something to tell her. He hadn't the first idea what that was going to be. He quickly pulled on his shoes, then moved to Mr. Newport's room.

Eloise caught sight of him first. "Uncle Hollis!" His name quavered on her lips as she ran to him.

He snatched her up and held her to him. Tears poured down her face. "My sweet girl."

"We had to run away, Uncle Hollis." She was shaking in his arms. "We had to run away."

Ana reached his side. "How are you here so quickly? Wallace only just left to get word to you."

"The fates are smiling on us today. I came for a visit, arriving just as Wallace was about to leave."

"A welcome spot of luck," Ana said.

"Indeed." He rocked Eloise in his arms, though he continued speaking to Ana. "What happened?"

"Someone was trying to break into your brother's house. Mr. Darby sounded afraid. The butler was stalwart but looked worried. Your brother is in danger. I'm certain of it."

Confound it. Hollis set Eloise down. "Stay here with Miss Newport." He turned to Wallace. "Stand sentinel at this house, man."

"I'll do for, guv."

Hollis slapped him on the shoulder before he hurried from the room.

"Hollis." Ana's voice called after him.

He stopped on the top step of the staircase and turned back, fighting the growing need to run home, to save his brother from the trouble he'd gotten himself into.

"Eloise heard your brother talking about card sharps. And, yesterday, I saw him go into the Thompsons' house with Mr. Lewiston. You've suspected he was gambling beyond what he ought. *I* suspect someone came today to collect on a debt."

Thugs. Hollis had seen for himself what Four-Finger Mike's roughs did to people. He'd best not go to Randolph's house alone.

"Do you know if Cora and Addison got out of the house safely?"

"They were gone for the day, visiting her parents."

Another welcome spot of luck. "Thank you for keeping Eloise safe."

"I'll thank you to keep yourself safe as well, Hollis Darby."

He tossed her a smile. "I am not unfamiliar with the shadows, Ana." He felt certain she wasn't either.

She leaned toward him and pressed a swift kiss to his cheek before hurrying back into her father's room.

Ana Newport was a growing mystery, and Hollis already had more of those than he could sort.

The door, three inches thick and solid oak, had been shattered off its hinges.

"Blimey." Hollis stepped gingerly into the vestibule, Fletcher on his heels. "If whoever did this hasn't killed my brother, *I* will."

The tables in the entry were overturned. A vase lay on the tile floor in dozens of pieces, flowers and water strewn about. Every door in sight had been thrown open. A few were barely hanging on their hinges.

"Fly me," Fletcher muttered. "What kind of mess did he land himself in?"

"A four-fingered one," Hollis said.

They stopped in the entryway, listening. No discussion of strategy was needed; they both understood the proper method of snooping. The type of roughs who'd leave a house in this state weren't trying to be stealthy. They'd not be this quiet.

"I'd wager they've left," Fletcher said.

"I'm sick to death of people wagering," Hollis said dryly.

They looked through each room, entering cautiously, leaving relieved. They found no thugs on the ground floor. None on the first floor, either. Or the second. Or third. All that remained was the servants' quarters and belowstairs.

"If the butler was the one protecting your brother, he might well have hidden him away in the area of the house he knows best," Fletcher said.

"And warned off the rest of the staff," Hollis said. "The house is too quiet for anyone to still be here."

The quiet of the house grew eerie as they took the stairs to its below-ground level. The silence in the servants' corridor was unnerving. This part of a London house was *never* quiet.

Fletcher halted him with a hand on his arm. "Do you hear that?" he whispered.

He did. A thumping. Distant, quiet, repeating.

"Toward the back." Fletcher motioned that way.

They moved slowly, keeping a careful eye on every shadowed corner and open door. Empty. All empty.

Yet the thumping continued.

"Something familiar in it," Fletcher muttered. "I know I've heard that before."

Hollis felt the same odd déjà vu.

As they approached the back of the house, the pounding grew louder. It sounded like wood against wood.

They reached the back door, the one leading out to the path cutting through the kitchen garden. The door was open. A stiff breeze from outside slammed it against the side of the house, over and over again. The pounding they'd heard.

Hollis dismissed the door as his gaze fell on something more ominous. The wall was charred, blackened with the scars of a fire hastily lit and hastily extinguished. Arson was Four-Finger Mike's calling card.

Fletcher eyed the scorch marks. Hollis checked the back garden. It was just as empty as the house.

"A close call, here," Fletcher said when Hollis stepped inside again. "It ain't like Four-Finger to let a fire be put out. I'd guess he wasn't tryin' to burn the place down. This was a warning."

"But where's the one he was warning?"

Fletcher tucked his hands in his jacket pocket. "Not to be morbid, mate, but I kept a lookout for blood. Didn't see a drop."

Hollis emptied his lungs. "Maybe Randolph got away."

"Parker's a reliable sort," Fletcher said. "The reason you added him to your network, no doubt. I'd guess he evacuated the staff, and that he spirited your no-good, lousy brother off somewhere safe."

If only they knew where that "somewhere safe" was. "Let's set the lads to sniffing out Randolph's whereabouts. I'll send word to Cora for her to stay at her parents' house."

Fletcher shook his head. "Convince her to go to Thurloe. I'll ask Móirín Donnelly to head there as well. Between her and Elizabeth, it'll be the safest spot for them all."

"Assuming, of course, they don't mind being featured in Mr. King's upcoming installments," Hollis said. "Though I'm enjoying 'his' latest work, I'm not certain I like watching my life play out on the page: a lonely gentleman sniffing out a thief and who's lost his heart to a lady who keeps him firmly in the role of a friend."

"Elizabeth writes what she sees in the world around her, like we all do."

Hollis eyed him. "Did you enjoy it when your life played out on our mutual friend's pages not long ago?"

"That tale ended well," Fletcher said. "When all was said and done, I didn't mind so much."

"If Elizabeth can keep Ana safe while we search out my brother, I might forgive her." He pushed out a breath as he eyed the scorch marks on the wall. "The roughs who came here might have seen Ana and might know who she is."

The fire had been a warning, yes. But Hollis had a terrible suspicion the warning had not been for Randolph but for anyone who came to help him.

A warning . . . for *him*.

CHAPTER 18

Ana had never met the fiery Irishwoman introduced to her as Móirín. She'd never once called
at Thurloe, yet, she and Elizabeth appeared to be
friends. Her attire was comfortably middle class, yet the
alarming details Mr. Walker was sharing of the state of things
at the Darby house didn't cause Móirín to so much as flinch.

"How much of this does *Mrs.* Darby know?" Móirín
asked.

"However much Hollis is up there telling her now," Mr.
Walker said. "Cain't say I know what that'll be. He don't
want to worry her, but he ain't looking to lie."

Poor Hollis. What a situation to find himself in.

"I've not heard any whispers of new gambling establishments among the folks I work with," Móirín said. "Sounds to
me like you've a criminal ring targeting, at least in part, the
fine and fancy."

"How do we get to the bottom of something like that?"
Elizabeth asked.

"You send in someone fine and fancy," Móirín said. She

hooked a thumb over her shoulder, pointing toward the doorway of Elizabeth's office. "Someone like that lad, there."

Sure enough, Hollis stood on the threshold, having arrived completely silently and without drawing the notice of anyone other than Móirín, who hadn't even looked backward. How had she known he was there?

Hollis came inside. "I've been thinking the same myself."

"Rest your bones." Móirín motioned to the only empty chair in the room, one, sadly, nowhere near Ana. "Tell us what you've in mind."

He dropped onto the chair. "I need to get myself invited to one of these games."

Everyone in the room nodded. Everyone but Ana. Those "games" were the reason Hollis's brother was missing, the reason his home had been ransacked, the reason a fire had been lit at the back door. How could they think diving into that cesspool was a good idea?

"You cain't go in alone," Mr. Walker said.

"But he, alone, has the standing," Móirín said. "We haven't another option."

"He can't." Heat spread over Ana's face when they all looked at her. "None of the gentlemen ever arrives alone."

Hollis nodded. "They arrive always and only in pairs."

Elizabeth stood and walked away, her expression mirroring the others in the group, all clearly deep in thought.

"I could wrangle someone to come with me," Hollis said, "but I won't place an innocent person in a dangerous situation."

"I suspect it doesn't work like that, anyway." Elizabeth paced back toward them. "If these were games anyone could walk into, you would have heard more whispers about them in Society."

"Makes sense," Mr. Walker said. "I'd guess the players arrive in pairs because one is bringing the other."

They were all catching on very quickly. She seemed to be the only one missing a piece of the puzzle.

"You're needing someone to get you in," Móirín said. "Your brother could, if he weren't cowering somewhere, hiding from the roughs that run the games. Did you recognize anyone else arriving at the fancy copper hell?"

"Lewiston," Hollis said. "But he arrived with my brother, which would make asking him to take *me* a little suspect."

"Ask Alistair Headley," Elizabeth said. "There's nothing else for it."

"He knows I don't like him."

"He knows *no one* likes him," Mr. Walker tossed in.

Elizabeth shushed him with a wave of her hand. "His gambling is better known than Mr. Lewiston's. If you tell him you're looking to improve your fortunes but don't care for the lower-class establishments, he'll take you to Thompsons'."

Hollis sighed. "I'm not certain I love my brother enough to join forces with Alistair Headley." There was a forced quality to the jest. He was, no doubt, nearly overwhelmed with worry. "When we find Randolph, I'll kill him."

A few chuckles rumbled around the room. They were all so comfortable with these inherently *uncomfortable* discussions. Dangers. Criminals. Derring-do. Perhaps Hollis being behind the Rollins's home hadn't been a mere coincidence. Perhaps he'd been undertaking something himself.

Mr. Walker rose and stood beside Elizabeth. "Do you want me to stay at the school tonight, dove?"

She shook her head. "Ol' Joe's here. He'll keep us safe."

"You do have an extra degree of risk with Mrs. Darby and the children staying here."

"That's why *I'm* here." Móirín rose. "I'm not as quick with my fists as he is, but I can wield a weapon with the best of 'em." She crossed to the door. "I'll settle in upstairs. Am I to keep my bein' here a secret from Mrs. Darby and the little ones?"

"For now," Hollis said. "I'd rather they were none the wiser about the precautions we're taking. No use alarming them more than they already are."

Móirín gave a quick nod and slipped out.

"I'll have a word with Ol' Joe before I hop off," Mr. Walker said. He and Elizabeth left as well.

Ana released the breath she'd been all but holding.

Hollis sat beside her. He wove his fingers through hers. "I wish I'd been at my brother's this morning like I was meant to be. You wouldn't have been required to face this alone."

"What happened this morning was frightening, yes, but it was not unfamiliar." She rested her head on his shoulder. "After my father's business failed and we'd sold our belongings to make good its debts, some who'd been defrauded decided getting their investments repaid was not enough. They, who had wealth beyond what we'd ever known, ransacked our house, taking anything that caught their eye."

"Then I am not the only one who is acquainted with the shadows."

She sighed and turned toward him, curving into his comforting strength. "What shadows are you familiar with?"

"I work amongst the poorest in London—rescue efforts and raising funds for education. It is dangerous at times."

"Is that what you and your Irish friend were doing the day you visited Father?" she asked.

"Why do you—" He stopped. She felt his chest move with a silent laugh. "Yes. That is what we were doing."

"You were very convincing," she said. "I'm not at all certain which parts of that day were lies."

"Lies?"

Her heart dropped, but she didn't shy away. "Your reason for being there. Your reason for staying. Your insistence you enjoyed your visit."

He slipped his hand from hers and wrapped his arms around her, tucking her closer. "Our initial reason for being in the neighborhood was not quite what we told you, but the rest was true."

Ana looked up at him. "And did you enjoy riding in the park with me and going to the theater and all of that?"

"'All of that' has been the highlight of the past months," he said.

"For me as well."

He leaned achingly closer.

"Hollis." Mr. Walker's voice pierced the moment.

"Oh, bother," Hollis whispered as he pulled back. He did not, though, drop his embrace.

"Ol' Joe needs a bit more information."

Hollis met her gaze again. "Remind me next time we

have a few minutes together to pick up where we're leaving off."

Heat touched her cheeks, but she smiled. "I will."

He rose and crossed the room. At the door, he paused and turned back. "And remind me as well to ask you how long you've been the Phantom Fox."

CHAPTER 19

A note was delivered to Hollis's flat the next day. He unfolded it, curious.

Hollis Darby, you rat.

His eyes jumped to the signature at the bottom of the page. *Elizabeth.* Why was she so put out with him?

> *I don't know what you said to Ana last evening,*
> *but when next I see you, I am going to throttle you.*

What had happened?

> *She quit. No warning. No explanation. Simply*
> *said she wanted what was best for the school and,*
> *therefore, was resigning her post. She has left already.*
> *I am without a music teacher and without my friend.*
> *Fix this.*
>
> *—Elizabeth*

Hollis tossed the note onto his desk, pacing away. He'd made his comment about Ana being a thief as a bit of teasing.

They'd shared a tender moment. He'd offered her a glimpse of his clandestine activities. Acknowledging that he knew a bit of hers had seemed fitting.

Instead he'd frightened her. She would be at her father's house; he was certain of it.

Hollis snatched his gloves off the desk. The door to his library opened before he could fetch anything else.

"Libby, I'll be—" But as he turned, he realized his housekeeper was not the one who had stepped inside. "Ana."

She snapped the door closed behind her, then pointed an accusatory finger at him. "I am not a thief." Her hand dropped. "Well, if one chooses to dwell on the technicalities, I *am*, but it's not as simple as that."

"Ana—"

"And it was rather brash of you to toss your discovery at me as you were walking away, offering me no opportunity to explain or respond."

"I—"

"Nor did you come back for one. I had no chance to defend myself or plead with you not to tell people what you knew—or *thought* you knew. That was terribly unfair of you."

"Darling." He slipped his arm around her. She didn't pull away. "I *did* come back to talk with you, but you'd retreated to your bedchamber. I didn't dare push that boundary of propriety."

"You revealed to anyone within earshot of Elizabeth's office last evening that I was a thief, one notorious enough to have a street name. Questionable meeting spots could hardly do more damage to my reputation." She was skittish as a foal in a field of snakes.

"The entryway was empty—even Fletcher had already slipped away. No one was on the stairs or across the way in the sitting room. I knew you alone would hear what I'd said. And"—he offered an apologetic look—"I thought I was being flirtatious."

She eyed him sideways. "You realized I was stealing things, and your response was to *flirt* with me about it?"

He shrugged. "Why not?"

Deep creases formed in her forehead. "You weren't horrified or disgusted?"

"Hardly."

Her lips twisted in dry amusement. "Thieves are your favorite sort of criminal, is that it?"

"*You* are my favorite sort of criminal." He dropped his hands to hers and held them. "And I am bursting with curiosity over what must be a very interesting reason for all this."

Some of the tension in her posture eased. "You didn't assume the worst in me, then?"

"Pessimism is not in my nature. Even my father, who did absolutely nothing to earn anyone's good opinion, kept mine far longer than he deserved."

Hollis kept hold of one of her hands and led her to the small sofa near the unlit fire. She sat beside him, not quite as cozy as she had the night before, but close and congenial.

"Now," he said, "how is it you came to join the League of Humble Housebreakers?"

She looked up at him. "Is that an actual organization?"

"It ought to be."

Her smile blossomed. "You are an unusual sort of gentleman, Hollis Darby."

"Yes, but am I your *favorite* sort of gentleman?"

Ana was a delight to tease. She enjoyed his silly jests, even blushed a little. And she didn't hold a grudge when they had a misunderstanding. She allowed him to explain, gave him the chance to make things right.

"Do you remember I told you that, after my father's business failed, some of his investors descended on our house and stole things?"

He nodded. "I remember."

"They *stole* those things. The debt owed to them had already been paid. They had no claim on the things they took." Her gaze dropped to their clasped hands. "So those things still belong to me, no matter that they are currently in someone else's possession. Stealing something doesn't change its rightful ownership."

"No, it doesn't."

"And a person can't steal something that already belongs to her."

Ah. "Your 'thieving' focuses on items that are already yours."

"Exclusively." She took a breath, her shoulders lifting. "I only take things that were stolen from my family, and only if they are still in the possession of the person who took them. If an item has since been sold to someone else, I don't . . . 'steal' it. The person who has it now is guilty only of paying for something that never should have been sold."

He rubbed her hand with his, hoping to encourage her and show her he was listening and not condemning.

"Those things my father's partner stole himself and then pawned or gambled away, I don't 'steal' either."

"Because the people who have those items aren't the ones who stole them in the first place?"

She nodded. "The things they have are still mine, but I would be punishing an innocent person by taking them back."

"Your heart must break, though, not having those things back."

Ana leaned against him. "I've been able to buy a few of them. That won't be possible for some time now, though. I don't have a job."

"Elizabeth told me—no, 'told' isn't the right word." He made a show of contemplating. "'Threatened.' *That's* the right one."

"She threatened you?"

He flashed her a smile. "It seems your departure did not meet with her approval."

Ana sighed. "*You* sorted out my questionable hobby. If anyone else did and word got around, it would destroy the reputation of her school. I cannot risk that. I never should have in the first place."

He put his free arm around her. "How long have you been in the thieving business?"

"Two years."

Two years. He'd only begun hearing of her exploits in the past two months, and only because a couple of street children had grown sloppy in their own efforts. That was, to be perfectly honest, impressive.

"I have every legal right to the items I've reclaimed," she

said, "but I have no guarantee the law would see it that way. And, of course, there's the matter of entering a house without permission. What I've done occupies a gray area of right and wrong. Lives are ruined by gray areas."

"I know."

She tucked her feet up on the sofa beside her, looking almost like a child. "You aid the less fortunate and rescue children. That is hardly a questionable activity."

"I've broken laws to do that, Ana," he said quietly.

"You have?"

"'Gray areas of right and wrong,'" he repeated. "Life is increasingly full of them."

She curled against his side. "You don't condemn me, then?"

"I, too, do some difficult things for my family. I keep up appearances in Society when I would rather be doing any number of other things. I chase down thugs in an attempt to rescue my brother. I make my living in secret, knowing my family would be embarrassed if my profession were known."

"You've told me you work for your subsistence. But you didn't tell me what you do exactly."

Nervousness and anticipation clutched his heart simultaneously. "Have you read Lafayette Jones's most recent work?"

She sat up straight, twisting to look at him more directly. Confusion filled her beautiful brown eyes. "I have."

"That is my secret activity, Ana."

Laughter shone in her face. "Hiding students in a school for ghosts?"

"No." He grinned. He was so much happier with her

in his life. "Writing stories about students being hidden in schools for ghosts."

For the length of a breath, she didn't say anything. Then, all at once, she said, "You are Lafayette Jones."

"I am. Very few people know that. Gentlemen *can* be writers without losing their claim to station and status, but not writing what I write."

She nodded slowly, understanding dawning on her face. "Should your endeavors be known and your brother's financial situation be revealed, your niece and nephew would find themselves on shaky ground."

"And so I keep up the pretense," he said. "One foot in each world, never truly part of either."

"We are peas in a pod, you and I."

From the far corner, Very Merry answered. "I'd say two cats in the cream."

Ana practically jumped off the sofa. She turned red as a strawberry.

Hollis leaned forward, resting his elbows on his knees and clasping his hands in front of him. "Very Merry, come over here and explain, you little imp."

She hopped up from her spot hidden behind a chair. Her self-assured saunter held a hint of worry.

"How long have you been in here?"

She shrugged a shoulder.

"You aren't in trouble, popsy." He patted the sofa beside him.

She didn't accept the seat he offered. "Even though I'm wise to your secrets now? And that I saw you sparkin'? And after I filched a scone from the kitchen? And—"

"Best quit listing things while you're still in my good graces." He motioned beside him again.

Very Merry accepted this time. The girl had so much gumption it was easy to forget how young she really was.

"Why were you hiding in here?" he asked again.

"On account of Libby an' Ambrose telling me I ain't s'pposed to have scones before supper. So I ate it in here."

Hollis bit back a grin. He didn't want to encourage her devilment.

Very Merry turned to look at Ana. "I ain't gonna tell no one about you being a thief. I'm not a snitch."

Ana's color went from red to pale.

"And I already knew you was a writerly sort," Very Merry said to him.

"You did?"

"Blimey, how couldn't I? You talk to yourself when you're in here making your stories."

Hollis dropped his face into his hands. "How often do you hide in this room?"

She shrugged. "I like scones."

He met Ana's eye. She pressed her lips closed, but the laugher in her eyes was unmistakable. "I told you this little heathen was a handful."

"I think I will leave you and your handful to sort everything out." Ana dipped a small curtsey, then offered the same to Very Merry. "My deepest gratitude for your discretion."

"Us thieves 'ave to look after each other," the girl said.

Though she blushed a little, Ana accepted the show of solidarity with good humor. Hollis walked her out of the room.

"You are very kind to her," Ana said.

"Because I'm afraid of her."

Ana bumped him with her shoulder. "Why, then, are you kind to *me*?"

"Because I adore you."

"A penniless thief?" She didn't hide her doubt.

He smiled. "A brave, determined, kindhearted, clever . . . thief." He raised her hand and kissed the back of it. "And a remarkable, caring, dedicated teacher. I hope you don't mean to give that up."

She didn't commit to any particular path but left on a note of hopeful uncertainty. Whatever her future plans, he prayed they included him.

THE GENTLEMAN AND THE THIEF

by Mr. King

Installment VI,
in which our Hero has a startling Revelation!

The little boy, whose name they had discovered was Pip, had made his declaration about stealing the blue flame, then had cried so ceaselessly he'd not managed another word. Not knowing exactly what harm the bluecap might bring, Wellington had thought it best that Pip, Mr. Combs, and Tillie all remove to the manor house. Of all things, he wished for them to be safe.

In return, he found greater joy in his house now than he'd known in years. He and Tillie, sometimes accompanied by Pip, made another search of the house, looking for the items the bluecap had nipped off with. Mr. Combs was of the opinion that the creature was inclined to stash his "payments" rather than spirit them off, but where that pile of treasures might be, they didn't know.

Pip was cheerful enough on their searches so long as neither of them brought up the topic of the bluecap. The reminder of the sprite he claimed to have stolen would turn him once more into a trembling heap. It made getting information from the child difficult, and they had no other help in finding the creature or the things it had taken.

Four days after they'd rescued the boy from the moors, Wellington walked alongside Tillie through the back corridors of the house, having come no closer to rooting out their mischievous visitor. Pip had fallen asleep, so they'd left him in his room and undertaken this search without him.

"I wish we could do somethin' for the little imp," Tillie said. "He's terrified of the creature he stole, and I suspect he's drowning in a sea of guilt as well."

"If only we could sort out how he caught it in the first place, we could rid ourselves of it."

"And of him?" she asked quietly, cautiously.

"He must be *from* somewhere," Wellington said. "And his family must be worried."

Tillie shook her head. "I don't think he has one."

Wellington motioned her out through the door of the music room; they hadn't found any missing items hidden there. "Why do you suspect that?"

She shrugged as she passed. "Because that's what Pip said when Papa asked him."

Tillie was a delight. He never laughed as much as he did when he was with her.

"Your father took the less-interesting approach." Wellington caught up to her. "Did he also happen to ask Pip where he came here from?"

"Ipsley, on the other side of Ipsley Moor," she said. "Slipped out of the workhouse, he did."

The workhouse. Mercy. "We can't send him back there."

Without warning, Tillie threw her arms around him. "Oh, Wellington! I had so hoped you would say that. I can't bear thinking of him in so miserable a place."

Something odd happened to Wellington Quincey in that moment. Something entirely unexpected. His heart, which had always been whole and entirely in his possession, gave itself over to his lifelong friend. Her arms around him felt like the warm embrace of home. He set his arms around her as well and held her, feeling his heart undertake its change of ownership.

"Papa and I can keep Pip at our cottage if need be," she said. "But he'd be happy as a cat in the cream here. He'd have long corridors to run through, and an entire nursery to make his own." She looked up at him. "Oh, Wellington! Say he can stay. Please."

"Of course, he can. This house has been far too empty for far too long."

In the instant after that declaration, the house suddenly filled with voices.

Tillie's head turned toward the noise, but she didn't drop her arms from around him. "Who's doing all that bellowing?"

He locked his hands behind her back. "I couldn't say. I never have visitors."

"You did a week ago," she said.

"I suppose I did."

Tillie leaned her head against his chest. "Could they be back?"

"I think they might be. They had said the house party they were attending would last a week."

She slipped back. "You should go greet 'em."

"You should come as well," he said. "Then they can meet you."

"They already have. They didn't like what they saw." Quick as anything, she hurried down the corridor without looking back.

Sometimes it seemed she was forever running from him! His heart ached for her to remain at his side.

He entered the drawing room and discovered his group of acquaintances there, dripping wet. The weather had turned whilst he and Tillie had been searching the house.

"Forgive the intrusion," Alsop said. "This deluge made the roads impassable. We find ourselves in need of your hospitality."

"Of course." Wellington would never turn anyone away in such circumstances. "We are short-staffed, so I cannot guarantee you the most comfortable of stays."

"If you can guarantee us a roof and a warm fire," Henson said, "we will be more than satisfied."

Mrs. Smith saw them all to the guest wing. Mr. Smith made certain each room had a fire burning. Wellington went in search of Tillie but did not find her. Pip was still sleeping in the nursery. His home was the busiest it had been in ages, yet he felt lonely again.

He went through the motions of being a proper host. The guests were checked on by Mrs. Smith and provided with a tray in their rooms so they could rest and warm themselves. He consulted with his housekeeper and butler about the trickiness of looking after five unexpected visitors with only the two of them on staff.

"Tillie will help," Mrs. Smith said. "She's a good 'un, she is."

"She is a guest here as well."

"Not the same, though, is it?" Mrs. Smith sighed. "She's your dear friend, yes, but the daughter of your steward. She's not one of your fine and elegant friends. They know it. And so does she."

"I could go the rest of my life without seeing any of to-day's arrivals again, and I would not be the worse for it," Wellington said. "But these past days, having Tillie's company so often, I know I could not say the same about her."

"She's not your equal," Mrs. Smith reminded him.

"No. She is a better person than I."

Mrs. Smith handed her husband the stacked linens he would be delivering to the guest rooms. "You and I know her worth, but Society wouldn't agree with us."

"We aren't in London. Those things don't matter much in the wilds of Yorkshire."

Mr. Smith watched Wellington with narrowed gaze. "You've lost your heart to the girl, haven't you?"

"She's been my friend all my life," he said. "But she's more than that to me now. She's everything."

"Not everyone'll see things the way you do," Mrs. Smith warned. "She'd not be welcomed with open arms in Town or at Society dos."

"I've never put a great deal of store by such things." A smile blossomed on his solemn face. "I would rather spend the rest of my life running around the moors with her than bowing and scraping my way through all the ballrooms in London."

"Then might I offer you a word of advice?" Mr. Smith asked.

Wellington nodded. He hadn't a father any longer to help point him in the right direction. He welcomed whatever wisdom was offered him.

"Make certain *she* knows that."

Wellington awoke to the sound of shouting. He'd slept later than expected, having been up longer than he'd wished. Preparations for breakfast for so many additional people in the house had required all their efforts. Tillie had undertaken hers from a distance, volunteering for every chore that would take her away from the visitors at the manor house.

He hadn't the opportunity to tell her of his feelings, and it seemed there would not be peace enough this morning for doing so any time soon.

All his guests were in an uproar, standing outside Miss Fairbanks's assigned bedchamber. The lady, herself, was flailing her arms, her words frantic. Tillie appeared on the scene a moment later, watching the group with the same expression of confusion he must have been wearing.

Miss Porter suddenly pointed an accusing finger at Tillie. "She took it. I know she did!"

Though Tillie paled, she didn't flinch. "I have a name, and you clearly have an accusation. See if you can't spit out both."

Wellington bit back a laugh. His light o' love was no shrinking violet. Still, fisticuffs erupting in the corridor hardly seemed advisable. "Miss Porter, what has been taken? Whatever it might be, I doubt Miss Combs was involved in its disappearance."

"We tried to warn you," Alsop said. "You're being robbed left and right, and you refuse to see the likely reason."

"I know the reason," he said firmly. "And Miss Combs is not part of it."

"You do not—" Alsop managed no more words as Wellington interrupted him.

"I have offered you my hospitality. I should hope you won't repay that by insulting my most honored guest, nor by casting aspersions on my judgment."

That brought the chaos to a swift end. Wellington took advantage of the silence.

"Miss Fairbanks, what has gone missing?"

"My diamond-and-pearl brooch. I set it on the bureau last evening when I retired to bed. It was not there when I awoke." She held up a hand to forestall any commentary. "I searched the room. It is gone."

Wellington looked to Tillie. "The little monster is at it again."

"So it would seem." Tillie frowned. "It was bad enough when we was the only ones being robbed. We can't let it go any longer now."

She was completely correct. This group, however, was not likely to give her the benefit of their good opinion.

Wellington set his shoulders and assumed his most authoritative air. "We know the identity of our thief. Thus far, though, the culprit has managed to evade capture. Miss

Combs and I will redouble our efforts to corner the criminal and reclaim all that has been taken."

That seemed to appease them a little. Very little.

"Now, if you will all take your time breaking your fast and enjoying one another's company, Miss Combs and I will recruit help from someone hereabout who can be trusted." He eyed them all individually. "I hope there will be no more unfounded accusations."

A few looked at least a little embarrassed to have been so unfeeling. The rest accepted the chastisement without showing the least remorse. So long as they stopped causing Tillie distress, he would let that be enough.

He offered her his arm. "Shall we, Miss Combs?"

"Yes, please." As they walked arm in arm down the corridor, she whispered. "What precisely do you mean to do?"

"Exactly what I said: catch a thief."

CHAPTER 20

"Was she pleased?" Hollis asked Elizabeth.

"I've never seen a lady's face light up so entirely at the mere sight of a ball gown. I suspect she has missed some of the frivolous aspects of Society more than she is willing to admit."

Hollis hadn't always appreciated having to maintain his Society connections. In that moment, though, knowing he'd brought a bit of joy to Ana, he was grateful that he had.

Móirín sat across the sitting room, adjusting the knife holster around her ankle. All the Dreadfuls were intimidated by Stone, but they likely ought to have treated Móirín with caution as well. She was too much like a sister for them to have anything but a deep, abiding fondness for her.

Elizabeth set her gloved hand on Hollis's arm. "How are you? Your brother's continued absence must weigh on your mind."

"From what I've been able to discover, Parker has him hidden. If I can corner Headley tonight and get myself included in the next game at Thompsons' then maybe this can be sorted enough for Randolph to come out of hiding."

"If you and Fletcher and Stone cornered him some-where," Móirín said, "I'd wager Headley'd spill every secret he has."

"And Fletch and I would be there mostly as an audience."

Móirín smiled. "Stone has a way of getting things done, yeah?"

"Decidedly," Elizabeth answered.

Hollis used his reflection in the sitting room window to straighten his lapel and smooth his jacket. "Unfortunately, Headley'll have to be treated with kid gloves. He's not who we're actually after, and we can't risk him tipping our hand to Four-Finger Mike."

"It's fortunate, then, you know how to slip about Society without being out of place," Móirín said. "Brogan can man-age it more or less, but not with the finesse you have."

"Fletcher puffed like a steam engine when I told him he'd best sit this one out," Elizabeth said. "The man does a fine job of affecting the manners of a gentleman, but Mr. Headley is an itch he cannot help but scratch. Pulls the urchin out in him every time."

"So, Achilles does have a heel after all," Hollis said.

"Two of them, in fact." Móirín wore an expression of pure mischief.

One never knew what she was going to say or do, except that she was reliable, fierce, and an unrelenting advocate for the vulnerable. And a little terrifying. Through her brother, she knew nearly all the Dreadfuls, and knew them well, but she didn't know about the Dread Penny Society, not in any detail. That was the agreement they all had among them-selves: the society was a secret one, even from their families. Their loved ones could know they were friends, that they spent time together, that they worked on behalf of the less fortunate, but, beyond that, even the people closest to them were kept in the dark.

Hollis heard the patter of feet on the stairs and the swish of a dress. He turned toward the sitting room door, smil-ing in anticipation. Ana had allowed him to hold her in his arms the last time they were together. It seemed his misstep in speaking aloud her thieving identity had been forgiven. The seemingly impossible dreams he'd indulged in after first meeting her were beginning to feel nearly within reach.

Móirín rose from her chair and moved casually toward him. "Seems *this* Achilles has a heel, as well."

"You're speaking of me, are you?"

Móirín smirked—*actually* smirked. "I know the look of a man in love."

"And you consider love a weakness?"

She shook her head. "Love can be a strength, but 'tis also a vulnerability."

"Is that why we've not ever known you to fall head over heels for anyone?" he asked.

"Feet on the ground; head out of the clouds." Móirín had said that before. It was something of a motto for her.

Ana stepped into the doorway, a vision in a light laven-der gown, scalloped ruffles adorning the full silk skirt. He'd learned more about fabrics and clothing from concocting dis-guises in the Dread Penny Society than in all his years before joining the group. He knew with perfect certainty this gown was in the first stare of fashion. But that was not what caught his eye.

Hollis couldn't pull his gaze away from Ana's absolutely elated expression. No one seeing her standing there, her fingers brushing over the lavender silk, turning a little from side to side as if barely preventing herself from twirling, could have the least doubt she was enchanted with the gown.

"Is it not the most beautiful dress you've ever seen?" she asked.

"Gorgeous."

Móirín gave him a nudge. "Feet on the ground, Hollis. Head out of the clouds."

"Keep your nose out of my clouds, Móirín Donnelly." He left her behind as he joined Ana by the door. "You are a vision."

She twisted enough to eye the scoop of ruffles on the side of her full skirt. "I used to love wearing dresses like this one." She twisted the other way. There was something so sweetly gleeful about her excitement. "I'm likely terribly shallow for being so pleased at wearing a beautiful gown and also for having missed it so much."

"Not at all." He took her hand in his. "When I first came to London, I had been wearing secondhand clothing for years. Lord Whitley provided me with a new wardrobe. I was working as his secretary, and, I would wager, he didn't want to look like he was being followed around by a pauper. I felt like I'd reclaimed part of my identity when I finally had better clothes."

She squeezed his fingers. "Precisely."

He looked back at Elizabeth, intending to ask her if she

was ready to leave for the ball. She and Móirín stood beside each other, watching him and Ana with nearly identical looks of amusement.

He chose to ignore it. "Shall we?"

"I think we'd better," Elizabeth said. She motioned them into the entryway, following them out of the room.

Hollis tucked Ana's arm through his, resting his hand atop hers. "You really do look lovely."

Her smile warmed him to his very core. How he wished he had the right—and the means—to provide her with the finest of gowns to wear all the time. To bring her such happiness would be an absolute honor.

Her glow hadn't diminished by the time they reached Lord and Lady Whitley's elegant home. Hollis's connection to the baron was the reason they'd managed three invitations to the evening's gathering of the upper crust. Headley was going to be there. This was Hollis's best opportunity to arrange an invitation to the next game at Thompsons'.

He walked with Ana and Elizabeth to greet their host and hostess. "Lady Whitley. Lord Whitley."

"My dear Hollis." Lady Whitley gave him a maternal smile. "We so seldom see you any longer."

"If your husband hadn't proven such a tyrant, I might still be in his employ."

She swatted at him playfully with her fan. "I am more of a tyrant than he is."

Hollis looked to Ana, assuming an expression of suffering. "Two tyrants in one household. Is it any wonder I don't reside here any longer?"

"The true miracle is that they didn't toss you out on your ear sooner for your ceaseless jesting."

That earned her a look of amused approval from the baron and baroness.

Hollis undertook the introductions. "Lord and Lady Whitley, this is Miss Ana Newport, of Pimlico, and"—he indicated Elizabeth—"Miss Elizabeth Black, headmistress of Thurloe Collegiate School."

Lady Whitley's gaze narrowed on Ana, not in disapproval but curiosity. "I believe you participated in Society gatherings a few years ago."

Ana froze. The color faded from her face.

"We are very fortunate she has rejoined us," Hollis said, tucking Ana's arm through his once more. "And doubly fortunate that you extended the invitation for this evening."

"You are always welcome," Lord Whitley said.

Hollis dipped his head and led Ana and Elizabeth away from the receiving line.

"That was expertly maneuvered," Elizabeth said quietly. "I'm impressed."

"Fletcher may be able to navigate the seediest streets in London with ease, but my specialty is avoiding the pitfalls and stumbling blocks of a proper ballroom." Then, dryly, he added, "Equally important abilities, of course."

Ana met his eye. "A half a moment ago, I found *your* ability far more important than his."

"Did you think I would stand idly by whilst someone, *anyone*, caused you distress?"

Her gaze softened. "I cannot imagine you standing idly by whilst anyone was in distress."

Elizabeth slipped around them, tossing back over her shoulder, "The two of you are a touch nauseating."

"Now you know how the rest of us feel around you and Fletch," Hollis said.

"And now *you* know how *I* feel around 'Fletch.'"

Such banter was generally frowned upon at fashionable gatherings like this one. "I believe that man is a bad influence on us even at a distance. We are hardly behaving ourselves."

"We've come with the sole purpose of tricking a gentleman neither of us is overly fond of into inviting you to participate in a dangerous game of chance," Elizabeth said. "'Behaving ourselves' was never on the evening's agenda."

All around them swirled the elegance of high society. Jewels sparkled. Ladies' fans fluttered. Men's shirts gleamed white as newly fallen snow. The voices were refined and spoke only of the most proper topics.

Hollis, Ana, and Elizabeth made a slow circuit of the room. They spotted Headley quickly, easily, and repeatedly as the evening wore on. He was always surrounded by others, deep in conversation. Headley would never discuss the very secretive games if he was surrounded by listening ears.

"This is frustrating," Hollis muttered under his breath after yet another failed attempt to catch Headley before he rejoined another group.

"Perhaps we should have brought Móirín, after all," Elizabeth said. "She'd have simply cornered him and demanded an invitation."

Móirín was actually far more sly than that, though she'd not sorted out the details of the Dread Penny Society. Not yet, anyway. None of them were at all confident she wouldn't unearth the secret sooner or later. She was too clever, too observant, and too stubborn by half.

"Forcefulness is not the only useful approach." Ana gave them both a look of slightly smug confidence. "Sometimes quiet finesse goes a lot further." She turned on her heel and slipped gracefully and unobtrusively back through the gathering.

"Where do you suppose she's going?" Hollis asked.

"I haven't a clue." Elizabeth watched her with narrowed gaze. "She's grown very bold since you've begun spending more time with her."

"I suspect she was always bold. We simply didn't see it."

"Ana is an exceptional person," Elizabeth said.

"That she is." He looked over the crowd of swirling colors and glittering jewels. "She is also a slippery person. I haven't the first idea where she's gone."

"She does that more often than you might think," Elizabeth said. "Until she finally told me about her visits to see her father, I suspected she might be living some kind of secret life."

That was truer than Elizabeth could possibly know.

Hollis and Elizabeth offered greetings and nods to various people as they passed, engaging in the kind of empty nothings that were expected at events such as this.

"Fletcher would have been miserable tonight," Elizabeth said during a lull.

"Which would have entertained me to no end," Hollis tossed back.

Ana returned a moment later, threading her arm through his. "Play along," she whispered.

He had no time to ask questions. She pulled him back through the crowd, heading directly for a group containing Alistair Headley. They stopped just outside the small gathering.

With a sweet smile, she addressed the man. "Forgive the interruption, Mr. Headley. I found this and thought I remembered you had one like it." She held up a brass pocket watch. "I wanted to ask if it was yours before turning it over to our hosts."

"Mercy." His eyes pulled wide as he pressed his palms over his waistcoat. "It must have slipped from my pocket."

Hollis couldn't even look at Ana, lest he risk bursting out laughing. She was not merely a thief; she was a pickpocket. He would bet every penny he had on it. What a bundle of entertaining surprises she was.

Ana set the pocket watch in Headley's hand. "I am so pleased to have returned it to its owner. Mr. Darby, here, was only just lamenting that balls are not always terribly exciting." She looked up at him, her expression one of sweet, naïve amusement. A thief, a pickpocket, *and* an actress. "Does this act of heroism help relieve a touch of the ennui, or are you still bored?"

Oh, she was shrewd! It was the perfect way to tip off Headley about his openness to more "exciting" pursuits without revealing his hand to all the others standing about.

"I am, of course, delighted with your company, Miss Newport," he said. "But a gentleman cannot help but wish for something a bit less sedate now and then."

The interest in Headley's eyes was unmistakable. "I agree.

A gentleman of action must want for something more than this."

Hollis allowed his curiosity to show a bit. "Do you have suggestions?"

"I might."

Ana laughed lightly. "I will leave you to discuss carriage races or boxing saloons or whatever it is that gentlemen prefer to balls and musicales." She slipped her arm from Hollis's. "Miss Black and I will be perfectly content with tonight's 'boring' activities."

She stepped away, the lavender silk of her dress catching glints of candlelight as she walked gracefully away.

"That Miss Newport is a beauty," Headley said. "And she seems a sweet lady."

"She is," Hollis said. "And decidedly ill-informed about what gentlemen consider exciting."

"Walk with me," Headley said. "I have a cure for boredom that I think you might find intriguing."

Bless Ana Newport. This was going to work tremendously well.

Hollis didn't bother entirely hiding his less-than-flattering opinion of the man. Headley knew Hollis wasn't fond of him, so pretending to suddenly enjoy his company would be suspicious.

"When did you last sit down to a game of cards?" Headley asked.

Hollis shrugged. "I do now and then with a few friends." Truth be told, he hadn't gambled since leaving Eton, but he had a role to play.

"I don't mean a casual game," Headley said. "A true game. Wagers. Stakes of some significance."

Hollis allowed a little more interest to enter his expression. "How significant?"

"The antes start low, but the winnings can be quite high."

Hollis dipped his head to a person he knew as they passed. He continued walking with Headley in a slow circuit but dropped his voice. "I have no interest in a copper hell."

Headley waved that off. "The games are held in a fine house in Pimlico. The players are gentlemen. The host provides brandy and port and fine bits to eat."

With liquor flowing at the Thompsons' place, no doubt the wagers soared high. "That sounds like the perfect antidote for the watery muck and stale finger foods one finds at evenings such as this." Heavens, he would have to apologize to Lady Whitley if word of that comment circulated back to her. "Where are these games held? I have half a mind to sit down to a hand or two."

"I can't tell you that." Headley's tone turned from eager to cautious. "One of the requirements of playing is that a fellow not share the location."

"Sounds a touch shady to me," Hollis said.

"Nothing underhanded." The answer came a little too quickly. "You should join us."

"How can I? You won't tell me where the games are held."

"But I'd take you to one," Headley said. "They only let you in if you come with someone who's already been given approval."

And Headley didn't think anyone would find this arrangement questionable? Even the most naïve of people would wonder about secret locations and members having to vouch for newcomers. It sounded like . . . Well, truth be told, it sounded like the Dread Penny Society. Little wonder people who'd heard whispers of them worried they were up to no good.

"Cora says Randolph's been out with you a lot lately. Has he been going to these games?"

Headley stiffened almost imperceptibly. "I can't tell you that."

Hollis held up his hands in a show of surrender. "Fair enough. If there's room in an upcoming game, I'd be interested in joining."

"There's always room."

Interesting.

"I can come to your place with a hackney tomorrow," Headley offered.

They quickly exchanged details. As they continued their circuit of the room, they drifted a pace from one another. Easy as that, Hollis had secured an invitation to a game that likely held the secret to more than one spot of difficulty in London.

CHAPTER 21

"We need to recruit another gentleman," Fletcher said. "It ain't safe sending only one of us off on a mission like this."

"Especially if that one is me?" Hollis asked dryly.

"You ain't exactly Stone." Fletcher motioned to the very man, standing nearby and watching them with his usual unreadable expression.

Hollis turned to him. "Do you have as little faith in me as this codger does?"

"You'll do." Coming from Stone, that was high praise.

Hollis wished he were that confident in himself. "Other than the friendly games with no stakes at headquarters, I've not taken up cards since I was paying for Eton."

Stone's gaze narrowed. "You won enough for that?"

Hollis nodded. "I was good."

Fletcher grinned. "You'll do."

Hollis pulled his money clip from his jacket and did a quick recount. The DPS was funding this mission, though they weren't exactly flush in the pockets. Every pound they had was hard-earned.

Stone, standing near the front window, peered around the side of the curtain. "Hackney's here."

Hollis snatched up his hat and set it jauntily on his head. "I'll report back what I discover."

"At headquarters," Stone said. "The fella's'll be there for parliament tomorrow."

Hollis eyed Fletcher. "How does Elizabeth feel about us still referencing each other as 'the fellows'?"

"She rolls her eyes," Fletcher said. "But I don't think it bothers her too terribly much. She knows old habits ain't broken easily."

They followed Hollis into the vestibule. He grabbed hold of the door handle. "Wish me luck."

Fletcher slapped a hand on his shoulder in a show of support. Stone just nodded. The two of them slipped out of view as Hollis pulled the door open and stepped out onto the walk, locking the door behind him. He was sure Stone and Fletcher could get back out and lock up after themselves despite not having a key.

Headley remained in the hackney. Considering they were headed for a gentlemen-only destination, the man ought to have been more civil than that. The contradiction, Hollis feared, was more a sign of what awaited him than a mere slip in manners.

The driver, at least, hopped down long enough to open the door for Hollis.

Hollis climbed in and sat across from Headley. "Ought I

to be blindfolded?" He asked the question with a laugh, but it died away when his companion produced a long, thick cloth.

This was proving even stranger than expected.

As the hired conveyance began moving forward, Hollis obliged and covered his eyes, tying the cloth snugly in place.

"You let me do the talking when we first arrive," Headley said. "There's a ritual to entry and you, obviously, don't know what it is." Headley somehow sounded equally authoritative and nervous. "You'll recognize people there, but don't acknowledge that you know them. Anonymity is a requirement, and anything that hints at breaking that will see you tossed out immediately."

Hollis nodded. "Anything else?"

"Outside of the house where the games are held, we don't talk in any detail about our activities."

"Anonymity," Hollis repeated.

"Precisely."

They made the rest of the journey in silence. Hollis couldn't help picturing Randolph making this same journey with this same man and, likely, this same blindfold. How could his brother not have backed out at the absurdity of it all? If Hollis weren't on a mission for the DPS *and* in need of rescuing his often-idiotic sibling, he'd have told Headley to forget the entire thing.

Upon pulling to a stop, Headley told Hollis to remove the blindfold. A truly observant participant would have pieced together where they were even without watching the route they'd taken. Perhaps the blindfolding was meant merely to intimidate.

As he walked with Headley toward the Thompsons'

door, the hackney drove off. It was precisely the scenario he'd watched from the window across the street. He had to fight down a laugh, knowing that Brogan was watching him now.

Headley took hold of the door knocker and clanked it in a specific rhythm: Clunk-clunk-pause. Clunk-pause-pause. Clunk-clunk. Did people not easily memorize the "secret knock"?

A peephole cover slid open, though who might have been on the other side wasn't at all clear.

"Napoleon was twice exiled," Headley said.

The cover slid back with a whack. A lock turned. In the next moment, the door opened, the person on the other side still in shadow.

Hollis followed Headley inside. The man who'd let them in stood in clear anticipation of something. He was dressed like a butler but was built like a prizefighter or a blacksmith.

"I have a new recruit," Headley said.

"The master's in 'is office."

Headley nodded and moved past the large front staircase to an ornate door. He gave the same knock he had when they'd first arrived. Looking back at Hollis, he motioned him over impatiently.

This door was opened by a wiry slip of a man who watched them over the rim of his thick spectacles.

"New recruit for approval," Headley said.

They were motioned in. Hollis eyed the beanpole's hands as he passed. Five fingers apiece.

The "office" had the look of a gentleman's library. The man behind the desk wore a suit of fine fabric in the latest fashion, but something in the fit was strange, as if the tailor had been talented but in a hurry.

The man set his neatly piled papers to one side and looked up at Headley. His eyes moved quickly to Hollis, assessing him.

Hollis didn't flinch, neither did he return the studying gaze with one of his own. He simply stood and waited with the assurance men of his standing were supposed to possess.

"You look familiar." The man's voice matched his suit: the impression of sophistication but executed with some sloppy details. "Have we met?"

"I don't know that we have," Hollis answered.

"He's Hollis Darby," Headley said.

The man nodded. "You resemble your brother."

"I have been told that before." Hollis suppressed the triumph he felt at hearing this man acknowledge that he knew Randolph. His brother's troubles had begun in this house; he was certain of it.

"Do you play?" the man asked.

"Play what, exactly?" Asserting a bit of confident ignorance would abate suspicion.

"Baccarat. Whist. Piquet. Whatever your pleasure, we likely have a table of it."

"Faro?" Hollis named a game often played by highborn gamblers.

The man nodded. "Of course." He looked to Headley. "He'll do."

"That's my quota met, then," Headley said.

Another slow, deliberate nod.

Headley left without a backward glance, without hesitation. He didn't quite run, but nearly.

"Johnson, here, will show you to a faro table," the man told Hollis.

"Excellent." He extended his hand. "I didn't catch your name."

"I did not offer it. I am called the Raven." He shook Hollis's hand. The man had all five fingers. Hollis's quarry was proving as elusive as Randolph. "And this"—he motioned toward the door—"is Serena, our housekeeper."

Housekeepers were never called by their Christian names. That alone would have told any observant visitor this was not a typical Pimlico home.

Hollis turned around. Serena was slight of frame and, if her expression was any indication, not at all at ease in her surroundings. He would place her age at somewhere circling thirty, though the heaviness in her expression and posture made her seem older.

She dipped a curtsey. "What is it you'll be drinking when you're here, sir?"

"Ginger cordial or lemonade."

She looked to the Raven, clearly confused.

Her employer responded with impatience. "Do we not have either of those?"

"We've lemonade," Serena said. "But none of the genn'elmen ever want . . . lemonade."

Most men, when gathering for games of chance and social interactions, preferred alcohol. That, of course, was part of the reason why so many lost so much.

"Mr. Darby wishes for lemonade." The Raven pushed

the words out through his teeth. "Is there a reason he cannot have it?"

She dipped another quick, anxious curtsey. "Of course not. I'll make certain we've ginger cordial in the larder for him the next time." With that, she slipped away.

The Raven's bony assistant showed Hollis out of the room. He was led back through the entryway and into what, in any other house, would have been a drawing room. In this one, it contained six tables, two of which were empty. At the others, fashionably dressed gentlemen sat, fully engrossed in card games. Glasses of liquor were at the ready. More than one cigar was being smoked. No one appeared to be wanting for food.

Hollis had no difficulty finding the faro table. The dealer eyed him as he sat in an empty seat at the table and watched.

The dealer flipped a card. "Ace loses." He flipped another. "Seven wins."

Groans and sedate cheers followed. The dealer paid out to those who'd placed their wagers on seven and their coppered wagers on the ace. More coins were placed on more cards. Another two cards were flipped over.

Hollis studied the upward facing cards already revealed, then back at the wagers. "The five's dead," he said.

A hush fell. All eyes darted to the upturned cards. With no more fives remaining in the deck, those bets were worthless, unless someone—like him—caught it and pointed it out

"So it is." The dealer dipped his head and handed Hollis the bets that had been placed on the five.

Serena arrived a moment later with his glass of lemonade on a tray. He accepted it with a nod. She answered with a curtsey, looking at him for the briefest of moments. Her gaze was haunted, afraid. Was she being mistreated, beyond the pompous dismissal of the Raven? Was she under the crushing thumb of Four-Finger Mike as well?

It seemed every time the Dreadfuls uncovered one dastardly corner of London's underbelly, they found more and more suffering in more and more shadows.

Hollis ended the night with a sizeable number of coins in his pocket. He'd discovered that every player in the room was, indeed, a gentleman of some standing. Shouts from distant rooms told him others were having more drastic experiences than he was.

Of all the things he learned that afternoon, though, the most important was that the Thompsons' house had indeed been transformed into the gambling den the Dreadfuls had been looking for.

"Everyone had all their fingers." Hollis wrapped up his report with that disappointing tidbit.

"Four-Finger had to've been there somewhere," Fletcher said. "Keeping up the appearance of being highbrow likely meant keeping the riffraff in the root cellar."

"The one calling himself 'the Raven,'" Stone said. "Somethin' sounds wrong about that fella."

Hollis nodded. "And it's more than dressing and speaking a little awkwardly."

"Mr. Headley said he had met his quota?" Elizabeth asked. "That part I cannot shake from my mind."

"They're recruiting," Martin said. "Those allowed to play are required to bring new players."

Hollis shook his head. "I wasn't asked to bring anyone."

"But you left the night ahead, yeah?" Fletcher said. "Recruiting might be offered as a way of having a debt forgiven."

"Then why did they tear my brother's house apart and send his family into exile?"

Fletcher slumped back in his throne, the way he did when thinking. "Could be your brother's rubbish at recruiting."

"And gambling," Martin tossed in.

The laughter was subdued. The matter of this gambling den was proving a heavy one. Mistreated staff, a connection to the criminal underworld, lives ruined.

"I've been invited back," Hollis said, "though I'm meant to come with someone already included in their numbers."

"Do it," Fletcher said. "Sooner rather than later. I've a feeling more than just your brother has been ruined by this business." He looked out over the others. "Penny for your thoughts."

Martin rose, taking the floor. "I'm following the trail of another little thief, but we've a bigger problem."

"How'd'ya mean?" Fletcher asked.

Some of the thefts they'd credited to children had actually been carried out by Ana. Hollis hadn't told the others that.

"I'm hearing whispers that our efforts ain't going unnoticed," Martin said. "We'll have more difficulty snatching up the little'ns moving forward."

"And we still have children up to their smudged little foreheads in trouble?" Fletcher guessed.

Martin nodded. "We need to bring down Four-Finger Mike before he gets all the urchins in London put away."

Thieves. Missing brothers. Shady games of chance. A slippery thief master.

London was many things, but it certainly wasn't boring.

HIGGLEBOTTOM'S SCHOOL FOR THE DEAD

A GHOST OF A CHANCE

by Lafayette Jones

Chapter IV

· Pudding sat on Snout's bed with a high-stacked plate of Bakewell tarts on his lap. He'd already eaten the bowl of boiled potatoes and chipped beef Bathwater had brought up from the dining hall.

"None of you want any?" Pudding held up one of the round pastries. "Best I ever had."

"If eating was one of the Spirit Trial challenges, we would have this competition wrapped up and tucked in our pockets." Snout watched Pudding with amazement. "How does he do it?"

"He's a Perishable," Ace said. "Some things come naturally to them."

Pudding set aside his tray of tarts and leaned against the headboard. "Can't believe you told everyone I'm going to be on your team for some sort of ghost challenge. What do I know about being a ghost?"

"Nothing really." Snout leaned his shoulder against the

bedpost but didn't quite do the thing properly. Half of him slipped through.

"You look like you've been impaled." Pudding cringed. "That would make a person run like a fox in hunting season."

"Good to know." Snout righted himself. "Fourth Forms have 'Terrify a Perishable to the Point of Hysteria or Loss of Consciousness' in their Spirit Trials. I'll have to remember the impaling."

"Do we have to scare peop—I mean, Perishables?" Pudding asked.

Ace shook his head. "First Forms are limited to dogs and cats."

"We have to scare dogs?"

"That test is called 'Artful Dodging,'" Bathwater said. "We have to sneak past a dog and a cat without either of them noticing us." Bathwater had struggled with that one. Even talking about it now he sounded nervous. "Animals see a lot more than Perishables do. And cats are malicious about it."

"Both of them would spot me straight off." Pudding's mouth twisted to one side.

Ace tried subtly mirroring Pudding's expression, but he couldn't quite get it. He'd learned to float through walls with only the occasional mishap, but he couldn't work his own face.

"There's also 'Churchyard Chase,'" Bathwater continued. "The student chases a stand-in for a Perishable all around a churchyard, with the aim of getting them to stop at a particular headstone."

Pudding slipped his hands behind his head. "I'm a fast runner."

"Won't work," Ace said. "If you fall, you'll scrape yourself up. Blood would be a dead giveaway."

"A not-dead giveaway, more like." Pudding had a way of making them laugh even when they were weighing heavy matters.

"If not Artful Dodging or Churchyard Chasing," Bathwater went on, "then maybe 'Is That the Wind, or Is This Place Haunted?'"

Pudding's eyes pulled wide. "That's the name of the test? That whole mouthful?"

"Rattlebag said it used to be called 'Ghostly Sounds, Beginner Level.'"

"Ghostly Sounds," Pudding repeated. "Like moaning and wailing and saying things like 'Who dares disturb my eternal slumber?'" He pulled the last word out long and singsongy, throwing his hands up like he was towering over something.

They all burst out laughing.

"Pathetic!" Ace said between chuckles.

Pudding pretended to be offended; no one seeing his exaggerated pout and pulled brows would believe he was in earnest. "If that was so bad, you try it."

Ace rose up from the bed—floating for effect—and hovered slowly closer to his new friend. He pitched his voice low and rumbling, dropping the volume and speaking almost painfully slowly. "Who dares disturb my eternal slumber?"

For just a moment, Pudding truly looked scared. But the fear dissolved on the instant. "That was brilliant! I could feel your voice shaking inside of me. Can you teach me to do that?"

"I don't know," Ace said, returning to his bed. Sitting on a bed without falling through was one of the first lessons at Higglebottom's.

"We don't have time for being wrong about what he can do," Snout said. "Pudding has to take one of the four tests. Which one do we give him?"

Ace gave it a moment's thought. "Snout, you're best at Artful Dodging. Bathwater, your strength is Churchyard Chase. I should probably take Is That the Wind, or Is This Place Haunted?"

"What does that leave me?" Pudding asked, another Bakewell tart disappearing into his mouth.

"Shroud Wearing," Ace said.

"And what does a fellow have to do in 'Shroud Wearing'?"

In unison, all three of them said, "Wear a shroud."

Pudding laughed. "No jesting. What's the challenge?"

"We're telling you the truth," Ace said. "The test is wearing a shroud."

"A fellow puts on a shroud and says, 'There you have it'?"

"Keeping something on that isn't made of phantom fabric is a difficult thing," Bathwater said. "My head still slips through at least half the time. Sometimes, I raise my arms to look bigger and more threatening, and the shroud doesn't come with me. Humiliating."

"Oh, blast it all, we're thick." Ace let himself drop through the bed and onto the floor beneath. This time, he didn't leave any pieces of himself behind. He slid out from under the bed, addressing them all. "Shroud wearing. Perishables don't need practice not floating through their clothes. We can toss a shroud on Pudding, here, and he could walk out, make the circuit, and come back the reigning king of First Form shroud wearers without having to learn a blasted thing."

Bathwater and Pudding whooped, both clearly seeing the genius in his suggestion.

Snout still looked skeptical. "A First Form shouldn't be perfect at it, though. That'd make the professors start thinking too hard about who this unfamiliar student is."

Ace nodded. It was a valid point. "So we figure out how to make it look like he's slipping into the ground a little. They'll assume he's concentrating so hard on staying inside the shroud that he's neglecting his feet a bit."

"And he'd be entirely covered up," Bathwater said.

Ace looked at each of his friends in turn. "What do you say?"

"It's brilliant!" Pudding declared. "And if it means staying here, out of the rain, with food to eat, I'll pretend to float through all the ground you want me to."

Ace was getting excited. They were going to sneak a Perishable into the Spirit Trials, and they were going to get away with it.

Ace, Snout, Bathwater, and Pudding were about to become Higglebottom legends!

CHAPTER 22

Ana held fast to Mother's paste brooch. It had been more difficult to find than the other items taken from them. Father wouldn't talk about the details of its loss. She'd only managed to learn two things: his former partner had stolen it and then had lost it in a game of cards.

The woman who had most recently acquired it had told a friend she was considering ridding her jewelry box of items she didn't overly care for. That friend had told a friend, whose lady's maid had overheard the conversation, and word of it had, through the servants' gossip network, reached Wallace, who had told Ana.

Mother had loved the little brooch. As Ana had heard the tale told, Father had purchased it in the first days of their marriage, when his business ventures were still small but growing. The token had been a monetary sacrifice, a purchase that had caused a noticeable financial pinch. That had added meaning for Mother and had made its loss all the more heart-breaking. It had little value beyond the sentimental.

Ana returned home with the treasure held in a desperate

grip, all the while keenly aware that Hollis was likely across the street attempting to rescue his brother while risking his own feeble fortune. She could hardly fault him for engaging in slightly underhanded endeavors for the sake of his family; she was guilty of the same.

Father was in his room, as always.

Ana sat beside him, then withdrew from her pocket the handkerchief-wrapped bundle. She slowly and carefully unfolded the linen. Seeing the blue-and-white cameo brooch again, even though she'd looked at it all the way from the home where she'd bought it, still brought a stirring of emotion. Mother had worn it so often, so proudly.

"Mercy," he said. "Is that Beatrice's?"

"It is." She set it in his hand.

"Where did you find it?"

In a pile of unwanted trinkets Mrs. Castleton sold for a pittance. "I was fortunate enough to come across it."

Wallace eyed her from over Father's shoulder. She met his gaze, amusedly daring him to press for more information. Though they'd not discussed it in any detail, she felt certain he realized she hadn't merely "found" many of the things she'd returned to this house.

"I hope you didn't pay too much for it," Father said. "It is merely paste after all."

"I paid what it is worth to those who haven't our attachment to it." She made the declaration as much to Wallace as to him. She had, after all, honestly paid for this reacquisition. "Mother would be so pleased to know we have it back again."

"That she would, assuming she had forgiven me for

losing it in the first place." He smiled sadly. "Her heart was broken already. Losing this only shattered it further."

"It was hardly your fault." Ana reached over and patted his arm. "None of us suspected Mr. Kellogg would do all the damage he did."

"He lost it on the turn of a card." Father pinned the brooch to his lapel. Anyone seeing it would think him utterly out of his mind, but to Ana, it was sweetly touching. "I've heard from many people who were there that they suspect the game was not a fair one."

What was this?

Father sighed and leaned back in his chair. "I would have felt bad for the horrid man, being cheated at cards, but he deserved every spot of bad luck he had, even if it did cost your mother this lovely little bauble."

"Cheated?" Ana hadn't heard a whisper about cheating at that infamous game.

"Wallace has it from the servants at White's." Father motioned to him. "The game wasn't fair or noble. Kellogg lost a great many things that day, but the only thing he likely should have lost was his dignity."

Cheating. Card sharps. Heavens, that sounded familiar.

"Who was he playing against?" she asked.

Father looked over his shoulder at his ever-faithful valet.

"Some bloke what called himself the Crow," Wallace said. "He weren't one of Mr. Kellogg's regular opponents. Ruined a handful of genn'elmen before White's took his membership and tossed him out."

That sounded very much like the sort of man Hollis was attempting to run to ground. Perhaps Wallace might remember something about "the Crow" that would help track down the man doing the same thing now.

"Kellogg ought to have known better," Father said. "A fellow who won't use his proper name to conduct business oughtn't be trusted."

Ana tossed him a smile. "I believe some of the penny dreadfuls you read are penned by people not using their proper names."

"That is different," Father insisted with a hint of amusement. "Noms de plume are long-established in the world of literature. Using one is not underhanded; it is tradition."

"I will grant you that." A bit of clamoring caught their attention. "There's our ghost again."

She'd heard the occasional something or other since moving back home. It wasn't a ghost, though. Nor was it vermin. She was absolutely certain *someone* was in the house. And she was further certain whoever the unknown occupant was, he or she was here with Wallace's blessing. A friend fallen on hard times, perhaps. Maybe a sweetheart who'd lost her position elsewhere.

How did one go about introducing so potentially tender a topic? He was hiding something of significance from his employers and making use of their house without permission. While Ana wished only to make the arrangements more comfortable for his guest, Wallace would think himself in trouble.

Her best course of action might well be to simply discover the hideaways and force the conversation.

She rose from her seat and took up her basket. "I will just put these things in the kitchen."

"I can do that, Miss Newport," Wallace said.

"I know you can, but you're seeing to the laundry just now. You keep to that."

He accepted her suggestion and continued placing Father's things in the clothes press. Ana hooked her arm through the basket handle and moved to the door. She knew perfectly well where the sound had come from: the bedchamber that had been her mother's.

She slipped from Father's room and moved to the one directly beside his. Careful to be as quiet as she could manage, she took hold of the handle and, in one quick movement, opened the door.

The room inside was not as empty as usual. The small table now boasted two chairs. The rug that had been in the sitting room now lay on the floor, with two bundles of blankets and two pillows set to one side. And, standing sentinel at the window, was Mr. O'Donnell.

He looked over at her in shock, that instantly gave way to amusement. That amusement grew to a grin, and, if she was not mistaken, he barely held back a laugh.

"Come in," he whispered, waving her closer. "And shut the door."

She did so without hesitation. Crossing toward him, she set her basket on the table. Two chairs. Two blanket bundles. Though he was alone now, he was not always.

"You are our ghost?" She stood on the opposite side of the window, facing him.

"Is that the explanation Wallace has been giving?"

"That is the explanation my father laughingly concocted—he has been reading Lafayette Jones's latest, after all—and we have all continued to embrace that explanation, though not one of us believes it."

"I bumped into the table a moment ago," Mr. O'Donnell said, his voice shockingly quiet despite the fact he was not actually whispering. How did he manage that?

She peeked around the curtain. "You are watching the Thompsons' place?"

He nodded. "Trying to sort out the gambling establishment that's been set up there. It's not precisely the aboveboard kind."

"Hollis is doing the same—" In a moment of lightning-quick clarity, she pieced together an entire puzzle. "He's the other one staying here. That's why he was so near at hand when I arrived with Eloise. He had not, in fact, arrived by coincidence."

"You've a mind for spy work, it seems."

She shrugged. "Clandestine undertakings are not unfamiliar to me."

That gained her a bit more scrutiny than she cared for.

"M' sister suspected as much," Mr. O'Donnell said. "She tells me you've a cool head and a steady hand. That's high praise from her."

"Your sister?" Again, pieces fell instantly into place. "Móirín."

He nodded. "She's a bit terrifying, i'n't she?"

"A little, yes."

"But hers is a heart of gold." Mr. O'Donnell turned his sights back to the house across the street. "Too many don't get to see that."

"Have you or Hollis learned anything useful about the activity at the Thompsons'?" she asked.

"We've our doubts the current occupant is actually Mr. Thompson's cousin. Hollis's certain this is where his brother got himself in trouble, he's worried the housekeeper is being mistreated—likely others on the staff as well—and he's concerned Mr. Lewiston is near to being ruined."

"Sounds like Mr. Kellogg and the Crow."

"The Crow?"

If Mr. O'Donnell was in league with Hollis, then Ana felt certain she could trust him. "My father's one-time business partner lost everything but his boots in a game of cards he thought was on the up-and-up, but as I understand it now, he'd played against a cheat. That man was known as the Crow, though he must have had an actual name. The game was held at a club. When his cheating was discovered, the Crow lost his membership and was tossed out, but by then he'd ruined a long chain of gentlemen in what turned out to be manipulated games."

Mr. O'Donnell stood frozen, brow pulled down in thought. "Could you take a message to Elizabeth at Thurloe?"

Mercy, was Elizabeth part of this network as well? Then again, of course she was. It all made perfect sense.

"I can," she answered.

"Tell her the Raven was likely once the Crow. Tell her Hollis needs to check the membership history at—which club held that infamous match?"

"White's."

He nodded. "The membership history at White's. If he

can find the identity of that card sharp, we'll know who we're dealing with now."

"Anything else?"

He offered a lopsided smile. "Offer m' sister a '*Dia dhuit*' from me."

Ana grinned. "I don't think I could repeat that if you paid me."

"Then just tell her to behave her troublesome self—not that she'll listen."

Of all the people who might have been hiding away in her house, Mr. O'Donnell was a fine option. And if his being there helped keep Hollis safe in the den of villainy across the street, Ana would see to it Mr. O'Donnell had everything he needed to remain precisely where he was.

THE GENTLEMAN
AND THE THIEF

by Mr. King

Installment VII,
in which our brave Hero and intrepid Heroine
face Danger and Mystery on the Moors!

Pip sat on Tillie's lap, wrapped in her protective arms while they reassured him he wouldn't be required to face down the sprite he'd stolen from its home.

"We simply need to know *how* you captured it," Wellington said. "It cannot continue roaming about, causing mischief. Its antics are causing people a great deal of distress."

Pip nodded. "It steals things."

"I'd wager it don't know it oughtn't take those things," Tillie said. "The little creature is away from the only place it knows, trying to make sense of somewhere so strange."

The boy looked up at her. "Do you think it's scared?"

"Might be. It's a frightening thing being surrounded by people you"—her eyes met Wellington's—"know you don't belong with. That's likely why it's hiding."

He fully understood the layer beneath her words. She

too had been hiding, ever since his Society acquaintances arrived. Just as Mr. and Mrs. Smith had observed, she "knew" she didn't belong among them. Oh, how his heart ached for her!

"If only our little thief realized we wouldn't harm it for all the world," Wellington said. "That we only want what is best for it."

"But having it here is causing so much trouble." She didn't look away, didn't drop her gaze. "What is 'best' is for it to return home."

"Is that why it's scared?" Pip asked. "It wants to go home?"

The thought of that idea applying to Tillie sat heavy on Wellington's heart. "Is it scared, dear?" he asked her.

She held the little boy closer. In a voice quiet and less confident than he'd ever heard it, she said, "Terrified."

Wellington sat near enough to reach out and gently brush his fingers along her cheek. "There is nothing to be afraid of."

Pip broke into what would otherwise have been a very tender moment. "But it's so far from home. All the way across the moors."

Tillie looked at the little boy. "You know where its home is?"

He nodded. "A mine, over near Ipsley."

A mine. Just as Mr. Combs had said.

"Do you suppose," Wellington said, "if we could catch it and return it to the Ipsley mine, it might remain there and stop causing mischief here?"

"If I had a home," Pip said, "I'd always want to be there."

Tillie held him closer. "You can have your home with me, Pip."

What would it take for her to offer him a home "with *us*"? How could Wellington show Tillie that such a future was not only possible but perfect?

"You'll not make me go back to the workhouse?" Pip looked from one of them to the other, worry and hope warring in his expression.

"No, Pip. We'd not want you so far away as Ipsley," Tillie said.

The boy sighed and leaned against her. He looked less burdened. "It likes things that are shiny. That's how I got it to come out of the mine—with shiny things. And I had a shiny box that it went into. And I closed the lid so it couldn't get out, and then I ran with it. But it wasn't happy in the shiny box. It bumped around inside. I ran and ran, but then I dropped the box and the lid came off and the blue flame came out and darted into your house." He looked to Wellington. "I should've told you, but I was afraid."

"How long were you out on the moors by yourself?" The creature had, after all, been undertaking its thefts for weeks.

"I hid in the stables." Pip curled into an ever-smaller ball on Tillie's lap. "The blue flame was angry. I didn't want it to find me."

"We'll lure it away," Tillie promised. "And we'll get it back home. Nothing will happen to you, dearie."

Pip climbed down. He assumed the determined stance of one attempting to be brave. "You'll need shiny things. And a box."

Tillie nodded solemnly. "We'll fetch 'em." She stood and

took Wellington's hand in hers. "Let's catch us a tiny blue monster." Tillie waved Pip along. "You can stay here with my papa."

"He likes me," Pip declared.

"We all do," Wellington said.

Tillie squeezed his hand and smiled up at him. A man could quickly grow accustomed to such a look from such a woman. Pip skipped off down the corridor, his joyfulness restored.

"What do your guests think of Pip?" Tillie asked. "They couldn't have missed that he's an urchin."

"I don't know that they've interacted with him yet."

Her gaze returned to the corridor, though he suspected she wasn't really looking at anything in particular. "Are you afraid they'll disapprove of him as well? Or accuse him of being the thief?"

"They might," he admitted. "Civility requires that I give them shelter from the rain, but there is no requirement that I allow them to be insulting."

"Pip and I are beneath them," she said. "Their behavior is expected."

"But it won't be endured. Should they cause you further pain, my dear, I will toss them out on their ears, rain or no rain."

Her expression softened. "Not many gentlemen would make that choice."

"They would if they knew *you*."

She swung their linked hands between them as they walked. "I think you've grown fond of me these past weeks."

"I've always been fond of you," he said.

"Fond enough to undertake ridiculous and likely dangerous adventures?"

He let his amusement show. "Increasingly so."

Tillie tugged him onward. "Let's go fetch some shiny things."

They'd been out on the moors for an hour without any sign of the elusive blue flame. Tillie was wearing every piece of shining, sparkling jewelry at Summerworth. Wellington kept near her with a wood-lined silver humidor at the ready. It was the shiniest box they could find.

And, yet, they'd had no success. To compound the difficulties, the skies above were turning leaden. Heaven help them if they were caught out in such a place under such circumstances!

"Perhaps we should come back another day," Wellington said. "I'd not want you to catch cold."

"Pip will not rest easy until the bluecap is home. And your guests aren't likely to leave until we recover the missing brooch."

He squared his shoulders. "That is all the motivation I need."

Tillie snorted, something a well-bred lady would never do, but which he enjoyed immensely. She was sunshine and fresh air.

She held up two fists full of dangling bracelets and chains of precious metal, bouncing them about so they sparkled. "Mr. Thief," she said in a singsong voice. "Come steal these fine things from us."

"That hasn't worked yet, it won't—"

A blue flame appeared, no more than fifty yards ahead of them. Wellington pulled in a tight breath.

Tillie shook the jewels.

The flame darted forward then disappeared.

"No, come back," Tillie whispered. She kept the jewels up high.

Wellington adjusted the silver box he held so the dim, cloud-infused sunlight glinted off it a little brighter as added incentive.

The blue flame reappeared, but for only a moment.

"We mean you no harm," Tillie called out. "Truly we don't."

"We want to take you back home," Wellington added.

Suddenly, the bluecap was visible again, closer this time. And it remained.

"We know you come from the mine by Ipsley," Tillie said. "We can take you back there."

Wellington opened the box. The flame disappeared.

"Perhaps it ain't fond of traveling in a box," Tillie said.

"I can't say I blame it." He tucked the silver humidor into the leather sack he'd borrowed from Mr. Combs. "Maybe we can convince the little sprite to follow us over the moors."

Tillie flourished the enticements again. "Mr. Bluecap! We want to take you home."

Nothing.

She looked at him. "Perhaps if we start walking in the direction of Ipsley, it'll follow?"

Wellington shrugged. "It's worth trying."

"I'd imagine it'll take an hour of walking," she warned. "And we've been out here an hour already."

He took the dangling jewels from her nearest hand, then slipped his fingers around hers. "I'm game for a long walk if you are."

They walked hand in hand, waving the sparkling lures about. The occasional backward glance revealed the blue flame following. But in the moment after they looked, it always disappeared.

"It is following us," Tillie whispered.

"I know."

On and on they walked. The sky overhead grew heavier and darker. The wind blew fiercer with each passing moment. The moors were no place to be in a storm. They were too far from Summerworth to turn back and too far from Ipsley to be at ease. A bone-chilling gust nearly knocked Tillie over.

"Perhaps we should've made this trek in the pony cart," she said.

"The flame would have spooked the pony. This could only be accomplished on foot."

After nearly an hour of winding through the moors, Ipsley came into view. The mine would be nearby. But where, exactly?

Tillie looked around, uncertainty in her face. She, apparently, didn't know either. "We cannot come this close only to fail. Where is it, Wellington?"

"The mine or the bluecap?"

"Either one," she said. The wind pulled at her hair and dress, yet she stood stalwart and fixed. How could anyone not see and admire the strength of this remarkable woman? She spun and motioned with her handful of jewelry. "There's the flame."

Wellington rushed alongside her toward their flickering quarry.

"Please," she called out. "We'll help you find your home."

"Truly." Wellington added his voice to hers. "Your mine is nearby; we know it is."

The blue flame flew further afield. They rushed after. They could not lose it. Not now. Not when they were so close to returning it to its home and ridding Summerfield of Alsop, Henson, and their lot!

The bluecap suddenly stopped. It hovered in place, flickering but not truly moving. In the instant before they reached it, the flame dropped straight down and vanished, not into thin air. Into a *hole*.

Wellington grabbed Tillie's arm and pulled her to a stop, her toes mere inches from the edge of a mine shaft. He drew her back to safety. The hole beneath their feet glowed an otherworldly blue.

"I believe our mysterious visitor is home at last," Wellington said.

Tillie leaned the tiniest bit forward and called down into the mine. "Could you return the things you stashed away? We've a shrew back at Summerworth who won't leave us in peace without her brooch."

The light grew brighter. Tillie stepped back. Wellington put his arm around her, unsure what was happening or what threat might arise next. The last weeks had taught him to expect what he could not possibly foresee.

A full dozen blue flames shot up out of the shaft and swirled around the two of them, whipping up even more wind than the storm brewing overhead. Tillie turned, burying her face against Wellington's chest. He set both his arms firmly and protectively about her as they were enveloped by the flames.

No heat emanated. Indeed, the flames were cold, like a draft from the dark corners of a . . . a mine. Stronger and stronger it blew, the pull of it twisting and turning. The vortex tugged at Tillie, threatening to yank her out of his arms.

"Wellington!"

He tightened his grip. "Kneel down." The wind carried his voice away. Had she even heard him? "If we're lower, it'll be harder to topple us."

The whirlwind pulled her further, stretching his fingers painfully.

"The wind is too strong." Tillie's voice pleaded with him.

With every ounce of strength he had, Wellington pulled her against him as he lowered himself—and her with him— to the muddy ground below, kneeling in the midst of the onslaught.

They hunched there as the blue whirlwind continued. They'd returned the wandering bluecap. Did its "family" think they'd kidnapped it in the first place?

Tillie was still sliding away. Her slight frame was no match against the pull of azure wind. She would be torn from him, perhaps tossed into the mine shaft. He wrapped the open sides of his jacket around her, then crouched over her, trying to shield her and weigh her down.

"We brought it home," he called out into the cold, blue cyclone. "We mean no harm. Let us go. Please."

With a flash of white, the flames disappeared. Only the gusts of humid moorland wind remained, and the first raindrops of the breaking storm.

Wellington kept still, waiting, watching for the bluecaps to return. Nothing emerged from the mine shaft. No light. No sound. No movement.

Tillie peeked out from her protective cocoon. "Are they gone?"

"I believe so."

She sat up straight, trembling and muddy. "I thought they'd blow me right off my feet and into the shaft."

"So did I." He kissed her temple. "You weren't hurt were you, my dear?"

"No lasting damage."

They scrambled to their feet, muddied but otherwise well.

"We make a fine team, Tillie Combs."

She smiled up at him, rain pelting her face. It was coming down harder now. They likely had time enough to reach Ipsley before the sky fully broke open, but only if they moved quickly.

"We'd best hurry," he said.

He kept her hand in his, and they moved swiftly toward the town. It wasn't until they were nearly there that Tillie stopped abruptly.

"Our sparklies."

He looked at her, unsure what she meant.

"All the jewels we were holding, to lure the bluecap onto the moors." She held up her empty hands. "They're gone."

He hadn't even noticed. His handful was missing as well. "Did we drop them?"

She shook her head. "I was clutching them tightly as I could manage."

He had been as well.

Tillie looked back in the direction of the mine. "They took it. They took the treasures." Her shoulders drooped. Rain dripped from her sodden hair. "I suppose this means Miss Fairbanks won't be getting her brooch back."

"Likely not." The wind blew rain up his sleeves and down his collar. They'd be soaked in another minute or two. "She'll rail and bluster, but I'll settle with her. Then she'll be on her way. They all will be."

"Is that a promise?"

"A solemn vow." He took her hand once more, the rain coming down in buckets. "But for now, my dear, it's time to run for cover."

CHAPTER 23

The only thing Hollis needed more than a nap was Ana's company. Unfortunately, he hadn't time for either.

He'd returned to Thurloe after the previous day's games to look in on his sister-in-law and her children. Not long before he'd arrived, word had come from Brogan that the records from White's needed perusing. Hollis had spent the rest of that day and into the night searching out a member who could get him the information he needed. Then he'd returned to the Thompsons' for more games and spying and snooping. Not willing to risk being caught out behaving in a suspicious way, he'd taken a hack all the way back to his flat, then another back to Pimlico, alighting several streets away and walking in the rain to the Newport house. He lock-picked his way through the back-garden door and slipped up to the lookout room.

"Welcome back, you lazy bum," Brogan greeted.

Hollis tossed his dripping coat on the table. "Your line

was 'Hollis, you look worn down. Please, take a nap while I continue as lookout.'"

Another voice answered. "And what's *my* line?"

He spun about, shocked to see Ana sitting at her leisure in a threadbare armchair, his latest penny dreadful in her hand, illuminated by a small candle on a copper candleholder. "I see this spot's grown cozier while I've been running all over Town doing the difficult work."

Ana raised an eyebrow and looked to Brogan. "Is he always this grumpy when he's tired?"

"I've not seen him tired before, truth be told. He's not usually the one doing the lifting."

Hollis pulled off his sodden gloves. "You make me sound like I've been out thieving."

"Shocking." Ana's theatrical tone pulled an exhausted smile to his lips.

He dropped his gloves in his hat and set it atop his coat. "I could use a hug if you have one to give."

"Hollis." Brogan pulled his name out long and singsong as he snatched Hollis into a bone-crushing embrace. "I've missed you, lad. Don't ever leave again. M' poor heart can't take it. I—"

"I *will* belt you, Donnelly."

Brogan laughed and dropped his arms. As he walked back to the window, he hooked his thumb over his shoulder in Hollis's direction. "Best of luck with that one, Ana. He's sore and sore."

"'Ana'?" Hollis eyed them both.

She rose from her chair and moved to him. "We've had a lot of time together, waiting for you. In addition to discovering his actual name, I've learned more about Dublin than I thought I'd ever know, and he is now an expert in the characteristics of various string instruments. And we are both now very familiar with the exploits of a certain one-time street urchin."

He pushed back his wet hair. "Fletch has been hanging about as well?"

"He has a message for you," Brogan said. "One he said he had to deliver in person."

"Which means *he* likely won't let me sleep either."

Ana brushed her hand against his, her fingers warm against his cold skin. She stood on her toes and kissed his cheek. Heat enveloped him on the instant.

He put his arms around her. She returned the embrace.

"You're damp," she said.

"I had to walk from Hugh Street and sneak in the back." No matter that he was ready to drop, he would not have traded the feel of her in his arms for even a moment's rest. "I'm convinced people were standing on the rooftops, emptying buckets of water on my head the entire way."

She rested her head against him, dampness and all. He breathed in the scent of her, a warm, soft vanilla. How had he not noticed that before?

"There ain't time for that." Fletcher made the pronouncement as he walked unceremoniously into the room.

Hollis didn't drop his arms away from Ana. Holding her gave him strength. "Brogan says you have a message for me."

Fletcher held out a sealed letter. A fleeting glance identified the stationery. For the first time in his two years as a

Dreadful, Hollis had been sent a direct correspondence from the Dread Master himself.

He kissed the top of Ana's head, then stepped away. She knew of his efforts at the Thompson house. She knew some of those involved in the mission. But she didn't know about the Dread Penny Society. It had to remain that way.

"You are near enough to my father's size," Ana said. "I'll gather you a change of clothes from his armoire. Then you won't be wet and cold."

"Thank you."

Once Ana left the room, Hollis broke the seal on the Dread Master's letter. The rainy skies outside provided very little light, so he crossed to Ana's candle, tipping the paper enough to see the neat writing.

"This isn't your penmanship," he said to Fletcher.

"I've told you myself that I ain't the Dread Master," he said. "Didn't you believe me?"

"I don't always know what to believe." He dropped his gaze once more to the brief letter.

> *Hollis.*
>
> *Received your report. We cannot ignore that the one-time Crow and the Raven are likely one and the same. Maneuver into a game with him. Catch him cheating. Gather proof. He must be stopped.*
>
> *DM*

Hollis pushed out a breath. This was what he'd wanted: the Dreadfuls to trust him with something other than scraping and bowing. The Dread Master's note gave him that in spades. Why, then, did he feel tired instead of excited?

Hollis tore the note in half, then half again, continuing the effort as the pieces grew ever smaller. Fletcher set an open flask on the table beside the candle. Hollis dropped the bits of paper into it. He'd seen Fletcher do that often enough after reading correspondence from the Dread Master to know the proper way of disposing of the paper. Fire was also considered an acceptable means of destruction, but this was easiest in the moment.

"Your Ana will return shortly," Fletcher said. "Any instructions we need before she gets back?"

"The Dread Master wants me to gather proof that the Raven cheats his patrons. That means going back. Getting in deeper. Likely breaking into areas of the house where I'm not actually allowed." Hollis rubbed at his face. "We'll eventually need to recruit a few more highborn Dreadfuls. This type of mission is beyond the scope of just one person."

Brogan spoke from the window while still watching the street. "How are you meant to play cards and sneak around the house at the same time? Does the Dread Master think you're actually a pair of twins?"

"Maybe he's hopin' you'll toss Very Merry into the efforts, let her do the snooping for you."

Though he knew Fletcher had made the suggestion in jest, Hollis still gave a serious answer. "Very Merry is safe where she is. I won't put her in any danger, no matter the enormity of all the Dread Master expects me to do."

A quick knock sounded at the door before it inched open.

Ana peeked inside. "I have dry clothes for you, Hollis."

"You're a worker of miracles."

She laughed and set the pile on the table. "Anything else I can do to keep my sainthood?"

"Do you know any talented sneak thieves?" Brogan asked, laughter in his tone.

Ana turned wide, worried eyes on Hollis. He knew what was weighing on her: *she* was a talented sneak thief, but they didn't know that.

"We're hoping to gather evidence that the games across the street are manipulated," Hollis said. "Brogan's proposing a more creative approach than I'm planning to take."

Some of the tension in her posture eased. She even managed a smile. "You mean to catch cheating as it happens, but he wants to break in and find marked cards or hidden compartments or, I suppose, a very convenient list of victims."

"That'd be grand," Brogan said.

Fletcher leaned against the wall near the window. "It's a right regular shame you didn't manage to catch the Phantom Fox, Hollis. You'd have precisely the skilled help you need."

The man didn't realize the legendary sneak thief was in the room.

Ana stepped closer to Hollis and, in an almost silent whisper, said, "He's not wrong. I *could* do it."

He shook his head. "It's too dangerous."

"I'd keep out of the public rooms."

"Ana." He pulled her to the side of the room. "Four-Finger Mike doesn't deal only in thieving children. One of his closest associates ran a vast prostitution ring, and very few of the women caught up in it were there willingly."

"I have slipped in and out of dozens of houses, some of which were full of people at the time, and I've only ever been caught by you. And even then, I still got away." Her gaze turned almost pleading. "I could do this, Hollis. I could help."

"If she's a skilled sneak thief, I think we ought to consider it," Fletcher said.

Hollis and Ana both jumped, looking over at him.

He gave them a look as dry as the Sahara. "We're in a tiny room with no other noises. Did you really think we couldn't hear you?"

Brogan added his thoughts. "Four-Finger Mike won't be expecting a woman thief."

"They agree with me," Ana said. "You're outvoted."

"This isn't Parliament, darling," Hollis said.

"This also isn't a dictatorship." She popped her fists on her hips. "So either you can include me in this and we'll formulate an approach together, or I'll simply wait until you're across the street and I'll get the information I need from these gentlemen, then do my part without you."

He eyed the others. "You'd do that to me?"

"The Raven has to be stopped," Fletcher said. "And you said yourself it's more than you can do on your own. Four-Finger Mike wouldn't recognize her, should she be seen. We can't say that for either of us."

Hollis paced away. He didn't like it. He didn't like it at all. But, no matter that the Dread Master had shown some faith in him, he knew he didn't have the clout to override the others. And he'd learned a little of Ana's stubbornness.

"This is dangerous." He said it as much to Ana as to the others, a last effort to change all their minds.

"If we bring down the Raven," Ana said, "we can likely bring down Four-Finger Mike as well. This neighborhood will be safer for it. The children of London will be safer for it. The women of London will be as well. It is dangerous, yes. But it must be done."

Fletcher gave a firm nod. Brogan mimed applause.

That was their fate sealed then. Ana would be sneaking into the lion's den, and there was nothing he could do to stop it.

"Swear to me you'll be careful." He brushed his thumb along her jaw.

"I swear."

He bent and brushed his lips over hers, a whisper of a kiss, unhurried and light as air. He'd caught her once, and he wasn't as wily as Four-Finger Mike. If anything happened to her, he'd never forgive himself.

O━━

The gambling rooms at the Thompsons' place were arranged according to the skill of the players and the height of the stakes. Hollis had begun in the lowest of the rooms—the ground-floor drawing room, sporting three-penny stakes and games dependent more on chance than skill—but he had already moved to the small sitting room on the first floor, four rooms advanced from where he'd begun.

Never in all his time there had he seen the Raven join

a game. He'd need to do something to catch the eye of that elusive fellow.

Hollis left every day with more money in his pocket than he'd arrived with, but that hadn't done the trick. He'd managed some impressive performances in various games. That hadn't either.

Skill alone wouldn't do it. He needed to borrow a page from Fletcher and swagger a little. The best game for that, in his experience, was baccarat. Tradition dictated that players could make quite a show out of revealing their cards. Some chose to simply flip them over. Others took their time, bending the cards, drawing out the drama.

Hollis sat at the baccarat table, determined to win handily and with flair. Baccarat involved a great deal of chance, but with six players and a dealer, a great many cards would be revealed. Hollis could track which ones remained in the deck and, thus, which ones were most likely to come up. He'd previously played with each of these gentlemen at other tables. He knew how to read them.

Each card he was dealt, he twisted loosely from one corner to the other, slowly making a pasteboard curl before laying it face up, perched on two corners. The drawn-out approach brought all eyes to him and built tension and expectation.

He played the table as much as the cards. Some of the gentlemen were cautious, making smaller bets, not easily persuaded to wager high. Others, though, needed only a couple of wins to toss caution to the wind. Hollis provided that, building their confidence and, with it, the pot.

No one would be ruined by him. He wouldn't allow the

wagers to reach that level. He simply pushed the game far enough for a few people to wander over and watch.

Hollis assumed an even more roguish posture and watched as the final opponent at the table turned over his cards, adding a small crease as he did. The first was a ten, which could prove either perfect or disastrous. The onlookers and the dealer watched closely as he turned his second card. An eight.

Whispers of excitement echoed around them. Only one pair of cards could beat a natural eight. But Hollis knew which cards were left, and he had a tremendously good chance of holding that pair.

Leaning on the arm of his chair, his posture unconcerned, he began curling back the first of his two cards, slowly revealing it. A ten. He tossed it to the dealer. The room watched and waited.

Out of the corner of his eye, Hollis spotted the Raven standing apart from the onlookers. But he was watching. He was most definitely watching.

Hollis undertook his card twisting with an extra degree of emphasis. The tiniest bit at a time, he wrapped it backward. The crowd bent forward, eager for a glance. Only one card would win.

He saw it before anyone else. Though most players kept their reactions subdued, this was not the moment for subtlety. He saw precisely the card he needed and grinned.

He tossed the curl of pasteboard to the dealer.

"A natural nine," the dealer declared. "Our winner, gentlemen."

Hollis stood, offered a dip of his head, and waited as the dealer gathered the impressive pile of coins Hollis had won.

Their host wove toward him, stopping beside him at the baccarat table.

"I suspect, Mr. Darby," the Raven said, "you may be bored with our games here."

"A little." He dropped his now much heavier purse in his jacket pocket, balancing the appearance of triumph with ennui. He had a very specific role to play, after all. "Do you know where I might find more of a challenge? I haven't a membership at any of the clubs."

The Raven waved that off. "They'll not challenge you there. What you need is a game in the front parlor."

"The front parlor *here*?" he asked.

The Raven nodded. "Very few are invited to play there. Your brother, in fact, never made it that far."

"My brother is not the brightest among us." He offered a nod to the table of gentlemen.

"But you, I would wager, are." The Raven assessed him. "What do you say, Mr. Darby? A greater challenge. Greater stakes. Greater privacy."

"Against whom would I be playing?"

The man's smile was somehow both oily and sincere. "Only the best."

"An undertaking on that level deserves an audience one can depend upon." He set his hands in his pockets, assuming a casual posture. "Allow me to bring my choice of companions, and I believe I will accept the challenge."

The Raven nodded. "Very well. Choose your support and choose your game. Simply tell me when."

"Tomorrow," Hollis said. "In the evening."

"I look forward to it."

Hollis put his hat on his head and, with one last nod, turned and left.

Tomorrow evening. His moment of truth.

CHAPTER 24

Watching Hollis knock on the door of the Thompsons' house, knowing he would soon be challenging a man whose card sharping was at the heart of her own family's pain, Ana could not be easy. Hollis had assured her he was an excellent cardsman. Fletcher had assured her Hollis was sharp as a razor blade and equally as dangerous when need be.

A turn of the Crow's cards had destroyed a great many lives. What if Hollis's was next?

"He knows what he's about, lass," Brogan said, standing near her by the window. "And securing permission to bring Fletcher along as a condition of the Raven's challenge was genius. The two of them together are more formidable than anyone'd likely guess. Everything'll be grand."

She stepped away from the window. "Fine words from a man who has filled the belowstairs of my house with police."

"For when the two of you catch that scoundrel red-handed," Brogan said. "He's inside now. 'Tis nearly time for you to sneak over."

Wallace stepped inside. "There's a girl here what needs to bend your ear, Miss Newport."

Odd. "I'll talk to her in the corridor."

It was not a student whom she saw there, though. It was Very Merry.

"What are you doing here, child? Your thief master frequents this neighborhood. You could be found out."

Worry sat deep in the girl's eyes, but she didn't turn away. "Mr. Hollis is in that gambling house, ain't he?"

"He is."

"Ambrose was talkin' with another servant what came to tell him things. I heard him say Mr. Hollis is for running to ground a criminal with four fingers, a man who makes children steal for him and who sells children to people who ought not buy children."

"*No one* should ever buy children."

The urchin looked downright cynical. "Fine fantasy world you're living in, miss. But I'm needing you in the real one long enough to save Mr. Hollis."

"Save him? He is in danger from this four-fingered man?"

"No, miss. He's in danger because he *thinks* that's who he's looking for. He's a bad'n Four-Finger Mike—I ain't arguing that—and he is connected to all this. But he's small pickings compared to some." Fear, blatant and unmistakable, accompanied the girl's every word.

"Who is it Mr. Hollis ought to be looking for?"

"I was stealing for the man who bought me," she said. "He'd kill me now if he could find me. It's what he did to t'others what disobeyed him and tried running off. He's killed grown people too. Heaps of 'em."

Mercy. "And this is who Hollis should be looking for?"

"No, miss. He should be running away. Except he don't know that man's nearby. He don't know what he's actually facing. If he did, he'd run. Least I hope he would."

Ana bent low, holding the girl's gaze. "Who is it?"

Very Merry paled. "The one they call the Mastiff."

Ana had heard Elizabeth and Mr. Walker whispering about someone who went by that name. She'd even heard Móirín mention him in quiet, tense tones. The Mastiff, she had gleaned even before Very Merry's worrying description of him, was a man any person of sense would be terrified of.

"And he's at this game?" Ana pressed.

"I cain't say for sure and certain. But he 'as a keen interest in what's happening at that house. It's the reason he had us busting into homes here. He wanted to know who lived nearby and what they lived like. Wanted to know if any of the homes was empty."

Ana's heart dropped. "Like this one."

"I were meant to bust in here, miss, but Mr. Hollis and his friends found me."

"They found you *here*?" Why had she not heard about this?

"The Mastiff'll know where I was caught. He'll believe that means it's filled with people. He'll keep clear of it."

She pressed a hand to her pounding heart. "Are you certain of that?"

"He don't waste his own time. He'll have staked his ground elsewhere."

Ana mentally checked off every house on that stretch of St. George's. "All the homes are occupied."

"I suspect he's inside the gambling house, miss. But Mr. Hollis will be keeping an eye out for Four-Finger Mike, and I know he's wary of the Raven. But they're dribbling babbies compared to the Mastiff."

How could she possibly get a warning to Hollis when he was inside a home more closely guarded than Buckingham Palace? There was really only one thing for it. When she broke in, she would have to do more than search for papers and evidence. She would have to find a way to get word to him.

Her already risky mission had just turned terrifyingly dangerous.

The Thompsons' house was not vastly different from her own, which meant the ways in and out were virtually identical. Ana slipped around back and, assuming an air of belonging, moved purposely up the garden walk. She'd scrounged up some clothes that would allow her to blend in amongst the servants.

Her original plan had been to avoid everyone and go unseen. Very Merry's revelation had changed that. This tactic was riskier, but it was her best hope.

A basket of freshly picked foodstuffs sat near the garden entrance. Ana scooped it up and walked inside as if she had every right to. She made her way up the corridor to the kitchen. The basket found a place near the washbasin. Ana snatched an apron off an obliging nail and tied it on.

Another woman, near to Ana's age and wearing an

identical apron, swooped over to the worktable and took up a tray.

"Lower card room," the cook barked out.

The maid left with a quick step.

Ana copied her actions and selected a tray of her own.

"East card room. First floor."

Ana spun and carried her load from the kitchen. Thank heavens these houses were so similar. She didn't draw undue attention fumbling around looking for the servants' stairs. The comparative calm of her forward movement allowed her to mentally take note of the comings and goings around her.

She saw only two maids. As she climbed the stairs, she crossed paths with a single footman and a harried-looking woman she guessed was the housekeeper. She'd not spotted a knife boy or a scullery maid whilst she was in the kitchen. For a house this size with such a steady influx of "guests," she'd expected a larger staff.

The first-floor servants' landing was empty. Ana stepped out and peeked through the first door she came across. The room was empty. The next room proved the same. Perhaps the staff was small today because the number of games was also small.

After a time, she found what had to be the east card room, no matter that cards were not being played. Men stood about chatting in what, on the surface, appeared to be friendly tones. When she looked more closely, the tension between them became obvious.

Ana set her tray on an end table, then distributed the plates of victuals to be within reach of the scattered gentlemen. As she did so, she unobtrusively eyed the gentlemen she passed. Hollis sat in a corner talking with Mr. Lewiston, whom they'd seen in the park a few weeks earlier. She couldn't very well drop a warning in his ear with Mr. Lewiston nearby.

As she returned to her empty tray, she caught sight of Fletcher, standing near the others but not deep in discussion. This was her chance. Best not give away the game, though.

She stepped near him and dipped a curtsey. "Beggin' yer pardon, sir. Was you the genn'elman what asked for a dram of brandy?"

Recognition flickered in his eyes for the briefest of moments. "I am, yes."

"We haven't four fingers' worth, sir. Ain't what we have here. I'd fetch it for you iffen I could. Swear to it, I do. I feel like a massive dog, though, not having what you're looking for. A dog, I tell you. A giant one."

He nodded, the gesture just the right degree of dismissive for him to blend in with the Society gents surrounding him. "Understood." He waved her away.

Did he understand? Truly?

She paused, watching him.

He raised an eyebrow. "Was there more? Beyond the four fingers of brandy and the massive dog?"

"Only that I hope you 'ave a very merry time here today, sir. You and any friends you might have come with."

"You are a very chatty sort, aren't you?" He eyed her with annoyance. "I don't suspect you'll hold on to a position for too long, running your mouth like you do." Fletcher looked away, pointedly dismissing her. The man could play a part.

She slipped out, telling herself Fletcher wouldn't allow Hollis to proceed without all the information she'd given. He cared about his friend, and he would do what needed doing.

So would she.

Using what information Hollis had offered about the house and making a few well-informed guesses, she navigated the servants' stairs and back corridors to the ground floor room serving as the Raven's office. The entire floor echoed with emptiness. She wouldn't have a better opportunity for searching than this.

Ana slipped inside and carefully, quietly, closed the door. That would give her a little warning if anyone came inside.

The Raven had no trinkets or mementos scattered about, nothing personal. Anyone at all might have used it. The space was neat and organized. Everything had a place— either piled, stacked, or laid out in straight lines. A man this meticulous wouldn't leave his profits, however ill-gotten, to chance.

The room had only one set of shelves, and they were filled with ledgers. Even in so busy an establishment, this had to have been years' worth of records.

She hadn't time to look through them for patterns of fraud or evidence of cheating, but she could tell the authorities where to find them once she gave them an iron-clad reason to burst in on the house.

Careful not to disturb the neat stacks, she flipped through

the papers on the desk. Insignificant correspondence. A list of goods to be purchased. Another list of repairs to be made to the house. An itemized accounting of recent purchases of furniture and dishware.

This was the man who had likely helped ruin her family. There had to be evidence of his dastardliness somewhere.

One by one, she opened the desk drawers. Packets of cards and bags of dice filled the long, narrow, top drawer. They already knew this house was a gambling establishment. Finding further proof of *that* wasn't helpful.

Ana examined the dice, but they didn't look or feel unusual. She dropped them back in their drawstring bags and returned them to the drawer.

The packs of cards were open, which was odd. To reassure players, packs were usually still sealed when brought to the tables. Ana took out the top pack and carefully fanned the cards. Instead of fifty-two different cards, the pack was made up entirely of aces. The faces were a little different on each card. The backs were of various designs, almost as if someone had gone through several dozen decks from different printers and gathered all the aces. The next pack contained all kings. Another, all nines. Yet another was filled with high cards, all in clubs, again with a variety of designs and styles.

While these might have been a collection of cards *removed* from several decks, it seemed far more likely that these were cards meant to be slipped *into* decks. The Raven could snatch from his collection specific cards that would prove most useful in whichever game he would be playing, matching them to whichever deck was being used.

Packs of cheat cards. If Hollis could catch the Raven in the act, the police would have all they needed. Ana flipped back the apron she was wearing and unbuttoned the hidden pocket in her drab dress. She opened her empty drawstring bag and set three of the card packs inside it.

Her loot secure, she closed the desk drawer. She checked that the room was precisely as she'd left it. No one would ever know she'd been there.

Quiet as a sleeping mouse, she pulled open the door, intent on slipping out of the room, the corridor, and the house. But the threshold was not empty.

The woman she guessed was the housekeeper stood there, quite as if she'd been waiting for Ana to open the door.

Ana froze for a fraction of an instant, then she dipped the half-curtsey she'd always seen upstairs maids give the monarch of the belowstairs realm. This housekeeper, however, did not continue on her way.

The woman, looking wearier than her thirty years, said, "You aren't one of ours."

Before Ana could even formulate a response, the woman pushed on.

"Are you here to steal something?"

An honest answer, she knew, was not the right one in that moment. "No, ma'am."

"Did a snatcher drop you here?" The housekeeper gave her a quick once-over. "They'd not 'ave chosen you to be a maid."

Ana wasn't certain the reason for the woman's surety on that score; it was the least of her worries. "Yet, 'ere I am."

"Why're you sneaking about the place?" the housekeeper pressed.

No immediate answer popped into her mind.

"You're trying to escape, ain't ya?"

For all her skill sneaking about, Ana hadn't developed a knack for lying. She stood there, silent.

"If I got you out, would you help the rest of us escape?" The woman's expression turned pleading. "Most of us ain't here 'cause we want to be. We cain't get away. We need help."

Brogan had mentioned Hollis's suspicion that the staff was being mistreated. He'd mentioned the housekeeper in particular. *This* housekeeper.

Ana knew dropping her role was dangerous, but she had already been discovered. And the woman before her was every bit as imprisoned as Very Merry had been. How could she say no?

"If all goes well," Ana said, "I can help. But I ain't in a position to tell you how."

"I have children. I cain't bear for them to live out their lives like this."

"I'll send help," Ana vowed, slipping past her. "But I cain't do anything if I don't get out o' here m'self."

"I can get you out." The housekeeper assumed a strong and unbowed posture, walking beside Ana toward the servants' stairs and then down into the belowstairs realm where the housekeeper reigned supreme.

"What's your name?" Ana asked quietly.

"Serena."

Ana would remember that, and she would find a means

of helping the woman and her children escape this imprisonment. Somehow, she would.

They moved toward the garden door, the same one Ana had used to get inside. She was nearly out when a mountain of a man appeared in the doorway, blocking most of the light spilling in. The housekeeper stopped on the spot. She watched this new arrival closely, wide-eyed, worried.

"Who's 'is?" The man's gravelly voice echoed with angry authority.

"A new maid." Serena's worry quavered in her voice. "I'm trainin' her. It's her first day."

Ana dipped a curtsey, mimicking the awkward but earnest efforts of inexperienced servants. She kept her gaze lowered enough to be deferent but not so much that she couldn't watch the encounter.

"She's a pretty 'un," the man said. "Wasted as a maid, she is."

"I think she'll do well here," Serena insisted. "The genn'elmen'll enjoy seein' a pretty face bringin' 'em their victuals and drinks."

The man studied Ana too closely for her comfort. Serena was shaking beside her, though she was doing a commendable job of hiding it.

"Pretty enough, I suppose." The man's tar-black whiskers twitched with a sneer. "Dressed as drab as a moth, though."

"Clothes can be changed," Serena said.

"Take 'er up to the dressing room," the man said. "Find something better."

Serena bobbed a curtsey. Ana did as well. For the first time, she was afforded a good look at the man's hands. He

had all his fingers. Very Merry had warned her the man behind this operation was not Four-Finger Mike as Hollis had
assumed. And this very much appeared to be the person in
charge: the infamous, dangerous, deadly Mastiff.

Ana was in a world of trouble.

~~H~~IGGLEBOTTOM'S ~~S~~CHOOL FOR THE ~~D~~EAD
A GHOST OF A CHANCE

by Lafayette Jones

Chapter V

The day of the Spirit Trials arrived cold and cloudy, but the school was in bright spirits. Spirit Trials were the highlight of the entire term.

Ace and his crew entered the cricket pitch with a great deal of swagger—Ace in front, Pudding directly behind him, with Bathwater and Snout on either side. The other First Form teams were assuming their places, but none with quite so much confidence.

Pudding pointed to the seats where the staff sat. "Which one of them is Higglebottom?"

Ace shrugged. "Couldn't say."

"You don't know?"

"No one knows. Might not be any of them. He runs the school, but no one sees him or knows who he is."

Pudding gave him a look thick with doubt. "The teachers and staff must know."

Ace shrugged. "If they do, none of them will say so."

The identity of Higglebottom was one of the afterlife's great mysteries.

"And that doesn't bother anyone?" Pudding was clearly having trouble accepting this.

"It is what it is," Ace said, repeating a phrase he'd heard more times than he could count during his own time as a Perishable. "School runs smoothly. The big decisions go over well. No use restringing a fiddle that plays in tune."

Pudding eyed the gathered staff through most of the welcome speech given by Professor Rattlebag as well as the instructions from Professor Dankworth. Ace was grateful Pudding's event would be last or else he might have been too distracted to even take part.

Artful Dodging was first. Ace slapped Snout on the back, managing to send his hand all the way through him.

He grimaced, knowing all too well how unnerving that sensation was. "Apologies."

But his teammate was too focused to take note of it. His gaze never left the animals gathered in the middle of the pitch. He watched the students who made the run before him, seeing what they did and how the animals reacted.

"You'll be brilliant," Pudding said quietly. "Even if I don't cheer out loud for you."

They'd all decided it'd be best if Pudding kept mum. His voice didn't echo or rattle enough. The others would notice if he spoke too often.

Snout's turn arrived. He closed his translucent eyelids, pressed his ethereal hands together. Slowly, the light drained from him. He could still be seen—total disappearance wasn't taught until Fourth Form—but he was much easier to miss.

With silent, careful step, he cautiously moved behind the redtick hound sitting at the ready. At one point, its ears perked, but it didn't turn around, didn't take notice.

"That's one success," Ace whispered to the rest of the team, watching from the edge of the field.

Snout took the same approach with the gray-and-white striped tabby. Again, a tiny twitch of an ear, the littlest bit of awareness, but no real notice. He was going to hand the team a full-marks finish.

At the last minute, the cat spun about and hissed, back arched and fur on end. Snout returned to his usual near-opacity, shoulders drooping. He'd been blasted close.

The cat who had snatched victory away swished its tail and sent Snout a sassy look. It had known what it was doing, making him think he'd bested it. Bathwater'd had the right of it when he said cats were malicious.

The score card was displayed. They were penalized only two points for the cat catching Snout, no doubt owing to his having crossed almost the entire distance.

Ace leaned toward Pudding. "Bathwater's bang up with Churchyard Chase. He'll fetch us full points easily."

And he did. The Perishable stand-in, a mop wearing a woman's dress and being flitted about by one of the professors to look almost like a living person, rushed about the churchyard, darting in one direction until Bathwater showed up and scared it back. In half the time of the other competitors, Bathwater had herded the mock-Perishable to the headstone of Kipper Kettlesworth, the destination he'd been given moments before the chase began.

Their team received full marks, placing them in a tie with Cropper's team.

"Next up," Rattlebag called out once the Churchyard Chase was completed, "'Is That the Wind, or Is This Place Haunted?' Teams, select your competitor."

"That'd be me." Ace tossed the others a cocky smile— he'd perfected that ghostly facial expression early on in his days at Higglebottom's.

The others heckled him, jesting that he would be the lowest-scoring First Form in history, but no one was actually worried. Ghostly sounds came easily to Ace.

His turn arrived. He met Rattlebag at the center of the pitch and waited for his instructions.

"Wind at a distance," Rattlebag requested.

Ace made precisely that sound. In another year or two, he would learn how to make his voice actually emerge at a distance, but the appropriate volume was all the Trials required of First Forms.

"Wind inside the house."

That one was trickier, since Perishables would know there was a jig afoot if they heard wind right beside them but felt nothing. Beginning haunters weren't meant to reveal that ghosts were nearby, simply lay the groundwork for the more advanced ghosts to build on. Still, Ace was not the least challenged by the request.

"Otherworldly gurgling," Rattlebag said.

Ace did so.

"Muttered gibberish that sounds vaguely like someone speaking a language other than the one the Perishable speaks."

That one was Ace's favorite. "Tippione traw groppier mantar." He kept the sound in the back of his throat and spoke without opening his lips. Sound could still emerge from a ghost's closed mouth, just more garbled and confusing. "Lessier noddle cooppinter."

Even Rattlebag looked impressed. He motioned Ace back to his team.

When the score was posted, it was the very top mark, a perfect score.

"That puts us in first place," Bathwater said. "As long as Pudding wears his shroud well, we have victory in the bag."

"And our ticket to Second Form," Ace said. "We'll be riding high."

Some twenty minutes later, after all the other teams had chosen and sent out their competitors, Pudding put the tattered shroud over his unghostly head and made the walk across the pitch.

They'd practiced for hours, trying to make him look like an expert without looking like too much of one. He was doing a fine job . . . for a Perishable, at least. Ace couldn't help thinking again what a shame it was Pudding wasn't actually dead.

Pudding changed up his pace a couple of times, sometimes slowing as if needing to regain his confidence. And he'd gained a real knack for bending at the knee, below the shroud so no one could see, and tipping to one side. It was the perfect picture of someone sinking a foot through the ground. He would recover, take a moment to collect himself, then walk forward again.

"A convincing performance," Bathwater said, his tone one of relief.

"I plan to call for an encore," Snout said.

"I plan to go straight to whichever Second Form dormitory catches my fancy and claim my bed." Ace wasn't delaying that move one moment longer than he had to.

Pudding was almost to the edge of the pitch when the heavy-laden skies burst open, and rain poured down like a waterfall. Rain wasn't generally of much concern among ghosts, but it did make the non-afterlife items they interacted with heavier and trickier to move.

At the end of the field, Pudding stood beneath an increasingly weighted shroud. It clung and grabbed at his form beneath it. So much for the subtlety of First Form hauntings. Still, subtle or not, Pudding had been by far the best in his test. They had their victory!

Cropper rushed across the pitch toward him. Rattlebag was drawing closer as well.

"C'mon, lads," Ace said. "Something's afoot."

They arrived in time to hear Cropper say, "A rain-soaked shroud is too heavy for a First Form to hold up. No First Form—not even Ace—could do this."

Gads, if the fellow wasn't right about that. They'd worried about Pudding giving away the game by being too good at his challenge. They hadn't counted on the rain making that glaringly obvious.

"He ain't an upper Form," Ace said. "My word of honor."

Cropper and Rattlebag looked at him, clearly attempting to find the gap in his words. More testers and onlookers had drawn nearer.

"He's not an upper Form," Rattlebag repeated. "But he doesn't seem to be a First Form, either. What, then, is he?"

Rattlebag reached for the edge of the shroud. Ace watched, worried. They would soon know if Pudding's chalk disguise was good enough to fool a professor at close range.

The shroud yanked off him and floated to the ground. Ace groaned at the sight before him. Rain had sent the chalk running down Pudding's face in translucent gray rivulets, revealing ample amounts of his Perishable complexion.

A collective gasp swirled around the crowd. Whispers began immediately.

Rattlebag's eyes took on a threatening glow. "All four of you. Higglebottom's office. Now."

CHAPTER 25

Never had Hollis waited so long for a game of cards. The Raven was making a show of greeting all the gentlemen who'd come to watch. Most mimicked his appearance of pleasure, though there was no mistaking the heaviness in their eyes. How many of them had been ruined within these walls? How many suspected they'd been cheated and hoped to sort out how? How many simply found enjoyment in seeing someone else lose everything he had?

Hollis had learned during his school years that appearing disinterested, even bored, set the perfect tone. His competitor would realize Hollis didn't care how many connections or supporters the man had, while also being convinced that Hollis wasn't the least nervous about the coming match.

He and Fletcher had undertaken a few brief greetings before sitting at the card table, silent and stoic, showing neither worry nor anger nor excitement, and waited.

At first, the Raven ignored them. But as the minutes passed, he began glancing their way, his expression growing increasingly curious, then frustrated. The man's efforts at displaying his vast network of supporters—most of whom Hollis knew weren't there to cheer the Raven on—grew ever more pointed.

Occasionally the two of them made comments to each other. Everyone made note of it, though most attempted to appear as if they hadn't.

"Very mild weather we're having at the moment," Hollis said at one point.

"Boringly so," Fletcher answered.

After another long stretch of silence between them, Fletcher spoke again. "The Metropolitan Railway is due to expand. That'll be a convenience."

"For those traveling that direction," Hollis said.

"Very mild weather in that direction," Fletcher observed.

"Boringly so," Hollis drawled.

They made a point of only discussing inane topics. It confused the people around them. Starting a game off-balance was a dangerous thing. That was most of Hollis's opponents' downfalls: they did not for a moment believe *he* was a dangerous thing.

Eventually, the Raven, his smile tight, suggested they get to the matter at hand. His eyes flashed in Hollis's direction, his anticipation easy to interpret: he expected Hollis to grow very suddenly worried.

"Excellent," Hollis said firmly.

The Raven sat in the chair directly across the table from Hollis. "What is your game?"

"I've mostly played faro here, though I do not object to other games. I enjoy baccarat. Some people prefer whist."

"Sitting-room variety games," the Raven said. "Surely you're familiar with something a bit more . . . challenging."

The chest-thumping was to begin early, it seemed. This called for a game requiring focus and skill as well as a healthy dose of luck. "Piquet, perhaps?"

"You consider yourself well enough versed in it to match me?" The Raven clearly doubted it.

"We could indulge in a game of beggar-my-neighbor, if that would make you more comfortable," Hollis casually tossed out.

Snickers and barely concealed smiles filled the room around them. Fletcher, actor extraordinaire that he was, didn't move a single muscle.

"You would insult me with a child's game?" The Raven said, his voice slow and tense.

Emotion would make the man less careful.

"You worried the other games were above my ability," Hollis answered, coolly. "I then suggested something very simple. A self-directed insult, you see."

The Raven narrowed his gaze, thinking that through. Emotion *and* confusion. Exactly as Hollis had intended.

"Shall we?" he suggested, not allowing even a hint of impatience or annoyance to enter his voice.

"We did not select a game."

Hollis shrugged. "Deal me in. I'll see if I can sort out what the game is quickly enough to beat you at it."

The Raven looked intrigued. For a self-proclaimed master gambler, he was utter rubbish at hiding his thoughts. Perhaps he did better once the game was being played. That was, after all, the reason Hollis undertook this bit of showmanship and banter before a match: he could learn to read his opponent while the man's guard was still down. He'd been doing that with the Raven since arriving at the Thompsons' place that day.

Narrowed gaze with mouth the tiniest bit agape: confusion.

Lips pressed on the right while the tiniest bit pursed on the left: frustration.

Small lift in the middle of the left brow: curiosity.

Hands on the table, index fingers steepled: excitement.

Slouching left: confidence.

Slouching right: *pretended* confidence.

There would be other giveaways, but those were the most crucial ones.

With a flourish, the Raven broke the seal on a new deck. He fanned the cards in a few different directions, cutting and shuffling the deck with one hand. Many people turned a simple game into a theatrical production. It wasted energy.

After a thorough shuffling, more flips of the cards, and several glances at the gathered crowd, the Raven dealt Hollis three cards, then three to himself, followed by another two to each of them. Then he turned over the top card in the remaining stack. An odd dealing pattern, but one that gave the game away.

"Écarté," Hollis said, his cards still facedown on the table. "A rare game."

"If you don't know how to play it," the Raven said, "I can select something else."

Hollis shrugged, casual and unconcerned. "I know how to play."

"Then place your first wager."

Hollis tossed in a half-guinea. "Three tricks."

The Raven matched it. "Three tricks."

Hollis took up his hand, organizing it. They each ex-changed a few cards before game play began. They took a slow pace, each adopting an attitude of minimal concern. Hollis knew the Raven was doing the same thing he was: studying his opponent. The stakes were lower than they would be as the evening progressed. Wagers weren't the point of the first game.

For all his showiness, the Raven really did know how to play. He gave away more clues than he ought, but all in all, he was proving a worthy opponent. The first round ended three tricks to two in the Raven's favor.

Hollis dealt the next hand. No flourishes. No showiness. Just business. The same bets were placed, and Hollis won back what he'd lost the previous hand.

The room filled as they played. Hollis recognized a few dealers from previous games. One of the footmen hovered nearby, his gloves dirtied and livery disheveled. The house-hold staff weren't precisely sticklers for propriety.

The wagers rose on the next hand. Hollis took the first trick. The Raven did an admirable job of hiding his feelings about that, though he did allow his mouth to purse a bit to the left. He hadn't expected to lose that trick.

Hollis didn't know how many hands they would need to complete this game, nor how many games they would play that night. But he knew he couldn't let the man grow too comfortable. Throwing him off-balance was a good thing.

"Shall we break a moment for a bite to eat?" the Raven suggested.

"I didn't come to eat." Hollis shuffled quickly, expertly, efficiently. "You're welcome to snack through the next trick if you can do so without mussing the cards or slowing the play."

"You aren't at all hungry?" The Raven slouched, but to the right. The man wasn't as sure of himself as he'd like to be.

"I can eat when we're done."

"A dram of brandy, then?" the Raven offered.

"I don't drink while I play." More shuffling, more pointed waiting.

"I happen to be able to do both." The slouch shifted to the left. An odd thing to take real pride in, but so be it.

Hollis motioned for him to proceed.

The Raven snapped at one of his staff and pointed to the empty spot on the table beside him. "Brandy, girl. Quick."

The man certainly didn't address his staff with any degree of consideration. Freeing them from this house felt as important as freeing his brother from exile.

Hollis kept shuffling, kept waiting. He'd learned long ago that equilibrium was essential to winning.

The maid, in a dress of startlingly bright blue, its fine fabric and less-than-serviceable style an odd choice for a servant, slipped over and set a glass of amber liquid at the Raven's elbow.

The Raven gave her an assessing once-over before tossing an all-too-slick gaze in Hollis's direction. "Once you graduate from the kiddie tables on the ground floor, you get to enjoy the company of our more . . . pleasant staff."

Considering Hollis knew of Four-Finger Mike's connection to people who ran brothels and prostituted women on the streets, the comment was not a particularly pleasing one. Equilibrium, he reminded himself.

"As I said, I'm here to play cards." Hollis cut the deck. "Everything else is just distraction."

The Raven examined the maid once more. "Some distractions are worth it."

The maid dipped a quick curtsey and stepped away. Doing so brought her face into view for the first time. If Hollis could get a good look at her, he might be able to describe her well enough to see if Móirín and Brogan could make certain she had somewhere safe to go.

He looked directly at her. For the first time in his long and storied career as a gambler, Hollis was completely upended.

The maid was Ana. *His* Ana.

The cards slipped a little in his hand, enough to throw off his shuffle but not enough for most to notice. The Raven did, though. He most certainly did.

This was not good.

Not good at all.

"That one's been about the place since we arrived," Fletcher said. "I could count on five fingers the number of times I've seen her."

So Fletcher had interacted with her already. Perhaps the situation wasn't as dire as it seemed. And "five fingers" was too pointed a phrase to be accidental. Four fingers would have made more sense, considering who they were attempting to find. Unless four was the wrong number.

SARAH M. EDEN

"Did she bring you anything?" Hollis asked.

"Brought me heartache, she did. Dropping a word of warning, like I was a great hairy dog."

Warning. Great hairy dog.

Blue blimey.

The Mastiff. He was connected to all this. Closely, apparently. Mercy, they were in trouble.

"Can't say I blame the bird," Hollis said to Fletcher. "You are a bit of a mutt."

Fletch shrugged and leaned back in his chair. "Are the two of you meaning to finish this game today, or ought we all find a corner for sleeping in tonight?"

"Oh, we're going to finish it." He looked across at the Raven. "We are going to finish this."

The Raven gestured to the table with a flourish. He always grew more elaborate when he was feeling cocky. That was a good thing at the moment. Hollis still felt more than a little off his game, seeing Ana nearby, trapped in this den of villainy. If the Raven was overconfident, that would even things up.

Hollis dealt. The room held its breath.

"Will you allow the exchange?" the Raven asked.

"No."

The room took a collective sharp breath. A dealer took a great risk in denying cards to be exchanged. If he lost the round, his opponent would receive an extra point, which could be enough to win the game.

"I'm declaring the king in the trump suit," the Raven said.

Hollis nodded in acknowledgment. That earned the

308

Raven a point, and it meant he was guaranteed to win at least one trick. Hollis wasn't in the most optimal position, but neither was he sunk. He held the ace, knave, and queen in the trump suit. His other cards weren't terrible.

The Raven played the seven in the trump suit. Hollis played the ace. One trick in his favor. He played the king in a lesser suit, knowing it would force the Raven to play any trumps he held.

For just an instant after the Raven pulled his chosen card from his hand, Hollis thought he counted five cards. The man ought to have been down to four. But the ten in the trump suit was dropped on top of Hollis's king, taking the trick, and leaving—Hollis counted—three cards visible in his hand.

A man who utilized all the flourishes the Raven did would most certainly be adept at sleight of hand. Was that how he cheated, a simple matter of slipping cards in and out of his hand?

The Raven played the ace in a lesser suit. As Hollis slipped the trump ace from his hand, he saw the same flash of extra cards in the Raven's hand. But they were gone in the next instant.

"When I first began seriously playing faro," Hollis said, rearranging his cards, "I often encountered players who improved their odds by tucking useful cards in their sleeves."

"A terrible thing," the Raven answered.

"It was, indeed. Those who would cheat at cards weren't welcome at future tables."

The Raven moved a card in his hand, slipping it first in front of the last card, then zigzagging it behind. At the same time, the hand holding his cards turned the tiniest bit, hiding his wrist from view. The perfect opportunity to slip a card up his cuff.

"Do you know how we guarded against that particular style of sharping?" Hollis managed to make the comment both offhand and pointed.

"How?" The Raven's lips pressed and pursed. He didn't care for the direction of this conversation. Good. Let him stew. Let him worry if he'd been caught out.

"We played with our jackets off and shirtsleeves rolled up past the elbows. Harder to tuck a card away. Harder to retrieve it."

He slouched. To the *right*. The man was on the defensive. "Why do we not simply strip from the waist up?" The Raven's laugh was forced. Others followed his lead, discomfort obvious throughout the room.

Hollis poked a little at that wound. He laid his remaining cards facedown on the table and began the task of rendering himself bare-chested. Heavens, this would be far easier to accomplish with equanimity if Ana weren't in the room. He had to pretend though.

Hollis tugged his necktie off, his eyes fixed on his opponent. "Are you afraid to take off your jacket? Something to hide?"

"I have nothing to hide."

Hollis caught Ana's eye as he pulled off his jacket. "Girl." He hated being so haughty with her, but what else could be done? They both had masks to maintain. "Open the curtains, shine some light on the situation."

"I like them closed," the Raven growled.

"You also like your jacket on, apparently." Hollis unbuttoned his cuffs, leaning his head toward Fletcher. "Make certain the light shines in the most helpful direction. I don't want anyone missing anything."

"Right you are, guv." Fletcher rose and joined Ana at the window. He would use the curtains to send a coded message across the street.

Hollis tossed his shirt onto the back of Fletcher's empty chair. He gestured to his own bare chest, then to the Raven. "You're the only one hiding anything now."

"I'm not hiding." The man yanked at his jacket with an odd, awkward movement. He was trying to remove his jacket without the sleeves hanging open. He nearly had his right sleeve off when the tiniest corner of a card peeked out.

Hollis all but dove across the table and snatched the sleeve, pinching it between his fingers with the card corner trapped and visible.

"Now, isn't this interesting?" He pulled the card the rest of the way out. A king of spades. "A high card, and a useful one."

"Are you accusing me of cheating?" The Raven spoke through clenched teeth.

"Are you expecting anyone in this room to believe that card was in your sleeve without your knowledge?" Hollis tightened his grip. "Or perhaps that playing cards grow in the fabric of your clothing? Or that you create such a hospitable climate for them that they crawl up your sleeves of their own accord in order to be closer to you?"

All eyes were on their host. "You're attempting to make me look a fool."

Hollis raised an eyebrow. "You don't need my help with that."

The Raven jumped to his feet, trying to pull free of Hollis's hold on his jacket. His hot, angry eyes bored directly into him. "I will not stand for this."

"Or *sit* for it, apparently." Hollis kept his cool by sheer willpower. He didn't like the anger he saw. If this man was the Mastiff, he was dangerous. Mightily so. Hollis and Fletcher weren't going to bring him down on their own. "Take off the jacket. Show us what else is hidden there."

"I will not be harassed in my—"

"Show us what else is hidden," Lewiston demanded. "You bested most of us in this room, and we deserve to know how."

The Raven met the eye of one of his dealers. "This ends," he growled coldly.

The room erupted. Servants and dealers dove to extricate the Raven from Hollis's hold. Gentlemen who now realized they'd been cheated jumped into the fray. Fists flew. Voices shouted. How long before knives were produced?

Ana needed to get out. They all did.

"Fletch," Hollis called out over the ruckus. "Get her safe."

The Raven rushed past him in that moment. Hollis lunged for him, grabbing the cheat by his collar and slamming him against the wall.

"You've won plenty of money," the man spat at him. "Enough to buy your silence."

"I can't be bought. I expect you to return the jewels and money and fortunes you've cheated men out of here."

"Cain't. It weren't mine to keep."

"This house wasn't yours to keep either." Hollis tightened his grip. "Run like a coward, if you must." He wouldn't get far. The lads across the street had been watching. "The money on the table is mine to redistribute."

"You cain't do that." For the first time, the man looked truly panicked. "I 'ave to make m'payment."

"To whom?"

The Raven didn't answer. He swallowed audibly, terror entering his eyes. He wasn't the Mastiff. How vast and complicated was this web?

"He'll find us," the Raven said. "He always finds us."

He'll kill me if he finds me. Very Merry had said that of the man who'd required her to steal and turn over her loot to him. The man who turned out to *not* be Four-Finger Mike but the Mastiff.

A pounding at the door below momentarily silenced the room. Someone pulled open the curtains of another window and looked below. "It's the police."

The Raven jerked out of Hollis's grasp.

"Help them find your boss," Hollis suggested. "They'd likely offer you protection."

"They're no protection against him."

In the next instant, the house filled with the sound of hard stomping of feet on the flagstone entryway. Even knowing he was on the right side of the encounter, Hollis was nervous.

The Raven flew from the room, trailed by many of those who'd come to watch and all of the staff. Hollis pulled his shirt on, then his jacket. He carefully tucked the thick pile of money from the table into his inner jacket pocket.

He met Fletcher's gaze. "Shall we?"

"I think we'd best." Fletcher offered his arm to Ana. "Care for a stroll, miss?"

"I don't think she was part of the wager," one of the few remaining spectators said.

"Would she like to be?" Fletcher had a way of asking potentially scandalous questions that made them sound more amusing than offensive.

"If it'll let me bunker off, I'll jump in." Ana could do a fantastic lower-class accent. A woman of vast talents.

The three of them walked casually from the room and onto the first-floor landing. The police were rounding up staff and players on the ground level below. It was chaos. The mess would eventually be sorted, but not without a great deal of hassle and annoyance. And it was entirely possible Hollis's winnings would be confiscated in the process.

"Anyone know of a secret passage out of here?" Hollis asked.

"What do I look like to you?" Fletcher asked. "A sneak thief?"

"I happen to know that is an item on your list of previous occupations."

"Not in this area of Town," Fletcher said. "I weren't that bold."

Ana took their hands and, with a mighty roll of her eyes, tugged them toward the servants' door. "I swear, gentlemen would be useless without women around."

Fletcher snickered. Hollis wasn't at ease enough to be amused.

"I hope, Ana, after we manage to get out of here, you'll explain how you came to be posing as a servant in this house," he said.

"I believe you mean 'a servant dressed very nearly like a harlot.'" She didn't shy away from the harsh description. "If we get out of here with our necks, I'll explain anything you want."

"Anything?" Fletcher asked, cheekily.

"*Nearly* anything."

"Hold her to that, Hollis," Fletcher whispered. "I suspect there's a whole heap she ain't telling us."

CHAPTER 26

f either of you turns around, I'll skin you alive." Ana tried to make the threat sound believable, but Fletcher's laugh told her how poor a job she'd done. "I'll have *Móirín* skin you alive."

That version held. Both men stood with their backs to her as she slipped out of the blue silk gown she'd been required to wear and into her own clothes. She wasn't neatly put together, but maneuvering would be easier in her flatter skirts and more accommodating bodice.

She buttoned up and tied off. "That's sorted."

"Are we safe to turn around now, or would we be risking our skins?" Hollis asked.

"Permission granted." She pulled from her hidden pocket the packets of cheat cards she'd found and held them out to him. "These were in the Raven's desk—cards designed to be slipped into decks."

Fletcher took the cards. "Did you find anything else?"

"More like these. And shelves of ledgers in his office," Ana said. "I'd guess they contain evidence."

"Brilliant."

She walked past them to the door of the third-floor bed-chamber and looked back over her shoulder at them. "Off with us."

The men followed. They were unusual, these two. Clearly they had fine heads on their shoulders and confidence enough for an entire battalion of soldiers. Yet they allowed her to take the lead without complaint or question.

She pulled them quickly to a well-hidden door at the back of the corridor and into a servants' stairwell, dark with shadows.

"I didn't see anyone using this one while I was in this part of the house," she said.

Hollis squeezed her hand. "Excellent."

"Most of the houses in this area have multiple corridors and exits belowstairs. One to the front, one through the garden, and, for houses like this one that share both sides with other homes, a second entrance in the back. Timing and patience is crucial to slipping out without being seen."

They kept moving slowly, following the stairs, listening and watching. The house was loud with voices, some shouting frantically, some authoritatively. The chaos wasn't likely to die down soon.

She looked to Hollis. "You're certain you couldn't simply explain to the police?"

"Not without trouble," Hollis said. "And that would draw attention. We don't want to be associated with the arrests."

"Even if you're the one who gathered the evidence during the game?" Ana pressed.

"Bung your eye," Fletcher muttered. "Evidence. The two of you get out. I need to guard the Raven's office."

"Guard it?" Hollis asked.

"We know this crowd has a love for fire. Cain't risk those ledgers going up in flames."

"Be careful," Ana said.

"I always am."

When they reached the ground floor, Fletcher slipped away, while Ana and Hollis kept moving downward until they reached the servants' wing.

"I can see the kitchen up that way," Hollis whispered, motioning ahead. "Looks like chaos."

"The garden entrance was just off the kitchens." Ana matched his low volume. "The other back door will be behind us. Head that way. You'll be in back of this row of houses and can easily navigate your way to the street."

"What do you mean *I* will be in back?"

"There's someone I have to find," she said. "I promised her I'd help her get out."

"Who?"

She nudged him in the direction of the door. "Your winnings tonight will help your brother and many others. We can't risk it being confiscated. And you need to be able to testify about the cheating."

"And *you* need to not get rounded up along with everyone else. There's a curio cabinet at your house the police ought not look into."

That was truer than she wished. The things were all hers, but they were also all reported as having been recently stolen. And yet . . .

"I made a promise, Hollis. I won't go back on that."

"Who do you need to find?"

"The housekeeper."

"Serena," he said. "I've seen her here often. Her situation worries me. I suspect she's not treated well."

"She isn't, and she's not working here voluntarily," Ana said. "And she has children who are in danger. She tried to get me out, but the man running all of this caught her out, and . . . I promised her."

"The Raven didn't know who you were when you slipped into the gambling room."

Ana nudged him again. He needed to get out without being seen.

Hollis spun back. "The Raven didn't recognize you because he wasn't the one who caught you, was he?"

She shook her head. "I suspect I know who that man was."

"The Mastiff?" Hollis whispered.

"I can't leave Serena here. She's terrified of him. They all are."

"You can't face down the Mastiff alone," Hollis said.

"I won't. I'll slip her out and avoid him." She stepped back. "Go. Quickly."

"Ana Newport, I admire your fire and your bravery, but your stubbornness on this will not outlast my determination." He took her hand and moved toward the kitchen. "We'll find her and her children, and we'll all slip out together."

She didn't want anything to happen to Hollis, but she had to admit, at least to herself, she was glad he hadn't left.

The chaos in the kitchen was even greater than she'd

anticipated. She and Hollis kept to corners and shadows, moving only when the nearest people were turned away and distracted. Ana studied every face. None were the man she suspected was the Mastiff. But none were the housekeeper either.

Where was Serena?

They reached the garden door without finding the woman they sought.

"Perhaps she got out already?" Hollis suggested.

"Or she was rounded up." Ana looked back once more, studying the people running back and forth. "What about her children?"

"I saw a little one at the back of the kitchen," Hollis said. "I assumed it was the knife boy."

"I didn't see a knife boy when I came through earlier."

Hollis moved back toward the fray. "I'll see if I can find him again."

Ana stepped out into the kitchen garden. She would check to make certain the path was clear so they could make quick work of their escape.

"We had none of this trouble before you, jam," a voice growled. An instant later, someone grabbed her.

Instinct took over. She bent and twisted as much as she could manage, then slammed her elbow into the stomach of the man holding her captive. The force was not sufficient enough to entirely loosen his grip, but it did allow her to get an arm free. She swung her elbow upward with every bit of strength she had, connecting with his face. That knocked him back enough for her to pull away. He, however, still stood between her and the garden gate.

She could seem him now. It wasn't the man she'd seen before. That was only minimally reassuring. He was enormous. And he was livid.

"This ain't none of my doing." She kept a distance, moving every time he did. "I'm runnin' same as you."

"You ain't running nowhere."

He lunged. She dove. He spun after her.

In a flash, Hollis was there, holding a knife like he'd been born to it. "This oughtta even the odds a touch."

The enormous mountain of a man looked from one of them to the other. A slow, sinister smile spread over his face. "This'll be fun."

"I certainly hope so," Hollis said.

Ana snatched up a large branch from the dirt near the door, arming herself with it. A knife would've been better, but she hadn't one at hand.

"Which one of us gets first whack at him?" Hollis asked.

"I'm willing to share." Ana circled.

The man kept his eye on Hollis. A knife was, after all, more dangerous than a branch, however thick. He fisted his hands. He was missing a finger.

Hollis feinted left. Four-Finger jumped back, hands up. Ana swung her stick, breaking it against the backs of his knees, buckling them. He fell forward. Hollis tossed his knife into his left hand and, with his right hand, landed a solid punch directly to the side of the man's face. He crumpled forward, not unconscious but stunned enough to be rendered temporarily still.

"Hasty retreat?" Hollis suggested to Ana with a grin.

"What else?"

They rushed for the back gate and out onto Warwick Square.

Hollis took her hand, swinging their arms between them as if they were simply out for a stroll. Ana's heart pounded in her temples, yet she did her best to appear entirely at ease. It would be best not to draw attention.

They wound their way back around to St. George's. A Black Maria sat outside the Thompsons' house. Police were escorting people from the house to the police wagon. Hollis pulled Ana gently to her house. They slipped in through the tradesmen's door. Compared to the home they'd just left, this one was a vacuous catacomb. Silent. Empty.

She closed the door behind them, turning the bolt.

They both leaned against the wood. "That was too close for comfort, Ana."

"I've had closer calls."

He slanted a look at her. "Have you?"

She shrugged a shoulder. "I was caught once making off with something I'd reacquired."

He bit back a smile, but she still saw it peeking out. "Were you?"

She nodded, grateful for the admittedly forced humor in the moment. Her heart still pounded, her thoughts spinning. "He told me I was unknowingly causing trouble for the urchins of London."

"Sounds like a remarkable man."

She emptied her lungs, attempting to release some of her tension. "He is."

"Hollis!" Brogan came bounding down the corridor. "We're for Thompsons'. Fletcher needs sneaking out."

Hollis met her eye. "Look after your father, and yourself, darling."

To Brogan, she said, "And you look after my Hollis. If anything happens to him, what I will do to you will make Four-Finger Mike seem like a pacifist."

Brogan grinned. "You've been spending too much time with m' sister. It's making you fierce."

Hollis shook his head. "She was already fierce."

The men left, rushing to their friend's aid. And, though Ana worried a little for her beloved, her heart held a degree of peace it hadn't in ages. She loved him and felt certain he loved her as well. For the first time in a long time, the future was a hopeful one.

ᚻIGGLEBOTTOM'S ᚄCHOOL FOR THE ᚦEAD

A GHOST OF A CHANCE

by Lafayette Jones

Chapter VI

Ace had pulled a lot of pranks and caused a lot of mischief in his time at Higglebottom's, but he'd never once been sent to the headmaster's office. He didn't know anyone who had been.

"We're in for it now," Bathwater said, as they made the trek up the cobweb-covered corridor that so few students ever saw.

"At least they can kill only one of us." Snout's bit of humor lightened all of them.

Even Pudding smiled. Then he looked to Ace. "We're in deep trouble, though, aren't we?"

"We're headed to Higglebottom's office. 'Trouble' doesn't begin to sum it up."

"I'm sorry," he said to all of them. "This is my fault. I shouldn't have stayed."

Ace shook his head. "Where else were you going to go?"

They'd established straight off that Pudding didn't have a home or a family waiting for him anywhere. Sneaking him around, sorting out a way for him to stay had been a lark, yes, but they'd also come to like him. Not one of them would want him tossed out to live under a rock or something.

Rattlebag, who'd been walking ahead of them, motioned toward a heavy wooden door. It opened. Moving things without touching them was something else Ace looked forward to learning.

They followed Rattlebag to the center of an empty room. Entirely empty. No furniture, no rug on the floor, no paintings on the wall. If there'd been chains and wrist cuffs on the wall, it would have looked exactly like a dungeon.

"Do we just wait here, or . . . ?" Ace let the sentence dangle.

"Hush," Rattlebag said. Then, in a suddenly booming voice, he called out, "Higglebottom, I've brought our troublesome students for your verdict."

Verdict. That didn't sound good.

A gust picked up in the room, swirling the dust around.

Under his breath, Pudding said, "Is that the wind, or is this place haunted?"

Ace and the others laughed for a moment before Rattlebag's glare silenced them.

The dust formed a whirlwind in front of them. Rattlebag, oddly enough, addressed it.

"These are the students and the Perishable they've been passing off as dead."

The swirl of dust broke apart and formed, in its place, words hovering in the air. *How did the Perishable get here?*

"I was lost in the rain," Pudding said. "I saw the school and slipped in to dry off."

How long have you been here?

"Just over a week, uh . . . sir."

Why did none of you report him here?

There was no voice to go with the questions, but it wasn't difficult to imagine the hard and angry voice behind them.

"He didn't have anywhere to go," Bathwater said. "And he was hungry. Perishables are fragile."

The question didn't change or disappear. Had Higglebottom—Ace was assuming this was the mysterious headmaster—not received the answer he wanted?

"And it was a challenge," Ace admitted out loud. "If we could hide a Perishable without being caught, that'd be something worth talking about for centuries."

You did get caught.

"I know, blast it," Ace muttered.

What do you suggest we do now?

The question was likely meant for Rattlebag, but Pudding answered.

"Let me stay?" He flashed an awkward but amusing smile.

"Let all of us stay?" Bathwater added.

The question didn't rewrite itself. Higglebottom hadn't heard what he wanted. Again.

Ace took a step closer and, likely for the first time since arriving at the school, took a stand on something other than the joys of mischief. "Pudding is a deuced good ghost, even if he's a bit too alive for our tastes. We have food here, which

326

he needs. We've a roof. Beds. Enough non-phantom fabric to make sure the boy ain't walking about in the altogether. He could learn what we learn, but he could also teach us about Perishables, things we might not know otherwise. If he stayed, it'd be good for all of us."

Still the question remained. The boys looked at each other, unsure what else they could say.

Into the silence, Rattlebag spoke. "These boys hood-winked all the students for a week. If not for the rain, they might have managed it even longer. Disguising a Perishable as a convincing ghost requires knowing what makes a ghost. And teaching a living boy enough to participate in the Spirit Trials is not a small feat."

Shocked silence gripped all of them. Rattlebag had defended them.

Professor Rattlebag and the Perishable will remain. The others will wait in the corridor.

Ace didn't like the idea of Pudding in here without a defender. "But we—"

Rattlebag's hardened expression warned him not to press the matter. So he, Bathwater, and Snout slipped out, waiting just on the other side of the door. If they'd had breath to hold, they'd have held it.

"What do you think Higglebottom will do to Pudding?" Bathwater paced, every third or fourth step slipping through the floor.

"What can a dirt whirlwind do?" Ace said with a shrug. His usual jovial tone fell flat. He wasn't sure what came next. None of their pranks had ever felt this . . . dangerous.

"If Pudding gets tossed out, I'm going too," Snout declared.

"So am I," Bathwater said.

Ace looked at both of them, feeling the strength that comes in numbers. "So am I. We're a group of four now. There's no going back on that."

In the next moment, the wooden door opened. Rattlebag floated out. His face gave no clues. Pudding was directly behind him.

All of them watched their friend, eager for anything he could tell them. He, too, was unreadable.

Ace couldn't wait another moment. He turned to Rattlebag. "Is Pudding being tossed out?"

"He is being kept on as a special consultant. An expert in Perishables, as it were." Rattlebag eyed the rest of them in turn. "The three of you will complete your First Form on the usual schedule, no matter that you took top prize in the Spirit Trials."

It was both disappointing and an utter relief.

"But we get to stay at school?" Snout said.

Rattlebag nodded. "Now, off with you. The Spirit Trials are still ongoing, despite the, shall we say, legendary disruption this morning." A hint of amusement tugged at the professor's lips. He was stern and often frightening, but Ace would wager Professor Rattlebag liked the mischief Ace and his friends undertook.

Bathwater, Snout, and Pudding offered their thanks and ran off, no doubt headed for the rugby pitch.

Ace stayed behind a moment. "Why did you stand up for us, professor? You had a chance to be rid of us."

"Never in my hundreds of years of teaching have I had a student even the least capable of hiding a Perishable in plain sight. You have potential. I'd hate to see that wasted."

"You like us," Ace said. "Admit it."

Rattlebag's expression hardened once more. "Do not press your luck."

Ace snapped a salute and sauntered down the same path his friends had taken. There were four of them now. Four friends with years of mischief ahead of them and a professor who, despite his gruffness, would take their part.

The afterlife was looking good, indeed.

CHAPTER 27

andolph arrived at Hollis's home thanks to the combined efforts of both their servants. Cora remained at Thurloe with the children.

Hollis sat in a chair by the fireplace, appreciative of the warmth of the low-burning fire, as Parker nudged Randolph through the door of the front sitting room.

"I didn't get your money back," Hollis said once Randolph was seated across from him. "But your debt has been cancelled. No roughs will be coming by your house to demand payment."

"How did you manage that?" Randolph had never been one for humble miens, yet, his current posture, expression, and tone could be described no other way.

"It's likely best if you don't ask too many questions," Hollis said. "Just know it's all sorted. You and Cora and the children can return home without worry."

"I've given you a great deal of grief over your activities these past years," Randolph said. "Yet, in the end, I'm the one who landed us in the suds."

Hollis felt too much empathy for his brother to lay into him as much as he'd have liked to. "We're family, Randolph. I'll always pull you out of the suds."

Randolph leaned forward, elbows on his knees. "The entire time I was tucked away, I kept thinking what a bit of unearned luck it was that Cora and Addison were away from the house that day. And when Parker told me he'd sent Eloise to *you* . . ." He took a deep, shaking breath. "Thank you, Hollis, for being steady all these years. I know I haven't always acknowledged it. I've accused you of being unreliable, yet I didn't worry the moment I knew my little girl was with you."

It was, quite possibly, the nicest thing his brother had ever said to him. "Miss Newport took exceptional care of her, bringing her to me and refusing to leave until we could safely reunite her with her mother."

Randolph looked up at him once more. "I've treated Miss Newport rather dismissively. I've worried so much about appearances that I stopped paying any heed to simply being a decent person."

"You've always been more than 'decent,'" Hollis said.

Randolph didn't appear reassured. "Is Cora disgusted with me?"

"She is worried about you. And she has missed you. Beyond that, I don't know her feelings."

Randolph squared his shoulders. "I'd best go begin mending what I've shattered."

Hollis nodded. "She and the children are at Thurloe Collegiate School. Miss Newport arranged with the headmistress to house and protect and care for them."

"Miss Newport seems a remarkable lady."

"She is precisely that," Hollis said.

They both rose, then stood a moment in awkward silence. Hollis hoped they would regain a degree of comfort with each other in time. Perhaps even overcome the tension that had marked their interactions for years.

"Off with you." Hollis tipped his head toward the door. "Cora will be eager to see you."

With another long and awkward nod, Randolph slipped out. Hollis wandered to the front-facing window and leaned against the frame, looking out on the street. London was turning colder. Hollis would have fewer Society events to attend. He hoped he'd gained enough of the Dreadfuls' confidence to remain busy on behalf of the DPS. And if all went according to the hopes of his heart, every free moment he had would be spent attempting to prove himself worthy of Ana's regard.

When he turned from the window to leave the room, he found Ana standing on the far side. She could not have come in through the doorway without his noticing. And she hadn't come up the front walk; he could see it quite clearly.

She'd sneaked in.

"Am I to play host to the Phantom Fox, then?" he asked with a smile.

"Your brother was taking absolutely forever to settle himself into his carriage. Climbing in through a window was faster."

He moved toward her. "None of my windows were open."

"They weren't *unlocked*, either," Ana said.

He tried to hold back his laughter but failed spectacularly.

"Not many gentlemen would be pleased to hear a lady had broken into his home," she said.

"Not many gentlemen are as brilliantly astute as I am." Hollis held his hand out to her. "What has brought you to visit? Besides, of course, the challenge of opening my locked windows."

She laid her hand in his. "I have checked the list of those taken up by the police last night. Serena, the housekeeper I promised to help, wasn't among them."

He walked with her to the small sofa. "Perhaps she escaped."

Ana shook her head as she sat. "She told me she had children, likely somewhere in that house. She wouldn't have simply slipped away without them." She released a pent-up breath and leaned against him. "The Mastiff likely dragged the lot of them to wherever he's doing his dirty work now."

He set his arm around her. "I wish I could say that was unlikely."

"I broke my word to her," Ana whispered. "She and her children are suffering because I failed her."

"You did all you could." He turned enough to pull her into a true embrace. "We'll keep an ear to the ground, darling. Someone will find her, and we'll get her out."

"Do you promise?"

He kissed the top of her head. "I swear to you. And I, too, know what she looks like. I'll watch for her myself."

She released a tight breath. "I just hate the thought of her and her little ones suffering."

"We will find her; I know we will."

Ana stretched up enough to kiss his jaw. "Thank you."

"You know, I enjoy your visits far more than my brother's."

She laughed. "I should hope so. And *he* doesn't even have to climb in windows on cold days."

The room *was* a little chilly. He stood and crossed to the fireplace. He stoked the embers with the poker.

"Is there evidence enough for the Raven to be put away?" Ana asked from the sofa.

"One never knows. But I think there might be."

She joined him at the fireplace. "I am glad Four-Finger Mike was apprehended."

"He has escaped before; I cannot guarantee he won't again."

Ana leaned into him, resting her head against his chest. "That was him, you know. The man we fought."

"I noticed the missing finger." Hollis held her, feeling the peace and completeness that came from having her close. "And I further noticed he was determined to hurt you." He whispered against her hair. "If he'd done you any harm—"

"But he didn't." She pressed her open palm against his heart as she leaned back and looked up at him. "We quelled him quite expertly."

"That we did, my darling, Ana." He kissed the tip of her nose, then touched his forehead to hers. "We make a good team, you and I."

"An astoundingly good team."

He slipped his hands up her back and shoulders and cupped her neck and head. Her eyes fluttered shut. He pressed his lips lightly to hers. A breath shuddered from her. He deepened the kiss, holding her as gently and firmly as one would a delicate and priceless treasure. Ana's fingers folded over his jacket lapel.

"I love you, my Ana." He trailed kisses along her jaw. "My darling, wonderful Ana."

She whispered against his lips what sounded like his name as her arms wrapped around his neck. He'd dreamed of this moment again and again over the months he'd known her. She'd claimed his heart from the beginning, and every day it became more irrevocably hers.

THE GENTLEMAN AND THE THIEF

by Mr. King

Installment VIII,
in which our brave Couple finds their Happiness!

Having procured a cart and pony at the coaching inn in Ipsley after waiting out the storm in a private dining room, Wellington made the drive back to Summerworth with an exhausted but joyful Tillie at his side.

"I am a bit disappointed." Her amused smile contradicted her declaration.

"What has disappointed you?"

"Our thief proved to be none of the things on m'original list." She shook her head and clicked her tongue.

He laughed. "You were hoping for ill-mannered dogs and well-coordinated magpies?"

"Oh, mercy, that would have been a lark to sort out."

He grinned at her. "I believe we had quite a lark regardless."

She sighed and leaned her head against his shoulder. "Chasing mythical creatures out onto the moors. What greater lark could there be?"

He pondered that for the length of a breath. "Mere weeks ago, I would not have thought racing over the moor was a worthy pursuit. I fear I was every bit the pompous bore you accused me of being."

"I really did call you that, didn't I?"

"You did, indeed." He led the cart around a bend in the path. "And you were utterly correct. I've spent too many years alone. The only company I'd kept with any degree of regularity was that of . . . well, people not unlike Mr. Alsop and Miss Fairbanks and their ilk. I'd lost sight of the Wellington I was when we were children."

"I loved *that* Wellington," she said. "He was my dearest friend."

"What do you think of *this* Wellington?"

She wrapped her arm around his. "I think he's wonderful."

"And I think *this* Tillie is rather remarkable as well."

They reached the front portico of Summerworth. His unwelcome guests would still be inside, likely moaning and groaning over Miss Fairbanks's missing jewelry. Wellington would do his best to settle the matter, offering to replace what was stolen and subtly pushing them out the door.

Mrs. Smith met them in the front entryway, her expression frantic. "What a scene!" She fanned herself with a dishrag. "You'd not believe what's happening."

Oh, mercy. Wellington met Tillie's eye. She clearly expected as much theatrics as he was anticipating.

"We'd best go face it," he said.

"And if they lob accusations at me again?"

Wellington set his shoulders. "Then I will toss them out with none of the civility I've been silently rehearsing."

She lifted an eyebrow and popped a fist on one hip. "I'm not afraid of a horde of creatures. We've faced down a number of them today already."

He took her hand in his, the lightness in his heart entirely at odds with the discomfort of the coming confrontation. On the first-floor landing, Pip found them. He bounced and jumped, grabbing for their hands.

"Come see. Come see."

"Come see what?" Tillie asked.

"All of it!" Pip dragged them up another flight of stairs and through the door to Wellington's rooms. "See. All of it!"

There, piled as high as Pip's knees, was a small mountain of jewelry, shiny metal boxes, silver brushes, and even the missing mirror and painting. Heavens, the Combses' spade was there as well, as was a hand plow and a milking bucket. The items Wellington and Tillie had taken out onto the moors, the ones that had disappeared from their hands during the blue whirlwind, were there also.

"All of it," Tillie said.

"One of these will be Miss Fairbanks's brooch." Wellington began digging for it.

Tillie dropped to her knees and joined the search. Mr. Combs, upon entering and hearing of their task, joined in the effort. As did Pip. And Mr. and Mrs. Smith.

Within the hour, Miss Fairbanks was in possession of her brooch, the rained-in houseguests were on their way, and Summerworth was peaceful and joyful again.

"They won't be the last visitors to disapprove of my

being here," Tillie warned as the traveling coach disappeared from view.

"I will remove anyone and anything that makes you less than happy, my Tillie. And soon enough, visitors, whether human or not, will learn that you matter to me more than they do."

"And Pip?" Tillie asked.

"He will learn that he matters to us too."

"*Us.*" She sighed. "I do like the sound of that."

"Then you are going to *love* this."

He kissed his beloved Tillie, holding her close as the wind whipped over the moors, cold and wild and tinted blue.

CHAPTER 28

"Fortunately for us, the Raven, once known as the Crow, kept meticulous records." Hollis addressed the meeting of the DPS, feeling for the first time like an equal rather than a second-class member. "He and his associates have been the ruin of many people in the past half-decade. Every asset he has was seized by the Metropolitan Police and will be used to help some of his victims recoup their losses. Unfortunately, the vastness of his villainy makes full restitution impossible."

Fletcher, lounging on his designated throne, nodded while still leaning his head against his propped-up fist. "The servants?"

"Some were found to be in cahoots with him. Some were victims, snatched off the streets or forced into employ upon arriving in London."

Kumar piped in. "That's more the methodology of Four-Finger Mike and his sort, not the stuffed-shirt Raven."

"Our lack-fingered friend was there, no doubt keeping the unwilling from leaving," Hollis said.

"The police apprehended him?" Irving asked.

"He slipped away again." Fletcher had sworn long and creatively when word of Four-Finger's escape reached them. "But he was part of it."

"All of it's connected, then?" Martin asked. "The arsonists from a few months ago, Mrs. George's ring of brothels, the children purchased by tradesmen, Four-Finger's network of thieves? All of that is connected to a highbrow gambling establishment full of sharps?"

"It appears that way, yes," Hollis said.

The men spoke amongst themselves in tones of unmistakable concern.

"We knew the efforts of Mrs. George and the street tradesmen were part of Four-Finger Mike's crime sphere. We now know people cheating at cards and ruining lives are part of the network as well."

"And the connection between them all?" Kumar pressed. "Other than a penchant for criminality, I mean."

Stone answered. "The Mastiff."

That didn't elicit murmurs, but complete silence.

"The baby thief we tracked to Pimlico confirmed the Mastiff has been directing thieves in the area," Fletcher said. "The impressive cat burglar we couldn't seem to find confirmed he was present at the Thompsons' place yesterday when the raid went down."

"Not merely present," Hollis corrected. "He kept tabs on the staff, his grip on all of them ironclad. His word was law, and they were afraid of him. Make no mistake, gentlemen"— he dipped his head to Elizabeth—"and distinguished lady, what we have uncovered in Pimlico is more than a gathering place for unfortunate gentlemen. We have discovered that we did not *end* a criminal enterprise when we foiled those arsonists earlier this year. And, I suspect, neither did we put an end to this gambling den. We are simply tugging on strands of a vast web."

"It's for us, lads—and lady—to trap the spider while freeing the flies," Fletcher said. "We've our work cut out for us."

"We're up for the challenge," Doc Milligan called out.

"There was a housekeeper at the gambling hole who tried to free our informant," Hollis said. "She indicated she had children who were also at the mercy of the Mastiff. I've posted her description in the library." He motioned toward the library two floors above them. "Keep your eyes peeled. If we can find her, we'll not only be saving her and her children, I suspect we'll be gaining an ally. And if this web proves much larger, we'll need all the help we can get."

"And the Phantom Fox?" Martin asked.

"She's an ally already."

With a mischievous glint in his eye, Fletcher said, "That ain't all she is."

Elizabeth joining their ranks had cooled some of the commentary they usually tossed around. Hollis appreciated it in that moment.

"That brings me to my last matter of business," he said. "We've gained more and more allies in our work, none of whom know the details of our society or endeavors. While many of you have managed to keep that secret from your wives, sisters, and children, I'm not certain how to proceed in my situation. I hope very much to secure the regard of my sweetheart. She'll know much of my comings and goings, but I can't tell her my reasons or anything about this group. How do I keep my promise of secrecy to the DPS without fully lying to the woman I hope will make a life with me? And how do I secure her help when I can't tell her the entire truth?"

If he couldn't find a way to continue with the crucial mission of the Dread Penny Society while still protecting Ana, he needed to know that now, before he'd committed himself to something he couldn't follow through with.

"'Tis something I've been tellin' the lot of you for years," Brogan said. "We're needing a means of letting our loved ones know a bit more than we can tell'm now. Not membership. Not full knowledge. Just something for those of us saddled with overly curious relations."

"Móirín's a lot of things," Fletcher said, "but 'overly curious' feels below the mark."

They laughed and needled Brogan good-naturedly. The Irishman took it in stride before taking up the topic again with emphasis. "I've proposed it before, but I'm doing so more strongly now. We're needing a sister organization. One that allows our closest family, who are qualified, willing, and eager, to offer a hand now and then in what we do."

Not everyone was in agreement. Arguments about accidentally revealing too much were tossed out alongside the insistence that such a group would eventually piece everything together. Some declared that keeping loved ones in the dark was making them only more curious, which was a risk unto itself. There was no consensus, no agreement.

"We've not enough here for a quorum," Fletcher said.

"Next full-membership meeting, we'll put it to a vote, and I'll consult the Dread Master."

"All the way to the top?" Hollis asked, both impressed and concerned.

"It's a matter that needs settling."

There was little else discussed among them. The matter of the gambling establishment and its broader implications were foremost in everyone's thoughts. The Mastiff had had his hand in this, just as he'd had in the arsons. Though they'd brought down the Raven, it felt like an empty victory. Four-Finger Mike had slipped away again. The Mastiff was still at large. People were still being hurt.

They were after a spider too venomous for ease or comfort, too wily to be trapped, too well-guarded for them to even know when he was nearby.

The meeting adjourned. Hollis didn't remain long enough to receive the congratulations coming his way. He had more pressing matters to see to. He popped out of the parliamentary room and into the entryway. The butler slumped in his chair as always. Hollis snatched up the penny he'd left on the end table, and the butler reached out a hand and pulled a lever, opening the front door automatically, without ever opening his eyes or changing his posture.

Hollis tipped his hat.

"Ye're welcome, sir."

He stepped out onto the walk and into the bustling press of humanity. An obliging hansom cab picked him up at the corner of Garrick and King Streets.

"Where to, guv'nuh?"

"St. George's Road. Pimlico." *With my heart in my throat and my head in the clouds.*

When he arrived, he went, not to the servants' door, where he'd entered before, but to the front door, like a proper suitor.

Wallace answered his knock. "Thought we might be seeing you, Mr. Darby."

"You did?" He hadn't made his intention known.

"Miss Newport's been watching for you. Cain't imagine you disappointing her."

"I never would. At least not on purpose."

"Best tell *her* that. Then her father. Then likely her again."

"Excellent advice." He followed the valet through the entryway, which had been recently dusted and swept, then up the stairs to the first-floor landing. "The ol' place looks nice."

"Miss Newport brought a li'l one over who's looking to learn to be a maid. The mouthy little thing is a delightful sort of hooligan. But she's done her work well."

A mouthy, delightful little hooligan. That rather perfectly described someone who'd recently shown herself to be a whirlwind in his house.

He entered Mr. Newport's room and found precisely the tiny thief he'd been expecting.

"Oy, sir." Very Merry snapped a jaunty salute. "Miss Newport said you wouldn't be in a huff if I came here to do a spot of learning. You ain't, are you?"

"Not at all, scamp."

"Scamp?" She put her fists on her hips again. That

seemed a favorite posture of hers. "I'm a proper maid now, you old put."

"A proper maid doesn't call anyone an 'old put,'" Hollis reminded her.

She shrugged and returned to her dusting. Very Merry was a handful, but a fellow couldn't help but like her.

He turned to Mr. Newport, seated by the low-burning fire. "Good afternoon to you. How are you enjoying your newest addition to the household?"

The kind-eyed man looked to Very Merry with real affection. "She is, quite possibly, my favorite person in all the world."

The little girl did something few urchins ever did: she blushed. Her smile, while still as full of mischief as ever, held a touch of fondness. Street children didn't trust easily. That Mr. Newport had earned hers already boded well for this arrangement.

"Ana has finally decided to move into the mistress's bedchamber," Mr. Newport said. "It's good for her to be finding her place in this home again. I'm hopeful her heart isn't hurting as terribly as it has these past years."

"You have a remarkable daughter," Hollis said.

"That you recognize that reflects well on you."

Hollis sat in the chair nearest his. "Does it reflect well enough that you'd not object if I started courting her?"

Amusement twinkled in Mr. Newport's eyes. "*Started* courting her?"

It was a point well made. "Started courting her in earnest."

"I have no objections, but the lady herself is just now

stepping in the room. Her objections are the ones you ought to be most concerned about."

His heart dropped. "She has objections?"

"Only one way to find out." Mr. Newport rose as his daughter approached.

Hollis did the same.

"Have you come to visit us, Hollis?" she asked.

"There's no 'us' about it, Ana," her father said. "He's come to visit *you*."

"How fortunate."

The simple observation made Hollis beam. *How fortunate.* She was pleased to have him there.

"I need help moving an armoire," she added.

Mr. Newport laughed out loud.

Ana grinned. "Come move the heavy piece of furniture, Hollis, and I'll say every flattering thing about you that you could possibly hope to hear."

"I will hold you to that," he warned.

She pressed a kiss to her father's neatly shaven cheek. "Do not spoil our Very Merry too much while I'm gone. I've seen you slipping her sweet biscuits."

"No such of a thing," Very Merry objected.

"She's quite right," Mr. Newport said. "They were jam tarts."

Ana looked content, something he'd not seen in her face the first months he'd known her, certainly not when she was here, fretting over her father and their home and lives. How Hollis loved seeing her so light and at peace.

He walked with her from the room to the adjacent one from which he and Brogan had surveilled the neighbors.

A large armoire sat in the middle of the room. She'd moved it far already, and on her own, apparently. When he'd first met her, he'd thought her fragile and perhaps too breakable. He hadn't minded the softness he saw, but he found he liked her combination of fire and lace even better.

He joined her at the tall piece of furniture. "Where are we taking this, darling?"

She pointed to the spot she was aiming for, and together they slid the armoire into place. In addition to that, her room now boasted a bed, a bedside table, a washstand, a large rug, and a chair near the window. It was a proper bedchamber again.

"I can't imagine you snuck the armoire out of someone's house the way you did the manicure set or silver snuffbox."

She laughed. "Wallace helped me repair a washstand and bedside table stored in the attic. The armoire was obtained secondhand in exchange for a few of the items I"—she cleared her throat—"repossessed. The bed, well, Wallace procured that, and I am choosing not to ask how."

Oh, dear.

Ana's moment of discomfort gave way to a look of contentment. "I mean to make my newfound independence a success, Hollis. Elizabeth is keeping me on three days a week, which will allow me to have some income while I increase my private teaching positions. And I get to live at home again."

"You sound excited," he said.

"I am." She reached out and took his hand. "I've been

living in shadows for a long time. I'm ready to step into the light."

He tucked her close to him and clasped his arms behind her. "I first met you while you were living, at least in part, in the shadows. I will miss seeing you there, darling."

She brushed her fingers along his jaw. "I could probably be persuaded to make a repeat appearance now and then."

"Could you, now?"

"Are you issuing an invitation?" There was the flirtatious tone he'd come to love in his mysterious thief.

"That's not the invitation I'd intended to make when I came here, but I'll not complain if you accept it."

She wrapped her arms around his neck. "What invitation were you going to make?"

"That you have dinner with me."

She smiled softly. "Tonight?"

"And tomorrow. And the day after that. And after that."

Ana leaned her head against him. "I'm detecting a pattern."

"I don't have a lot to offer," he said. "A nonexistent inheritance. A snooty brother with a gambling problem. Questionable activities I don't intend to give up but neither am I at liberty to explain, even to you. And I am caught between the demands of Society and the pull of low literature. An ideal suitor, really."

"A *perfect* suitor."

He laughed. She didn't.

"My list of assets isn't terribly different," she said. "We might very well be the two best-matched people in the kingdom." She rose up on her toes and pressed the tiniest whisper of a kiss to his lips.

"Would you let me court you properly, Ana? Come call on you? Scrape and bow to your father in an attempt to gain his good opinion? Nervously ask you to dance at balls and ride with me in the park and sip tepid tea while sitting in awkward, nervous silence?"

Her smile melted him as it always did. "Have we not passed that phase already?"

He slid his hands down her sides, resting them at her hips. Hollis bent close, a mere breath between them. "I love you, Ana Newport." He kissed her quickly, lightly.

"I began loving you the first time I met you, but I didn't dare let it show." She brushed her fingertips over his cheek. "You are a gentleman from a fine family. I am the penniless daughter of a bankrupt businessman."

"And a thief," he reminded her.

She smiled and blushed. "Do you truly wish to court a thief?"

"I can think of nothing I wish for more ardently."

Ana linked her arms behind his neck again. "I love you, Hollis Darby."

There was nothing tentative about the way she kissed him, and nothing indifferent about his response. He kissed her lips. Her cheek. He took his time pressing kisses to her neck, reveling in the feel of her in his arms.

For years, he'd wondered if he would ever have enough or be enough for anyone to wish to build a life with him. Ana knew his double life; he knew hers. Together they could build a new life, together, with all their contradictions and struggles. He kissed her with the promise of that future. He kissed her with all the dreams he had for tomorrow.

Theirs would be a very happy, never dull, ever after. Together. The gentleman and the thief.

ACKNOWLEDGMENTS

Invaluable sources of information and insight into this fascinating era and people:

- Susie Dent's many brilliant books on dialect and etymology.
- Normanby Hall's exhibit on Victorian-era clothing.
- *A Treatise on the Game of Ecarté, as Played in the First Circles of London and Paris,* published in 1824.
- *The Handbook of Games,* published in 1867.
- *Sharps & Flats,* published in 1894.
- The fantastic faro demonstration at the Sharlot Hall Museum in Prescott, Arizona.
- *A Book of Remarkable Criminals,* by HB Irving, published 1918.
- *The Battered Body Beneath the Flagstones, and Other Victorian Scandals,* by Michelle Morgan, published 2018.

Invaluable sources of encouragement, advice, and support:

- Annette, Emily, and Luisa, my Tuesday writing gals.
- My family, for helping me with random research,

ACKNOWLEDGMENTS

putting up with my focus on such oddities as Victorian-era card games and the difficulties of climbing walls in 19th-century clothing, and cheering me on.

- Lisa Mangum and the team at Shadow Mountain for making the final product a fabulous one we can all be proud of.
- Pam Pho, agent extraordinaire, who makes navigating this industry more pleasant and far more possible.
- Kneaders™ banana-and-walnut oatmeal, for getting me through more writing sessions than I can count.

DISCUSSION QUESTIONS

1. Hollis feels like he has more to offer to the Dread Penny Society than they know. What talents or skills do you have that are not well-known to your friends?

2. Ana went to great lengths to reacquire items that had been stolen from her family. Was she justified in stealing back those things, or should she have found another way to secure justice?

3. Mr. King's penny dreadful featured a bluecap—a creature from English folklore. Had you heard of a bluecap before? What did you learn about them from this story?

4. During this time, boarding schools were reserved for the wealthy and well-connected, yet Hollis's stories were designed to appeal to poorer children who could never attend such a school. How did he make his story relatable for his readers who had a very different personal experience? What about his story made it enjoyable for readers of all ages?

5. Ana and Hollis both kept secrets from each other. Did keeping those secrets help draw the couple closer together

or keep them further apart? Is it ever okay to keep a secret from someone you love?

6. Gambling and card games were a common pastime during the Victorian era. What games are you proficient at?

7. Who do you think the Dread Master is?

ABOUT THE AUTHOR

Sarah M. Eden is a *USA Today*™ best-selling author of historical romances. Her previous Proper Romance novel *Longing for Home* won the Foreword Reviews 2013 IndieFab Book of the Year award for romance. *Hope Springs* won the 2014 Whitney Award for "Best Novel of the Year," and *Ashes on the Moor* was a Foreword Reviews 2018 Book of the Year silver medalist for romance.

Combining her obsession with history and an affinity for tender love stories, Sarah loves crafting witty characters and heartfelt romances. She happily spends hours perusing the reference shelves of her local library and dreams of one day traveling to all the places she reads about. Sarah is represented by Pam Pho at D4EO Literary Agency.

Visit Sarah at www.sarahmeden.com.

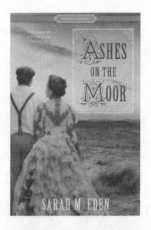
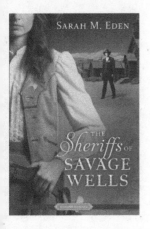

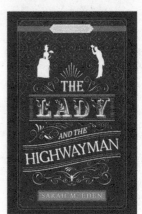